The Treasure of the Hills

By
Harold H. Milton

Llumina
PRESS

ISBN: 978-1-62550-263-6

978-1-62550-264-3

Printed in the United States of America by Llumina Press

Library of Congress Control Number: 2015918232

Dedicated to my father and mother,

Charles Henry Milton & Eva Marilla Farley Milton

and to my daughter, Nancy J. Milton and my niece,

Janice Louise Blanton, whom I raised as my

daughter & whom made my books possible.

Preface

T he production of lumber has always been an industry of vital importance to our nation as timber is one of our greatest natural resources. This is an old industry, dating back to when the first settlers marched into the wilderness and carved out homes for themselves and their families.

First one state and then another would lead in lumber production, and in 1909, West Virginia outdistanced all competitors with a production of well over one billion board feet.

The following story is based upon this year of peak lumber production. It was a colorful era, one in which the men who toiled in the virgin forests of the Allegheny Mountains were as rough and rugged and the country in which they worked.

In writing of those lusty days, I need only draw upon my memory of the stirring tales told by the old timers who lived and worked in the mountains during that time. Many and varied were the tales they told: tales of love, hate, jealousy, and greed. But the most often told stories were about violence and bloodshed.

Those men of the ax, the crosscut saw, the sledge, wedge, and cant hook were famous for their brawling. Though they loved nothing so much as a good fight, for the most part, they were honest, hard-working men who didn't necessarily need to have their blocks knocked off. All that was required was that they look as though they needed it. Before long, some lumberjack would accommodate them.

In practically every lumber camp, there would be a man who prided himself upon being the *Bull* of the woods. More often than not, such an individual would lord it over his fellows like a dictator. The word of the *Bull* was invariably accepted as law by everyone in his camp. If the *Bull* was a fair-minded man, then all would be well. On the other hand, if he was tyrannical, then all hell would usually break out, quite frequently.

The following story originates in the mountains of the Cheat River watershed. Its plot and characters are completely fictional. However, I have strived diligently to write it in such a way that it does justice to this land and the people who inhabited it in those days.

I submit this story with fear and trembling, and with pride. My fervent hope is that the reader will visualize this great country through the appreciative eye of the author, and even regret not having been privileged to have participated in those bygone days of rugged adventure.

With all sincerity,

Harold H. Milton

November, 1953

Foreword

Deep in the forests of mountainous West Virginia, far from the haunts of men, wild ginseng still grows undisturbed, as it grew centuries ago. For many years, the exportation of ginseng roots from the United States of America to China was big business. The returns from this product annually run into many hundreds of thousands of dollars.

The people of China hold ginseng roots in high esteem. They have great faith in its healthful benefits. Consequently, the demand for the root far exceeds the supply. The population of China exceeds four hundred and fifty million, and they all use ginseng root, from the highest class of people on down to the lowest class. It is easy to understand how ginseng trade affords a handsome profit to local buyers as well as to exporters.

The following story is based upon a legend a West Virginia mountaineer told me more than twenty years ago. I named this story *The Treasure of the Hills*. To many people living in the hill country, ginseng has indeed been a treasure. During the summer months, the money derived from gathering and selling these precious roots has often alleviated the pinch of poverty, being a source of income that requires no investment or qualifications, other than an average knowledge of the herb and a generous supply of patience and persistence in gathering it. Armed with those two commodities, the backcountry "seng digger" has often been able to line his pockets.

I speak on this matter with authority, for I speak from my own experiences. In my boyhood in southern Ohio, I learned ginseng and its value from my father. From 1929 until the start of the Second World War, work in the rural districts, other than seasonal farm work, was almost exclusively confined to government projects.

During those lean years of the Great Depression, wild ginseng was a heaven-sent boon to my family. How often did my father and I roam the woodlands, near and far, gathering this precious root? Now, as I draw aside the curtain of time and look back, I come face to face with a startling fact. Surely, the good lord directed our steps through the woods to help us find enough ginseng to be sufficient for our needs. Rare indeed were the days my father and I returned home empty-handed. We were fortunate enough to always return with a nice amount of roots and happy hearts.

In writing *"The Treasure of the Hills"* I have permitted my imagination to hold full sway. However, in presenting this story I have make every effort to portray my characters as people really are in real life; and not as I would have them to be. To do so I had but to call upon that which I have learned from the hard school of life in more than two score years of living. With kindest regards and best wishes, I remain.

Harold H. Milton

May 6 1955

The Treasure of the Hills

Chapter I

*B*en Waters paused as he lurched down the mountain and wearily sank onto a moss-covered rock. With shaking hands, he unstrapped the knapsack and, opening the flap, viewed its meager contents through bloodshot eyes. His food supply was exhausted. Another day would see its finish. Buckling the flap of the knapsack securely shut, he raised his head and gazed about him. The forest stretched in all directions. Ahead, it dropped away gradually, sweeping down and down, until at last it became lost in the gloomy haze that hung low under the trees. Back up the sloping spur, down which the weary man had just staggered, the view was shot off by bulging shoulders. The forest was largely second-growth timber. How long ago the virgin stand had been timbered off, he had no way of knowing, nor did he care. However, it had to have been at least a third of a century before.

The man was lost. For six days, he'd traveled ridges, staggering up and down slopes, fording streams, trying to find his way out of the woods, but all his efforts had been in vain. He was still no nearer civilization than he had been days ago.

Rising from the stone, he pulled on his battered felt hat and began pacing while bitter denunciations rolled from his lips. Waters was lanky six-footer around thirty years of age. He had a thatch of light brown hair that hung over his ears and forehead in wild disorder. His face was long and homely, but his jaw was square and craggy. Big ears and a long nose did not add to his beauty. His dominant feature was his eyes. Under normal circumstances, they were a piercing light grey. At the moment, they were dull and bloodshot. Despair was mirrored in those eyes as Ben once more sat on the mossy rock.

"Waters, what a fool you've been," he said, nearly sobbing in despair. "Reckon you've learned some late that these mountain woods ain't to be compared to the rabbit patches you were used to back in Wood County. Hunting seng in them woods was a cinch. I miscalculated this country. If I get out of this predicament with my life, it'll be nothing short of a miracle. If the way things've been going lately is any sign, I'll leave my bones bleaching in these damned mountains. I ain't never been what you'd call the praying type, but God, if you're in hearing distance, hear me now. I need your help like I've never needed it before. If you head me out of these woods, I give you my word I'll try to be a better person than I've been in the past. My situation is desperate. I'm on my last legs. Two more days of this will see my finish. I'd like powerful much to take out some of the seng I've seen in these woods since I've been lost, but without your help, I don't reckon I will. So again I say, help me, or all is lost."

After making his plea, Ben hung his head and slouched on the mossy rocks, the picture of despair. As he sat with bowed head, his life passed through his mind in review.

It was late June, 1933. Four years of the Depression had rolled over the heads of the American people. Work was as scarce as hens' teeth, and what little work there was paid very poorly. Employers commonly picked men with families to support over hiring a single man. This was, in one sense, a fair practice, but a single man, not the head of the family, was almost certain to find himself largely unemployed.

Ben Waters was single. He had been born and raised in Wood County, West Virginia. The first twenty years of his life had been spent on a rented, eighty-acre farm about five miles up the Little Kanawha River from Parkersburg. In those twenty years, Ben acquired knowledge of the things that make up life in a rural community. Farming and its many mysteries had always come easy to him. Mother Nature must have recognized him as a child of the sod, because he and his father's crops were amongst the finest in the neighborhood. Things seemed to take a special delight in growing for them. Their garden was always the most bounteous, and their money crops bore the heaviest yields of the entire neighborhood. Their fruit trees were pruned, dug around, and sprayed. This type of care put new life in the old trees, and it did wonders for the younger ones. Bar frost, the fruit trees were prodigious in their bearing. The neighbors of Ben Waters and his father summed up the two men's agricultural ability in one word. They possessed that which is commonly known in rural districts as "the touch."

As much as he loved farming, young Waters was never as happy as when he was roaming the woods. Over the years, he came to know nearly every herb and forest plant by name. He could always be depended on to find particularly scarce herbs. His special delight was spending a long summer day in the fastness of a secluded woodland gathering wild ginseng and yellow root. Sometimes his father accompanied him on these hunts. At other times, a neighbor boy was his companion. Not infrequently, however, young Waters tramped the woods alone, and it was not all unusual for him to spend the night alone in some far off wilderness, miles from his home. Often, his root gathering trips were very profitable. He dug and sold many pounds of dry ginseng root and yellow root. If the market was good, he often made more money in his spare time, than the young fellows who worked for local farmers.

When he was twenty years old, his mother died. A year later, his father remarried and moved into Parkersburg. From the day his mother passed away, Ben's life was full of hard knocks. Life at home was not the same. He accompanied his father and stepmother into town and for five years worked in local factories and stayed with them. One day, a month after his twenty-fifth birthday, the wanderlust seized him. He decided to see something of life up and down the broad Ohio River. For the next three years, he worked as a regular man on a packet boat between New Orleans and Pittsburg.

In 1929, the Great Depression struck. Almost immediately, Ben found himself out of work. For the next three years, he must have worked for a hundred different men. A day here, a day there, sometimes he got a month of steady work, but such an occasion was rare. Men by the thousands left the cities and returned to rural districts. Ben Waters, his father and stepmother, and an older married sister and her family were in the ranks of those who returned to the land. In those days, money, even for the direst necessities, was a luxury. Often, for whole months at a time, hardly any money at all changed hands between farmers and local merchants. Most transactions took the form of bartering. Eggs, cream, and other farm produce were exchanged for commodities from the store. In those lean times, people learned the meaning of neighborliness. What one man didn't have, in all probability, he could get from a neighbor by trading something his neighbor needed. And so it went.

Once he'd returned to his boyhood community, it seemed natural for Ben to revert to his old ways and activities. Since work for wages were impossible to find, he again became a root digger. Eventually, he acquired a dilapidated touring car and traveled far and wide. He became known in the area as the "seng digger." That was how Ben spent his summers. In winters, he ran a trap line, and between these two activities, he managed to get by. Though he enjoyed his wild, free life, some intangible thing was lacking. He finally concluded that he was not getting anywhere in life by going from one year to the next. If he should meet a nice girl and fall in love with her, he could not, in all fairness to the girl, ask her to marry him. It would not be right. His future was far too uncertain to entertain thoughts of marriage.

Ben resolved to better himself, and here again, his old standby, ginseng hunting, came to his aid. His best bet for success was to be self-employed, and ginseng paid more money than anything else he could turn his hand to. The big problem was finding it in sufficient quantity. He would have to hunt in the wide, wild woods. The woodlands in Wood County or any of the adjoining counties, did not measure up. They were far too small and had been hunted too thoroughly. Ben had to strike out and travel until he found a section of country the filled the bill. First, he talked the whole thing over with his father. The result of that talk was illuminating.

"Well, now, Ben," Amos Waters had said. "Reckon I can't blame y'all for wantin to better yourself. It's natural. The important thing is to make a good try doin something about it. I like your spirit, son. Now, about this seng diggin. You're on the right track, iffin you can find enough. So you're lookin for a big wood to hunt in? Ben, my boy, this old state of ours has some mighty powerful big woods in it. It's the mountain section I'm speaking of. You don't have to leave West Virginia to get your fill of wild and lonely places. Years ago, I cut timber back there on the Gauley River watershed. It's a wild country, an no mistake. Why don't you wait till a bit later in the summer? Maybe I could spare a couple of weeks away from the crops an go with you. I hate like sixty to see y'all traipse off by yourself. It ain't safe for a man to go in them woods alone. Don't laugh, son. I know you're a good woodsman, but you ain't ever tackled woods fifty miles square. That's the kind of woods I'm thinkin of. It's that big one at the head of the Gauley. It takes in a good-sized hunk of five counties. That is one wild, lonely piece of country. There's bears, deer, elk, wild cats, an even panthers in there, to say nothing of findin rattlers wrapped around ever' other bush. It's all mountain country. Some of them big hills are well over four thousand feet high. You'll find a few mountaineers back from the main roads, but they're few an far between. Mostly they live on the traveled road. They're a fine, upstanding lot of people. They'll take you in, feed you their best, an treat you like a king, but a mountaineer won't stand for much monkey business. I ain't saying this cause I'm figgering y'all might try to pull a fast one out there in them hills. Reckon I know my own son better than that. I'm just wanting you to get good picture of that country an its people.

"Well, there you have it, Ben. If you go, watch you don't get lost. Only the good Lord would know where to look for you. It is the gospel truth that there's many a man what's left his bones bleachin on one of them mountain ridges. Have a care y'all don't add your bones to that list. Reckon that's all. When, an if, you do hit them woods, head up a stream an come back down the same way. Never jump ridges. That's a bad policy, even for a seasoned mountaineer. For a greenhorn to that country, it's plumb suicide. I wish you the best of luck, good weather, no mishaps, an seng like you never dreamed. That's the best your old dad can do for you."

Ben thanked his father for all he told him. His mistake was in not taking his parent's cautions seriously. He'd laughed at all that talk of getting lost. The idea was preposterous. Wasn't he the best woodsman in Wood County, or any adjoining county? Hadn't he traveled every wood in his part of the state, day or night, with never the slightest difficulty? He wondered why his father had warned him of the danger of getting lost. Finally, after mulling it over for several days, Ben had concluded that the only logical explanation was that his father was getting old. He dismissed the entire matter. He wasn't a boy any longer. He had been taking care of himself for more than ten years. He could take care of himself in any woods that West Virginia boasted. His chest swelled with pride. A man had to have confidence in his abilities, even if others were skeptical.

Ben spoke to his father in the early spring of 1933. From that day forward, he began preparing for the coming summer and his quest into the mountains. He bought heavy clothes and high-topped leather boots. The small mattock he carried for digging ginseng was fitted with a new white hickory handle. He bought a new belt ax and heavy clasp knife. For his foodstuffs, Ben bought a knapsack and treated it with a waterproof solution. As the spring went by, he added to the list of the things he felt were essential to the success of the trip.

By the time the trees were in full leaf, Ben was ready to hit the trail, but upon consulting literature on the mountainous section of his native state, he decided to tarry another month. The bulletins warned that the mountain section of West Virginia opened a full two weeks later than did the surrounding countryside.

At last, the day of his departure was at hand. It was on a Monday. The Sunday before, numerous friends had dropped by the Waters home to wish him well. Many a sly grin and good-natured jab followed their well wishes. To them, Ben's mountain seng hunt was a wild goose chase. To the old timers, it was the dream of an ambitious youth. They nodded their silvery heads and kept a still tongue. Let the boy have his try, they reasoned. They, too, had had dreams of sudden wealth in their younger days. Amos Waters wrung his son's hand at their parting, a misty-eyed grin on his leathery countenance.

"Bennie-boy," he said in a tremulous voice. "I don't need to tell ya how much I hope your dreams will be justified. However, if you don't hit it this trip, you're young and can always go again. Them old hills out there are big, mighty big. Don't be ashamed if they fool you the first time in. It takes time to learn your way around that country. The seng's there, of that I'm certain. All you got to do is to get back in the woods. That's the big secret in a nutshell. My only regret is that I can't go with you on this first hunt, but there'll be other trips. Then I'll get to see that country again. This is only the middle of June. Fall is a long ways off. Please be careful."

Chapter 2

*B*en waved a cheery hand to his folks. He cranked up his trusty touring car and started on his first big adventure with a wheeze, a chuckle, a rattle, and a roar. His folks hadn't said much at his departure, but he knew they all were praying for him. His sister, her husband, and their kids were there to see him off. Outward displays of emotions are seldom evidenced by those who till the soil, but their hearts are in the right places. When they wish a person good luck, it comes from the heart. Ben accepted their well wishes in the spirit in which they were given and held his peace.

US Route 21 swept down from the shores of Lake Erie and crossed the nation to the Atlantic seaboard in South Carolina. When Ben started on his way, the summer sun was three hours high. By early afternoon, he had reached Charleston, the state capitol, and the Big Kanawha River, the largest waterway in West Virginia. Here US Route 60 joined Route 21. The two national highways ran as one for more than forty miles up the Big Kanawha River. This stream was markedly different from the placid waters of Little Kanawha. Only in the flood had there been any turmoil in the waterway upon whose banks Ben had grown to manhood. It had always flowed unhurried as calm and serene as a summer's day.

The river Ben was traveling held a sinister fascination. The highways followed it mile after mile after mile. The Big Kanawha was almost continual rapids, interspersed with broad pools, where dark, swirling waters were anything but inviting. As he drove along, Ben reflected on the waterway. It was reputed to be one of the longest and oldest rivers on the North American continent. From Point Pleasant on the Ohio River Valley, it meandered through West Virginia, Old Virginia, and deep into North Carolina, with its shed reaching clear to the slopes of Mount

Mitchell, the highest mountain in North America east of the Rocky Mountains. The total length of the river ran into the hundreds of miles.

In some places, the river had carved its way through hundreds of feet of solid rock, forming deep gorges with varicolored stratus glistening in the sun. In other places, islands of solid rock appeared in the middle of the river, the dark current swirling around them. Great blocks and shafts of rock rose out of the river near its banks in the form of rugged bluffs hundreds of feet high.

Ben saw very little bottomland on his way upriver from Charleston. Mostly, the road had been carved out of the side of the frowning river bluffs. Truly, this was a river of mystery, Ben mused, as it gurgled, moaned, growled, and roared on its long journey. Somewhere on the headwaters of one of its branches, Ben hoped to make his fortune.

With each mile that sped by, he saw changes in the topography of the country. The rugged hills gave way to high ridges that climbed into the blue June sky to inspiring heights. They swooped down to meet the chugging, wheezing old touring car. He began to realize his father had been right. The mountains were gigantic, stupendous, colossal. The woods clothed their broad, high slopes and crests in a solid stand as far as the eye could see. Ben Waters felt a thrill along the length of his frame. Before him was the kind of woodland he had always dreamed of searching for ginseng in. He laughed joyously as he envisioned the patches of old, well developed "seng" he would comb out of those hills.

At Gauley Bridge, the waterway branched. Here the Big Kanawha River ended. The branch from the left was the Gauley River, and the fork from the right was known as New River. The road followed the rock-infested New River. If the Big Kanawha had been awe-inspiring, Ben thought, how much more so was the stream he now followed? New River was frightening, to say the least. It resembled a liquid monster as it rolled along, leaping, swirling, howling, and roaring against the confines of its rocky bed. At last, the highway left the river and began climbing the mountain. Shortly thereafter, the federal highway branched, with US Route 21 swinging to the right, and US Route 60 swinging to the left. Ben left 21 and stayed on 60. Eventually, after much twisting and turning, always up and up, he drove around a sharp bend and pulled to a stop. Far below, the New River roared and moaned. The gorge it ran through was at least a thousand feet deep with almost perpendicular sides. He looked up New River Canyon, about which he had heard so many stirring tales. Far ahead was a foaming rapid in the river. Directly beyond, the canyon swung sharply to the right, and the view was cut off by a six hundred-foot-high cliff with a sheer drop down its frowning face. After a last look, Ben drove on with apprehensive tingles running up and down his spine.

Twilight found him at Lewisburg, less than fifty miles from his jumping off place. Marlinton was his destination. Once there, he would stash his car in responsible hands, then into the woods he would plunge. The great forest at the head of the Gauley River lay directly west and north from Marlinton. He spent the night at Lewisburg. An old man with a kind face and keen blue eyes ran the only hostelry that the mountain village boasted. He inquired of Ben's business in such an easy, casual way that Ben found himself telling the oldster all about his big venture and high hopes.

"Sure now, son," the old fellow drawled with a strong southern accent. "Here's wishin y'all good luck. Reckon you've picked the biggest wilderness hereabouts for your seng hunt. It's in there, if you're lucky enough to stumble into the right cover. My name's Clem Nickols. What's yours, son?"

"I'm right pleased to meet you, Mr. Nickols," Ben replied. "I'm Ben Waters. Born an raised in Wood County. My father, Amos Waters, used to cut timber in these woods."

"I helped timber that section off myself," Nickols said. "Maybe I run into your dad. Who knows? Anyway, Ben, I'm powerful pleased I met up with you. Before you head into the woods, go up to Marlinton and stop at the West Virginia State Forestry Office. That country is all state forest now. You need a permit from the forestry people to go in and build fires an all that. It's okay, son. It is only a formality to keep check on who's in the woods. If the rangers spot any smoke that can't be explained, they're duty-bound to investigate it. They have a few fire towers on ridges around the edges of that tract. There's none in the center, though. From some of the towers you can see better'n fifty miles on clear day. You're goin into an almighty big country. Be extra careful. It's as easy to get balled up in there as fallin off a log. Anyways, son, I'll just say good night now, and good luck."

Bidding Clem Nickols good night, Ben retired to his room. Since he'd arrived at the hotel after the supper hour, he'd had to eat a warmed over meal, but the food had been very good, and there was plenty of it.

He fell asleep almost as soon as he stretched out between the clean, cool sheets. The long hours of darkness passed as if they had been only a moment. Old Sol was just topping the crest of a timbered ridge to the east when he woke. He sprang out of bed and quickly dressed. He walked to the window facing east and sized up the weather with the experienced eye of a farmer. The sky was as clear as a bell and held the promise of another fine summer day.

In an hour and a half, he was on his way. The innkeeper came out just before he drove away. He walked out to the touring car with Ben and shook hands with him then invited Ben to stop again. Nickols impressed Ben as honest and sincere, and he liked the old fellow.

By nine o'clock, he was in Marlinton, a mountain hamlet of less than thousand inhabitants. An hour after arriving, he had secured a permit from the forestry service to cover his activities, and he was ready to take to the woods. His touring car had been placed under the care of a man who ran local garage and livery. He charged Ben three dollars, whether he was in the woods a day, a week, or a month.

By ten-thirty, Ben was in the woods, embarked upon the greatest adventure, or mistake, of his life. He ignored his father's advice and crossed two hogbacks in quick succession, and at sundown, was as turned around as if he had been in the heart of Africa. It looked alike to him in every direction. An icy tingle of apprehension ran up and down his spine as he came to the realization that he was in over his head. Reluctantly, he acknowledged that he'd acted like an amateur. He was lost, and he knew it.

Ben built a lean-to shelter for the night then gathered wood to cook his supper and breakfast. He camped on a small flat area beside a gurgling stream. The water from the tiny brook was so cold it made his teeth ache. This was the most abundantly watered country he had ever seen. Nearly every gully and hollow he'd crossed had had a stream of clear water. The miniature waterways babbled, laughed, and sang as they flashed over and among the mossy rocks.

Full darkness had descended by the time Ben cooked and ate his supper. The night was as dark as pitch, but he eventually picked out a few twinkling stars through the branches of the trees around his campsite. It was very lonely by his flickering fire. The punkies descended upon him at sundown and fairly ate him alive. Ben cursed and swore as he rubbed his hands, face, and neck, vainly trying to rid himself of the winged cannibals. His first night in the Gauley River mountain country was fraught with strange sounds. He slept fitfully, consulting the illuminated dial of his cheap pocket watch every time he woke. As the first grey streaks of dawn heralded the approach of another day, a piercing scream cut through the silence of the slumbering forest. He sat up in his blanket, shaking like a leaf and bathed in cold sweat from head to foot.

Ben listened anxiously, wondering if he had actually heard the blood-chilling scream, or if it had been a figment of his imagination. He didn't have long to wait. Sharp and clear, the scream came again, and his blood became as ice in his veins. Again and again, the agonizing shriek rose in the motionless, predawn air. It came from far up the slope behind his camp. Soon he heard answering cries from a distant ridge. Two somethings were serenading the fading stars. Ben Waters had never, in all his years of roaming the woods, heard a sound like it. They were blood-curdling shrieks of agony most of the time, but they were interspersed with weird mewing sounds. This went on for a full twenty minutes before it died away to a deathlike silence. At last, after what seemed an eternity, full daylight came, and with it the slowly ascending sun. Even with the early morning sun shining in long, slanting shafts through the woodland, Ben was so unnerved that he could hardly cook his breakfast. He fancied he still heard those awful screams. He looked around, half expecting something to confront him.

Thereafter, for nearly a week, the days and nights for Ben Waters were nothing short of nightmare. He tried to find his way through a wood that was as vast as an ocean—up a slope and down the other side, wading streams that were as cold as ice and swift as mill races. Or then again, he might fight his way through a tangled laurel bed. Some of the patches of evergreen were tremendous, literally covering acres. The shrubs grew big, tall, and luxuriant. Its scaly trunks and long, wide, thick leaves of deep green reminded Ben of jungle foliage. Sometimes it took him an hour or more to fight his way through a bed.

On the second day in the Gauley River woods, he began to find ginseng the size and quantity of which he had long dreamed. Many of the ginseng stalks were waist-high. Ben had never seen "seng" stalks with more than four prongs to its top. Now he passed any number of stalks that had five and six prongs on top. At first, he dug up some of the bigger plants. The roots on the five- and six-prong stalks far exceeded any roots he had ever seen. They were old, wrinkled, and notchy, and Ben believed that some weighed close to a pound, just as they come from the ground.

Then, laughing like a madman, he flung the great root from him and plunged through the woods. It was ironic. He had traveled more than a hundred and fifty miles to find woodland of sufficient magnitude to serve his needs. He had found the woods, God, yes. Also, he had found ginseng, the likes of which he had never seen before. Then he had gotten himself completely turned around and panicked. The trip Ben had looked forward to for so long had turned into failure. He would be fortunate to get out with his life, let alone a load of ginseng roots. Waters shook himself and prepared to resume his search for a way out of the woods. Strapping his knapsack on his back, he rose from the mossy rock and continued down the slope.

The seventh day of his wandering saw the end of his food. Towards the middle of that day, he found himself once again in a section where the laurel grew in big patches. Huge sandstone boulders were strewn amongst the laurel beds. Ben had unconsciously picked a place to cross a ridge that was a tremendous natural saddle. Once into the saddle proper, he ran into the biggest laurel bed he'd encountered, but instead of fighting his way through the bed, he followed a game trail that cut through the center of the laurel patch and the saddle. He was very grateful for this. Ben was in no condition to notice his surroundings. He was weak and exhausted and shuffled slowly along, his eyes on the ground most of the time.

Without noticing, he came to a plot of open land, and he decided in a hazy sort of way that he would lean against one of the trees beside the trail and rest for a while. Something, he knew not what, compelled him to observe more closely the tree against which he leaned. When he saw that it was a huge black walnut, he gazed about him in quickening excitement. Back where he had grown up, a black walnut tree was a most welcome sight to a "seng" hunter. Some chemical substance leached from black walnuts enriched the soil. One always found a walnut tree in the center of a particularly rich spot, more often than not accompanied by spicewood bushes, alders, and other vegetation.

Ginseng seemed to like to grow around black walnuts. Ben Waters had found some of the finest "seng" he had ever dug growing strong under black walnuts. Gazing around, he realized he stood near the center of a large grove of walnut trees. He estimated that it embraced two acres or more. It was a natural forest amphitheater, with the branches of the great trees interlocking overhead to form a canopy. Then Ben let his wandering glance drop to the ground. A full minute lapsed before the significance of what he saw registered. It was what every ginseng hunter dreams of finding but never expects to see. The floor of the black walnut grove was covered with wild ginseng. It stood waist high in a solid patch from one edge of the laurel bed to the other.

Hardly believing his eyes, Ben stumbled amongst the big "seng" stalks. Big seed stems with bunches of greenish seeds stuck up above the tops of the stalks. Some of the seed bunches were almost as big as Ben's doubled fist. He was in the presence of a fortune, and in a dim sort of way, he was aware of it. All around him was the answer to his dreams. He had found more ginseng in the center of that laurel bed than he would have thought possible to find in any one patch in the whole state of West Virginia. There were acres of it. Big stuff. God only knew how old and well developed that patch of ginseng was. Thousands and thousands of dollars' worth of roots, and he knew that he would never live to harvest this great discovery or market it. With a laugh that was scarcely more than a croak, Ben stumbled through the black walnut grove. He entered the laurel thicket, and as he passed along the game trail, the evergreen foliage closed behind him, shutting off his view of the walnut grove as completely as if it had never existed. For a moment, the ancient hills had bared one of their treasures, but only for a moment.

Three days later, Ben Waters struck a waterway of goodly proportion that flowed northwest. More dead than alive, he staggered and crawled along its south bank. He had crossed a lot of country since finding the big ginseng bed, and he was delirious. He had been for two days. It was midday. Less than an hour after he struck the stream, he slumped forward onto his face on the narrow game trail that ran along the mountain river. To all appearances, he had reached the end of his trail.

Chapter 3

Alice Randall came out on the front porch of her home and sat down in an old, steer-hide   rocking chair. The chair was very comfortable, despite its age. The young woman rocked slowly back and forth, unconscious of the creaking and groaning of the venerable, homemade rocker.

Alice was twenty years old. She was slightly above average height, with a beautiful face and figure that caught the eye of every eligible young male for miles around. Her lovely features were framed by an abundant mass of wavy, glossy hair that hung low on her shoulders and was as dark as a raven's wing. Her eyes were big, brown, and widely spaced, and they were fixed meditatively on the lofty mountain ridges and domes that surrounded her home.

She mulled over the misfortune that had dogged the Randall family for the past four years. Five years before, her father, Grant Randall, had mortgaged his thousand-acre farm for five thousand dollars. He put the money into cattle and improvements. The first year, by dint of hard work and much scraping and saving, the Randalls paid off half of the lien on their home, with interest. The following year, 1929, the bottom dropped out of all markets.

Since the beginning of the Depression, Grant Randall had been unable to pay a single dollar of the mortgage on his property, or the interest on the loan. Three years before, he had talked the bank president at Richwood into extending the time limit on the mortgage until Oct. 1, 1934, hoping that a miracle would prevent foreclosure. Time was running out, and Alice Randall saw no prospect ahead but the loss of the home she had known since birth. Either that or she could consent to enter into something loathsome beyond words. As she rocked slowly to and fro, she shuddered at what might lay ahead.

Her older brother, Walt, had brought home a little money from time to time, such as he had been able to acquire, but it could not be used to pay off the mortgage. It was immediately eaten up by the expense of keeping a home. Alice, her mother, and her younger sister Lynn had taken care of the housework, the garden, and the canning. While doing so, they had watched the lean years come and go, unable to do anything to better the situation except hope and pray.

She reflected upon all these things, and her thoughts drifted to her father. Grant Randall was a sorry specimen. Financial difficulties were breaking his spirit. Faced with ruin, he had taken a drink. For more than a year now, every time he returned home from a trip into Richwood, the county seat, he was so drunk he could hardly sit in the saddle. In the past six months, her father had fallen under the influence of Jesse Savage, a wealthy businessman of unsavory reputation, with vast holdings around Richwood.

On a few occasions, Savage had driven her father home in his big, low-slung car, and his bold, hard eyes had casually appraised her from head to toe in undisguised admiration and desire. Jess Savage was the most disgusting man she had ever met. He was an ogre. Alice blushed as she recalled him mentally undressing her. She saw him now, in her mind's eye, his stocky figure reared back, riding roughshod over everybody and everything in his way. Savage was overbearing, ungentlemanly, and unscrupulous.

To add to her distaste, Alice had only to recall some of the gossip that had come to her ears concerning his unholy carryings-on. Savage was a bachelor, in his late forties, with plenty of grey at the temples and a reputation for being quite the lady's man. If local gossip could be taken seriously, many married women found his attentions not at all unwelcome.

Ordinarily, Savage would have no bearing upon Alice's future happiness, ten days before, her father told her that Savage now held the mortgage on their home, which was dismaying, but the crowning blow fell when he informed his daughter that Savage had offered to tear up the mortgage in exchange for her hand in marriage.

At first, anger had consumed her, and she lashed out at her father for not knocking the man's block off. He had been indignant at Savage's scheme, but his anger had not swayed Savage. Alice blushed, remembering how her father had pleaded with her to consider his position. The ultimatum had been short and to the point. If her hand were not forthcoming in marriage by the date the mortgage fell due, October 16, 1934, he would demand payment in full of the lien to the last cent, with compounded interest. Otherwise, he would foreclose upon the property and by legal force, if need be, throw the entire Randall family—big, little, old, and young, bag and baggage—right out into the public road.

Alice bowed her head at the thought of how far her father had drifted from the stalwart, upstanding, two-fisted man she remembered. Grand had lost his eldest daughter's respect. He pressed upon her the importance of taking everything into consideration before she flew off the handle and came to a rash decision. After all, he argued, the man was willing to make her his wife. That showed that he wished to do the honorable thing by her. He suggested that she look at the practical side. Forget the wagging tongues and think of the wealth and position that would be hers as Mrs. Jesse Savage. Her father's final argument was that Alice had the means to put an end to all the financial difficulties that had harassed the Randalls for the past four years.

Since that talk days before, Alice had kept this new development bottled up inside her. Her mother, sister, and brother were unaware of Savage's intervention in the Randall family fortune, but as days went by, the burden of her problem began to weigh heavily upon her. She needed someone to confide her troubles to. Who would understand and sympathize? Alice ruled out confiding in her mother or her brother Walt. She knew from experience that her mother might disagree with her father at first, but in the end, he would convert her. Her mother was a good woman, but Beatrice Randall was brought up to accept any decision made by her husband. It was futile to expect her mother to brush aside a lifetime of training and obedience.

Alice also knew what to expect from Walt Randall. Her brother was twenty-three years old. He was tall and strong, with light hair, blue eyes, and a fiery temper. Walt Randall was fond of his beautiful sister, and he would rip off a string of blistering oaths, call Jess Savage every name he could lay his tongue to, then saddle his mare and ride hell-bent for Richwood to confront Savage. The result would be a knockdown, drag-out fight. Therefore, Alice kept Jess Savage's unscrupulous plan from him. The situation was bad enough without her brother landing in jail on an assault and battery charge.

This left only her younger sister, Lynn. Of the three, Alice could most put trust in her to share her problems without fear of consequences. The afternoon was perfect for a walk in the woods. Why not coax her sister into a long walk? She would take Lynn into her confidence. With this resolution, Alice rose from the ancient rocker and went to search for her sister.

The Randall home was one of the oldest dwellings in Nicholas County. It was a massive, sprawling affair of hewed legs, stone, and mortar, built by Preston Randall, her great grandfather, nearly a century before. It stood atop a beautiful knoll that was situated on the banks of the Cranberry River. When he settled on the Cranberry, Preston purchased a thousand acres of virgin timberland for the ridiculously low price of a dollar and a half per acre. In those days, the headwaters of Gauley River, of which the Cranberry was a branch, was a howling wilderness. It was to this country that Preston Randall brought his bride and built his home.

As the seasons came and went, the hardy settler slowly cleared a good portion of the forest, and he became pioneer, hunter, farmer, and the father of two sons. At the beginning of the War Between the States, both of Preston Randall's sons shouldered arms and marched away to war. Only one returned. Morgan Randall passed on at Gettysburg without leaving on heir. Five years after his return from war, Frank Randall took unto himself a wife. He brought his bride to the sprawling log home on the banks of the Cranberry. And in the strange way fate has of following a pattern, two sons were born of his union, also.

In 1886, Preston Randall went the way of all on this earth. He had seen more than four score of years roll over his head. He was old and very tired the cold winter night that the grim reaper knocked at his door. A year later, his wife followed him in death. With the passing of his parents, Frank Randall became the sole owner of the thousand-acre homestead. In time, his two sons, Grant and Marion, grew to manhood. At the call for volunteers at the onset of the Spanish-American conflict, they also stepped forward to serve their country. Again, war took its toll on the Randalls. Grant marched back to his home on the Cranberry alone. His brother Marion had fallen victim to malaria in Panama. Here again, history repeated itself. Marion Randall died a bachelor.

During the very early years of the twentieth century, another bride came to reign in the old log homestead. To the union of Grant Randall and his wife were born three children—Walter, Alice, and Lynn. Originally, the Randall holding had embraced a thousand acres of virgin timberland. Except for two hundred acres that had been cleared during Preston Randall's life, the original stand of timber remained intact until shortly after the close of the Spanish-American War. Prices skyrocketed in nearly everything, and timber followed suit.

Frank Randall decided that he would take advantage of the high price for timber and sold every stick of timber he owned to a big eastern concern. The timber deal caused his death. The trusting old backwoods farmer had been taken in by a gang of timber sharks. Acre by acre, they slaughtered his woods, and he received a pittance of the amount originally stipulated.

Thinking to recover his loss through the courts, Randall brought legal action against the company. His return was a worthless judgement. The timber company went into bankruptcy the week before his case against them came to trial. The money he was paid on his timber was eaten up by court costs and attorney fees. He still had his thousand acres, but Frank Randall went to his grave a land-poor man.

It was a sort of religion with Grant Randall to stay clear of debt. Conditions were not always easy for him and his wife as they brought up their three children. Though it was slim pickings sometimes, he always managed to get by and keep the homestead free of encumbrances. True, he had inherited a thousand acres. However, three-fourths of the land lay in shambles. More than seven hundred acres were laid waste in the wake of the timber butchers. In places, it had been cut in so thickly that a rabbit would have had trouble crawling through it. At first, the wasteland was covered in immense blackberry patches. Gradually, as the years passed, the briars gave way to a host of seedlings. A brand new stand of timber was on its way.

After the Great War with Germany, prices boomed again. For more than nine years, Randall ran his farm with a conservative hand. Eventually, as is human nature, he became fed up with sitting on the sidelines, watching other fellows make money while he just squeezed by. He had the land. All he needed was a few thousand dollars to stock his place. With that and the new stand of timber that would be ready to market in a few years, he was in a position to safely borrow money.

Grant Randall wasted no time. In 1928, he mortgaged the old homestead for five thousand dollars. One year later, the bottom dropped out of everything. Things seemed to go from bad to worse. Now they were at the mercy of an unscrupulous scoundrel. Truly, the Randall household had fallen upon evil days.

Chapter 4

*T*he interior of the Randall home was furnished in a rustic fashion. Much of the furniture was home made. The rooms were large and airy. Several deer heads hung on the walls of the huge living room. The dominant piece was a magnificent elk head with great, spreading antlers, upon which a number of long guns hung. It had been mounted above the stone mantle of the yawning fireplace by Preston Randall shortly after he settled on the Cranberry.

The elk head was beginning to show the ravages of time. It was faded and full of dust. And to add to its unsightly appearance, several spots had lost hair. However, despite its decrepit appearance, the Randalls would not part with it. It had assumed the proportions of a family heirloom, and they looked beyond its unsightly appearance.

Alice found her sister in the kitchen, helping their mother do the dinner dishes. She waved a soapy hand at Alice. "Hi, there, Ally. You're just in time to pitch in with the dishes. What say?"

"It's a deal, Lynn," Alice replied, "providing you'll take stroll up the river with me after we're through. Would you mind, Mom?"

"Go ahead, girls. I don't care," replied Mrs. Randall, a tall, spare woman in her middle fifties. Her hair was almost totally gray. The tired eyes were big and dark, and the faded features bespoke a beauty that had long since fled. One look at the mother was sufficient to determine where Alice had gotten her good looks. She was a replica of what her mother thirty years before.

Lynn Randall was seventeen. She was a tomboyish, long-legged girl with the coloring of her Randall ancestors. Her hair was blond, and her eyes were sky-blue. She was a finely chiseled beauty with a saucy pertness that spelled distraction to every teenage boy for miles around. Lynn was as tall as Alice was, but her figure was not as well rounded. At the moment, she was wearing a pair of faded blue jeans and an   old, white blouse. Her jeans were rolled up halfway to her knees, displaying her trim ankles and well-shaped feet. She was washing the dinner dishes, and Mrs. Randall was drying them. Wiping the suds from her arms and hands, she turned and cast a mischievous glance at Alice.

"Sure, sis. We'll take a little stroll up the old Cranberry," she laughed. "I'll bet you want my opinion of them two moon-eyed ginks Walt bought home with him from Holcomb last night."

"Could be you're on the right track," Alice answered dryly. "I'll say this. You'll probably know one way or the other before we get back." Turning to her mother, she took the drying cloth Mrs. Randall had been using. "Mom, go out on the front porch and take it easy. Me and Lynn'll soon wrap these dishes up. Don't you worry. We'll get back in plenty of time to do the chores and have supper on the table by the time Dad and Walt get home. We won't be gone long."

"All right, girls," Mrs. Randall said as she began walking through the house towards the front porch. "Don't forget what your pa always told you kids when you went for a walk in the woods. Put on your shoes. Both of you. Don't you dare let me ever catch either of you girls traipsing off into the woods barefoot. There's plenty of rattlers in these here woods. Stay out of the river. I know it's almost July, but the water in the Cranberry is still too cold for wading or messing around in. It has too many big springs feeding it."

Both girls assured their mother that they would be very careful on their stroll.

"Another thing, girls," Mrs. Randall added. "Take a couple of Walt's good-for-nothing hounds along. You never can tell. Them lazy mutts might come in handy one of these days for something besides keeping bread from spoiling. A person never can tell. They might surprise us after all."

Flying into the dishes, the two sisters had them done in no time. They went into the huge bedroom they shared and put on heavy shoes that looked much worse for wear. Alice pulled on a pair of her brother's overalls and turned up the cuffs several times. They donned wide-brimmed straw hats and were on their way, waving to their mother as they whistled for the dogs. Two long-eared, lazy looking hounds came loping around the house. In a twinkling, the sisters and the dogs had quitted the yard and were walking along a path that led up-river.

The Cranberry River was practically identical to other watercourses in that part of the mountain country. However, there was a considerable drop to its drainage all along its length. Most of the time, it ran as a gurgling, roaring riffle. Occasionally, though, one came to pools of considerable size and depth, where the water swirled and eddied, leaving a trail of foam along the banks. The waters of the Cranberry were light amber, but perfectly clear in every respect. Due to certain conditions in the mountain country, the waters that drained out of the vast timberlands were stained or colored by rotting logs, decaying leaves, and the immense laurel beds through which they had to filter. The waters of the Cranberry were no exception.

A few minutes after leaving the house, Alice and Lynn entered the woods, the hounds loping ahead. Lynn began plying her older sister with questions. At first, Alice was non-committal. Maybe she shouldn't tell her sister of her troubles, but she was miserable, and misery loves company.

"Lynn, I didn't ask you out for a walk just to gab about some moon-eyed fellow."

"Oh, no?"

"No."

"What did you want to talk about then? Don't tell me you needed the exercise."

"No, honey," Alice said. "It wasn't exercise I needed. It goes much deeper than that. What I want to tell you is of grave importance to all of us."

"See here, Alice," Lynn said, stopping in the footpath and throwing an arm around her older sister's waist. "Why so mysterious? Out with it. You and me never keep things from each other. You're worried about something. Otherwise, you wouldn't look and act so spooked."

"Okay, here goes, but I warn you. Hold onto your straw hat. No, let's not sit down. I can't explain, but I think I'd feel better if I was on the move while I get this off my chest."

"Boy, you are a mysterious one. Never mind, we'll walk. Anything you say, sis. Only spill it. You've got me on pins and needles."

"Well, you know how Dad's in debt on our home?"

"Sure, but what's that got to do with the bad news that's got your hip pockets dipping sand? That ain't news to me. You'll have to do better than that to get me excited."

"Just hold your horses, girl. Don't be so impatient. I'm coming to the details. The mortgage is what this deal hinges on. The mortgage and the interest are due next October 16. This debt is driving Dad into an early grave. He was always careful with money. He didn't believe in going into debt for anything. It seems downright unfair that the first time Dad went into debt to try to better himself, the bottom dropped out of everything. Anyways, the bank at Richwood gave Dad the loan and took a mortgage out on our home."

"I know all this," Lynn said impatiently. "Let me have the bad news. Stop beating around the bush."

"All right, all right, I was leading up to it. Ten days ago, I learned that the mortgage on our home has changed hands."

"Changed hands?" Lynn repeated. "I don't understand. Explain yourself, Allie."

"Somebody bought the mortgage on our home from the bank. That lets the bank out. From now on, Dad will have to deal with the new owner of the mortgage. Understand?"

"Perfectly. Who is the two-legged rat that'd pull off a cute little trick like that?"

"Jess Savage," Alice answered.

Lynn Randall jumped, as if stung. Whirling around, she faced Alice in blazing wrath.

"Jess Savage? What the hell does that sneaking woman-chaser want? He has more than enough property in Richwood to keep him busy. I don't get it. Are you sure you got this straight, Allie?"

"I got it straight, all right," Alice assured her.

"Are you sure someone wasn't pulling your leg? Say as a big joke?"

"It couldn't have come any straighter."

"I still don't believe it," Lynn maintained. "The bank at Richwood wouldn't sell Dad out. Us Randalls are one of the oldest families around. I just don't believe it. Who fed you this beautiful cock and bull story?"

"All right, Lynnie. Here it comes, and with both barrels. Remember what I said about holding onto your hat. I heard it ten days ago, from our father."

"Dad told you?"

"That's exactly right," Alice said. "Dad came out to the pasture one evening last week when I was milking the cows and told me."

"That means that from now on, we'll be dealing with Jess Savage?"

"That's the situation in a nut shell," said Alice.

"Well, I'll be lop-eared son-of-a-bitch," Lynn swore.

"Lynnie! Such language," Alice cried, aghast. "Honestly, sis, the way you cuss anymore, I'm positively ashamed of you. It ain't a bit ladylike."

Though Alice scolded her younger sister, she couldn't help but admire her fiery spirit. It was a well-known fact around the Randall household that when the occasion so demanded, little Lynn could cuss with the best of them. Her vocabulary would have put to shame a veteran streetwalker. Alice often wondered where she'd picked up all the spicy language.

"Sorry, Ally." Lynn shrugged. "I didn't mean to curl your hair, but that's the way I feel right now. When the mortgage on our home comes due next time, we'll be up shit creek without a paddle, unless we're prepared to fork over better than three thousand dollars. I hate to say this, sis, but we don't stand a China man's chance of having that kind of money. Looks like us Randalls have really hit a snag this time. You can bet your sweet life that our dear friend Jess Savage has that all figured out. Oh, he's the foxy type. It ain't no secret to him how hard times have been for people in debt these last four years. It's been plenty tough just getting by, let alone paying off a mortgage. I'm willing to lay you two to one odds that before this mortgage deal is over, Jess Savage will come up with one of them underhanded deals he's so well known for."

"He already has," Alice answered miserably.

Lynn threw back her head and gave a mirthless laugh. "Ha, ha. Well, I must say, our esteemed friend didn't waste any time. Did Dad tell you all this, too?"

"He did," said Alice.

"It seems mighty strange that Dad would blab all this to you and not whisper a single word to the rest of his family. That's not like him at all."

"Well, that's how it was."

"Seeing that you're the only one of us that's in our father's confidence, maybe I ought not ask too many questions, but I'm going to ask them, never fear. Now look, Ally. What say we come clean? You're holding out again. If that's the way you want it, go right ahead. I'm getting damn good and tired of your hemming, hawing, and beating around the bush. Spit out what's got you walking bowlegged, or I'm turning around right here and heading for home."

Alice sank down on an old log by the footpath, covered her face with her hands, and burst into tears. Lynn looked down at her sister, stunned. She had never seen Alice like this. This must be more serious than she suspected. Could Alice be making mountains out of molehills? Things were not nearly as bad as they sometimes seemed. Jess Savage was at the bottom of all this, of that she positive. The man was a rascal. From all the reports, the crummier the deal he could pull off, the better it suited him.

Someday the wind would shift. It always did. She knelt by her sister's side and tried to comfort her.

"Ally, Ally. Please stop crying. I didn't mean to hurt your feelings. I'm sorry I was nasty. I'm not mad at you at all. I only want to help, but I can't do a thing unless you trust me. Buck up, sis. We'll face whatever it is together, but you have to tell me what that brigand offered Dad. You ain't said so yet, but that must be what's got you so down in the dumps. Please stop crying and tell me all about it. I'll help you any way I can."

Alice's sobbing slowed, she raised a tear-stained face, and with a halfhearted smile, she rose to her feet. "Lynnie," she said, wiping away her tears. "Forgive me for breaking down. Ever since Dad and I had that talk, I hardly know whether I'm coming or going. Please, be patient. I'll tell you everything, but I was so shocked and hurt."

"Atta girl, sis," Lynn said. "Get it off your chest. I'm on your side all the way. It really doesn't matter what kind of a scheme Jess Savage talked Dad into. You and I don't have to live up to it. Our father ain't himself anymore. He worries and drinks too much. Never mind that now. Let's sit down right here on this old log and have this thing out in the open."

"No, Lynnie," Alice replied. "I'm not in any mood to tell you this sitting down. Let's walk on up the river."

"Maybe we better start back," Lynn said. "Up ahead the river forks and we ain't ever been farther up than that. Dad told us to never go beyond the forks. Remember all them tales about people getting lost in the woods? Walt says them tales are true. Not long ago, he told me that these woods were the biggest in the state. Better than fifty miles wide in places, he claimed. I think we better be heading back. Mom might get worried if we're gone much longer."

"We'll not be gone that long," Alice assured her. "I don't care if Dad did tell us never to go beyond the forks. I'm in no mood to turn back now. Of late, I've begun to think that our father's advice ain't so hot. I bet when you hear my news, you'll think so, too. So let's be reckless and walk up the right-hand branch a-ways. I'll tell you the good news as we go."

Chapter 5

The two Randall sisters strolled further up the Cranberry River than they had ever gone   before that bright afternoon in late June 1933. When they came to where the river forked, they turned onto a narrow game trail that ran along the south bank of the right-hand branch. The two hounds swung onto the trail ahead of them as Alice began.

"Sis," she said, in a voice fraught with shame and misery. "You might as well hear it from me, because it's bound to come out into the open sooner or later. To make it short and sweet, he offered to tear up the mortgage on one condition."

Lynn sighed. "That sounds like our Mister Savage. What was   the condition? I'll bet it's a lulu."

"It is that," Alice said. "He told Dad that he would tear up the mortgage if I became his wife. What do you think of that?"

Placing a hand on each of her trim hips, Lynn gave vent to several of her most shocking expressions as she whirled around and faced Alice on the narrow trail. For once, Alice didn't scold as her younger sister stomped around, fumed, and cussed.

"Ally, I'm so mad I can hardly talk," she said at last from between clenched teeth. "The very idea. No wonder you've been so down in the dumps lately. I must have been blind these last few days, or I would've noticed how worried you've been. Talk about brass. Why, compared to that no-good, a brass monkey would look like a cast iron pig. I'd like to be a big, strong man for just ten minutes and have that bastard right here in the woods with us. It'd be a pleasure to kick his dirty, stinking rear end clear between his shoulders. Don't think I wouldn't do it. If I ever had the opportunity, what a pleasure that would give me."

"I know, sis, I know," Alice agreed. "I feel the same way, but we're only a couple of girls. Honey, I've still got the worst part of this ugly mess to tell you."

"Out with it, Ally," cried her younger sister with blazing eyes. "I've a sickly feeling in the pit of my stomach that I've already guessed the worst part, but I want to hear it from your own lips."

"Here is the hardest part of the whole dirty deal," Alice said, a wretched look on her beautiful face. "I'd rather take a beating than have to tell you this, but it's gospel truth, I'm ashamed to say. When Dad told me about Savage buying our mortgage and his proposition, I blew my top. Dad just stood there and looked so miserable that I felt like crying. I raked him over the coals for not knocking Jess's block off. Dad said that he tried to stand up to Savage, but Savage laid down an ultimatum. He told Dad that if I didn't marry him before the lien was due, he would demand payment in full to the last cent or throw us out of our home, lock, stock, and barrel."

"He would, too, Alice, and enjoy every minute of it," growled her younger sister.

"There's more to tell, and it's the worst of all," Alice admitted. "Dad tells me I'd be doing the family a favor by marrying Jess Savage. Lynnie, I nearly fell off the milking stool. He even pointed out the advantages that would be mine as Mrs. Jesse Savage. That rendered me speechless, and I ain't much better yet. Sis, it's an awful thing for a father to save his fortune at the expense of his daughter's womanhood. It's like being sold on a block."

"Honestly, sis, I don't know what to say," said Lynn. "This has knocked the wind out of yours truly. It's an ugly mess. Dad's really got me buffaloed. He ain't the father that we used to know, not by a long shot. He'd have knocked Jess Savage out the minute he opened his yap."

"Maybe the moonshine he's been swilling so much of lately has undermined his principles," Alice suggested. "I'll bet that's it. That and the fear that he's going to lose the old homestead."

"I believe you're right, sis," Lynn conceded. "I can't think of anything else. Have you said anything to Mom or Walt yet?"

"Not a word. I'm not going to tell them till I have to. Walt would explode like a stick of dynamite and get himself into trouble. As for Mother, well, she would bounce Dad about it, I know, but in the end, he would overrule any argument and bring her around to his way of thinking. I've studied this from all angles, and I feel that best bet is to sit tight and keep mum."

"Okay, sis. I'm with you till the cows come home with bulls on their backs. We'll sit tight and keep our traps shut. Maybe a miracle will happen. Like Jess Savage taking poison, for instance. We'll work something out. It's a long time till October16, 1934. If we can't do any better, you and I can hit the road. I'll be nineteen by then."

"Hush, child. Leaving home is the last resort. I'm not sure what I'll do when pinch comes. I'll have to wait and see. I owe something to my parents for the sacrifices they've made for me."

"Us kids owe Mother and Dad something for their sacrifices, and I'm willing to do all I can for them, but when it comes to a deal like the one Jess Savage proposes, I draw the line. If we're going to lose our home, wouldn't it be better to step away from it as a family rather than knuckle under to something that would cost us our pride?"

"Of course it would, Lynnie," Alice agreed. "But try and tell that to our father. He's old and scared, and feels that if we don't meet these terms, he'll lose everything he's worked for all his life. Dad has closed his eyes to the kind of man he's asking me to marry. Jess Savage is old enough to be my father. That is bad enough, but compared to his reputation as a woman chaser, his age is of secondary importance. If all we've heard about is true, I'll bet there's a dozen married men around Richwood that he's made cuckolds of. Just think how excited and proud I'd be to call him my husband. How wonderful it would be on my wedding night to strip off my clothes and creep into his eager, waiting arms. Wouldn't that be a beautiful moment? After one hour in that slimy rat's arms, I don't think I'd ever feel clean again."

"Ugh," Lynn said. "The thought makes me gag. I'd just as soon kiss a snake as have him lay a dirty paw on any part of my body. I'd rather mate with an ape than become his wife. But enough of this. We'll face it together, just you and me, no matter what comes. What say we head for home? It's getting late. We've walked up this branch at least a mile. I don't relish going any farther. It's getting wild looking. I'll whistle for the dogs."

Alice nodded. Throwing back her head, Lynn pursed her lips in a shrill whistle. Just then, the dogs set up a clamor around a bend in the stream ahead. The two girls looked at each other in a fright. For a moment, they debated turning and running, thinking that the dogs had surprised a mother bear and her cubs. Each knew that anything could happen, and flight was the wisest decision to make, but they didn't hear the sounds of a fight or chase. The baying hounds seemed stationary. Maybe the dogs had run onto a rattlesnake. If so, they had to investigate before one of the hounds ventured too close and got bit. They summoned their courage and cautiously started upstream.

The sisters rounded the bend, their eyes darting here and there, expecting to see they knew not what. They breathed easier when no raging mother bear confronted them. Everywhere they looked was only the peaceful forest. After a moment, they spotted the dogs in the trail about fifty yards ahead. The girls called and whistled, but the hounds pointed their muzzles skyward and gave long, drawn out howls, their attention centered on something on the trail beyond them.

Alice and Lynn stepped hesitantly forward, Alice ahead of her sister by a good five paces. When they were fifty feet from the dogs, Alice turned to her sister with bulging eyes.

"Good lord, Lynnie," she gasped. "There's somebody lying in the trail up there."

"A dead man, by all that's holy," Lynn said, standing on tiptoe and straining her eyes to better see the figure in the trail ahead. "Ally, let's head home and report this. Dad and Walt should be home in a little while. We'll let them come up here and investigate. I ain't got no stomach for looking over a corpse."

"No, Lynnie," Alice said firmly. "I'm going to see if he is alive before we head home. Maybe he is alive, but badly hurt and in need of help. Come on. Let's go see."

"I'm scared stiff," Lynn replied in a shaky whisper.

"Then stay here. I'm going to see if anything can be done for him."

Alice strode to the side of the man on the trail. The dogs whined and moved to one side. Lynn followed slowly. As Alice bent down for a better look at the haggard, bearded face, the man moaned and stirred. Then he opened his eyes. They were bloodshot and vacant. She sprang to her feet and turned to her sister standing a dozen feet away.

"Lynnie," she cried excitedly. "It's a young man. He's alive, but in bad shape. He needs help. Come and look at him."

In an instant, Lynn was at her side. She bent down and looked at the man at her feet.

Alice said, "Lynnie, I'll stay here. Take one of the dogs and go for help. Don't be afraid. Everything will be all right. Bring help as quickly as you can. He looks starved to death."

"Right, Ally," Lynn cried. "I'm not afraid anymore. I'll go for help and bring it quick or bust a gut trying. We'll save this man's life or know the reason why. He's come into our lives when we was in dire need of a friend. Yes, I'll help, and then we'll take him home and nurse him back to health. By the good Lord above, I've the strangest feeling about this man. Something tells me that the day will come when he'll throw a monkey wrench into Jess Savage's rotten scheme."

Chapter 6

*B*en Waters looked at the sisters with a speculative eye. He was hard put to remember when he had looked upon two more pleasing specimens of young womanhood. Each sister was as pretty as a picture, and though the older one possessed the more rounded figure, he knew that underneath her gingham dress, the younger sister hid a surprising lot of femininity. She was much more slender than her older sister, with a winsomeness that was pleasing to behold.

Ben mentally undressed them, envisioning the proud thrust of their well-developed breasts and the satiny smoothness of their skin. He imagined the exciting way their lovely bodies tapered down to delightfully slim waists, sweeping out and down in the rounded loveliness of hips and thighs. Ben had no difficulty imagining their dimpled navels or the tangled mats that cloaked their loins.

At the onset of his employment on the river, the ways and doings of his fellow workers while ashore had jarred upon him. As time wore on and he tasted of the relaxed love life in the river towns, he changed his views toward women. He found, after bitter disappointments and hard knocks, that he was a far happier man when he took the fair sex as they really were, and not as he would have them be.

In time, Ben Waters changed from an inexperienced farm boy to a man well versed in the intrinsic mysteries of womanhood. He could tell at almost the first glance whether a woman was on the make and whether it would be worth his time trying to roll her. All he needed was a certain gleam in her eyes. Be that as it may, Ben hoped to put his best foot forward in his relationship with the sisters. Maybe mountain women were different from women he had known in the past. Maybe they had a stricter code of honor. He hoped so. Time would tell.

At the moment, he was sitting on the edge of the front porch of the Randall home. A month had lapsed since the sisters found him in the woods up the Cranberry. With the help of their brother Walt and a neighbor, they had brought him home, more dead than alive. For ten days, his life had hung by a thread. Then he began to mend. His recovery was slow, but with each passing day, he came closer to his former good health.

He had been up and around for three days, but he was still shaky and weak. He had begun to sleep and eat well, and the tide of his recovery was fast turning in his favor. At first, after he was brought to the Randall home, he thought he was still lost in the woods. During such moments, he raved and carried on like insane person. As he improved, this condition subsided until the fear of being lost faded even from his dreams.

A week later, he dictated a letter to his folks and one to the man at Marlinton, who was keeping his touring car for him. Alice wrote the letters for him. In the one to his folks, he told of his close brush with death, and then added that they shouldn't worry because he was in the best hands and on his way to recovery. As to when he would come home, he wrote that he would let them know for sure about that later.

Ben refrained from mentioning the patch of ginseng. He was afraid they might think it a figment of his imagination. Ben had come too close to death to appreciate any jokes about what he had seen in the forest. Even now, he found it difficult to grasp the vastness of West Virginia's mountain woodlands. They were colossal and terrifying, even to a seasoned woodsman. The woods had won the first round. In the future, he vowed to take every precaution.

Grant Randall and his wife extended to Ben the hospitality of their home, a gesture typical of mountain families, if all the reports he had heard were authentic. However, aside from his initial welcome, Randall ignored him. Randall was tall and broad, but there was a gauntness about the man's frame and features that did not speak well of his health. He brooded. More than once, Ben saw him standing and staring out across his mountain domain with a haunted look in his eyes. Trying not to seem conspicuously curious, Ben asked Alice if her father was worried about something. She looked at him a moment, as though debating her answer. Then, with a sad smile touching the corners of her lovely lips, she informed him that her father was worrying himself into an early grave because of the mortgage hanging over their home.

Since then, Ben had been thinking. Now, as he gazed upon the Randall sisters, a plan was beginning to form. He hoped to be able to help the good people who had saved his life.

"Well, girls," he inquired. "How do I look today?"

"Better all the time," they laughed, coming over and seating themselves on the porch steps.

"I take it then that you hold out hope of my recovery."

"That's right," they assured him with big smiles on their faces. "We're afraid now that you're really going to live."

"Is that good or bad?" he asked with twinkling eyes.

"In some cases, I'd have to say that that would be very bad," Lynn replied merrily. "However, in your case, I believe it's going to be good."

"What do you think, Alice?" Ben asked the older sister, who was regarding him with a thoughtful look in her big brown eyes. "Do you agree with Lynn?"

"Yes, I do, Ben," she answered. "It's good to see you on the way to recovery. I hope you never have such an experience again. Next time, you might not be so lucky."

"That's right," Ben agreed. "Anyway, girls, thanks a lot for your kind words and well wishes. You make me feel good inside. Them old hills sure gave yours truly a mighty nice working over. I was more than lucky to get out with my life. If you girls hadn't found me when you did, I wouldn't be sitting here talking to you. The next time I go in, I'll know what to expect. I hope this first bad go won't scare me out. How far is it through these woods to Marlinton?"

"It's a good fifty miles by road, going by the way of Richwood," Alice said. "Through the woods, up and down over them awful ridges, I expect it's at least that far. Maybe farther. Why do you ask?"

"Marlinton was my jumping-off place when I entered the woods," he said. "That little town seems clean across on the other side of the world from us here."

"Well, it is a heck of a ways off," Lynn laughed. "Ben, we ain't wanting to appear nosey or meddling, but ever since that day we found you, I've been awful curious as to what you was doing in them woods all by yourself. Come clean. Are you running from the law?"

"Certainly not," Ben said. "I'm definitely not on the dodge. I went into them woods to look for ginseng."

"Did you find any?"

"Yes, quite a lot in spots," he replied. "But I was lost when I found it, so I just kept right on walking."

"Dad and Walt used to dig some seng," Alice said. "That was a few years back, as I remember. Seng seems scarce around here. They never did find much. Not enough to pay for their time and trouble. Is that why you were in these woods, and why you came out here from Wood County?"

"That's right," Ben said. "I hunted seng a lot in the woods back home, and I did real well at it. In the past four years, work has been scarce, so I turned back to my boyhood activity. I hit some pretty big woods back there, but they were rabbit patches compared to the woods here. These woods are endless."

"How come you quit hunting roots at home and come way out here if you was doing so well?" Lynn asked.

"Because I wasn't doing as well as I wanted," was his reply. "I figured if I could get into vast woodlands, I could find seng as I'd always dreamed of finding it. Dad suggested this part of the country, so here I am."

"I suppose when you're feeling yourself again, you'll go flittin back home and give your seng digging idea up as a wild goose chase?" Alice asked, looking him squarely in the eye. Her lovely features had gone pale. Ben returned her gaze and tried to read what was going on in the mind behind those wide-spaced eyes. After a moment, she smiled and dropped her gaze to the flagstone walk.

"No," he replied, leaning back against one of the porch posts. "I've plans up my sleeve that don't include giving my seng digging up."

"Glad to hear it," Lynn said. "That's the spirit. Never say die. Have you always been a root hunter?"

"Not always."

"What else have you done?" Alice asked.

"I've farmed most of my life," he answered. "For three years, I was a helper on a packet boat that made runs from New Orleans to Pittsburgh. When the Depression struck, I was out of a job."

"So you've worked on the Mississippi River?" Lynn asked with shining eyes. As Ben had expected, the mention of work on the river spelled romance to her young heart. He laughed aloud.

"Yes, I have," he said casually. A riverboat, and all those far-off southern cities were ample material for the imaginations of young women, and the Randall sisters were no exceptions.

"Did the boat you worked on tie up at any of them wicked river towns?" Alice asked.

"All of them," he grinned.

"Did you men spend the evening in town?"

"Every man able to navigate went ashore every chance he got," Ben replied, but as innocent as his act was, he knew exactly what the sisters were dying to ask him. He smiled and continued to play dumb. Experience told him that feminine curiosity would not let the doubt in their minds go unsatisfied for long.

"We did anything we could find to do in the way of entertainment," Ben answered. He looked at Lynn. She had gotten up from the porch step and moved to within arm's reach. A broad, provocative smile wreathed her face.

"Would much of the entertainment you men were looking for in those towns include girls?" she asked boldly. Alice was silent, but she was keen to hear his answer.

"Could be, Lynnie." Ben grinned at her. "You girls can make an evening a lot more pleasant for us men."

"Uh-huh, I see what you mean," she replied. "Are those Southern girls pretty?"

"Pretty as picture."

"Ever meet up with any of them Creole girls down there in New Orleans?"

"Sure. Almost every time we hit old New Orleans."

"How are they for looks?"

"You'll pardon me for saying this, Lynnie," he said, "but you asked for the truth. I seen thousands of pretty girls during the three years I worked on the river, but the Creole girls of Louisiana walked off with the cake every time. Those babes could really knock your eyes out. Mmmm-boy. Ha, ha."

Alice and Lynn joined in, and then Lynn gave him a measuring, calculating look. "Were these Southern beauties easy to meet?"

"In some cases, yes, while in other cases no," he said. Turning his head, he looked at Alice and winked broadly.

Lynn barged ahead, determined not to be outdone. "Mr. Waters, did you find them attractive?"

"Oh, naturally," he laughed.

"To what extent?" she asked.

At this bold query, Ben realized that Lynn had all the earmarks of being completely uninhibited. She wanted to know if he had had sexual relations with the girls that he'd met in the river towns. To hell with beating around the bush. Women loved a direct answer.

"Ben, quit daydreaming," Lynn prodded. "I asked you a question."

"I was just thinking that you girls might get a bad opinion of me if I tell too much of my past life. Can't I just act as if I didn't hear your question?"

"Definitely not," Lynn said in mock anger. "You've been with us a month, but you're still a stranger. Alice and I are innocent country girls. I think we should know if we've a wolf in our midst. Don't you agree?"

"Oh, sure, sure," Ben replied. "Far be it from me to take   advantage of innocent girls, though. That ain't my racket. Fire away. I hope my escapades don't shock you girls. Now, about them Creole girls and others I met up with in them river towns."

"Yes, yes," Lynn prompted.

"I'll say this," Ben continued. "I never let any of them suffer when they were around me. Does that answer your questions?"

"Perfectly."

"Satisfied?"

"Yes, siree," Lynn grinned. "You and them Southern belles made whoopee every chance you got."

With a merry laugh, she shook her right leg in a tantalizing manner. Her round hips rolled like those of a burlesque dancer. With another trilling laugh, she shook her upper body until her full breasts quivered and surged, fighting the confinement of her dress.

Ben gazed at her, spellbound. He was positive she was a virgin, yet she was performing like the sexiest kind of a bump and grind artist. Though young and innocent, Lynn Randall knew just what the facts of life were. Her demonstration was sensational. When Ben had worked on the river, that sort of thing had been old hat, but he could not remember when he had seen it presented with more zest, abandon, and enjoyment.

Eventually, Lynn brought to a climax her wiggling, rolling hips, and quivering, vibrating breasts. She threw back her blonde head, and snapped her hips forwards and up. She laughed at the blank look on her older sister's face, and the wiles of Satan shone forth in her sparkling blue eyes. Lynn was in her late teens, but she was a woman, a beautiful, young, vibrantly alive woman, who would never permit her desires to be hampered by conventional behavior.

As he watched her wiggle and shake for his approval, he divined that he was slated to teach Lynn Randall the facts of life. He had hoped to put that wild phase behind him. Now he wasn't sure he could. Oh, well, to hell with it. Ben was a fatalist. He believed that whatever was to be would be. No man could change fate, and there was no need to try.

"Lynn Randall," Alice said severely. "What a way to act. What a shameful, disgraceful spectacle to make of yourself. Surely, you're ashamed of yourself. I know I am. After such an exhibition, I feel like hiding my face. It wasn't a bit nice."

"Aw, hell, Ally," Lynn laughed merrily. "Loosen up a bit and enjoy life while you're still in the pink. It was only in fun. I'm sorry if I shocked you. After Ben told us how beautiful and desirable them Deep South girls were I couldn't resist shaking it up a bit. I'm not one to take a back seat to any female, regardless of how well she's stacked or able to present her charms."

"Okay, okay," Alice replied, exasperated. "So you're a ravaging blonde that no man will be able to resist once you've debuted. I say bunk and boloney. Dad would blister your rear end if he ever seen you shaking around like that."

"All right, sis," Lynn said. "In the future, I'll keep my foolishness under my hat. Ben, how did you like my presentation?"

"Lynnie," he said sincerely. "I think it was put over with real class. I couldn't have enjoyed it more if I'd have bought a ticket to see it. You've got it, kid, that's all I can say. You've sure enough got it."

"I can't see anything to get excited about," Alice said flatly, an indignant look in her big eyes.

"I reckon that depends on how you look at that sort of thing. In all fairness, though, your sister has as much class and intrigue, as any I've ever seen. I'm sure that ain't the point Lynn wanted to make. She simply wanted to show me that a nice country girl possesses all the talents them burlesque queens put so much store in and she put her point across very well."

"I might have known that you'd take up for her after that disgraceful spectacle," Alice said with flashing eyes. "You're a man, and I ain't never yet met a man who didn't enjoy seeing a pretty young thing wiggle and twist. You men are all alike."

"I plead guilty, Alice." Ben laughed as he winked at Lynn, who had an impish grin on her face. "Watching them parade their charms is a weakness all men have. It's that way with us from the youngest, right on up to the very oldest. We can't help ourselves. Alice, the good lord planted the appreciation of a beautiful woman in the hearts of all men when he created Adam, and it's been there ever since. Who am I to fight such a thing?"

"Ben Waters, you're impossible," Alice answered severely, though there was a smile tugging at the corner of her mouth. Then a merry laugh burst from her lips as she shook her head and shrugged in hopeless resignation. Lynn and Ben joined in and laughed with her.

When they had stopped laughing, Ben looked at the sisters. It was time to have a sincere talk with them. He wanted to help the mountain family who had done so much for him. They had snatched him from the grave and ministered to his every need and want. His debt to the Randall family was incalculable. However, he was going to try to help them out of the morass of debt if they would only trust him and let him try.

"Girls, I'd like very much to talk with both of you this afternoon. Is there some place close where we could talk without disturbing your mother?"

"Sure," Lynn said. "Me'n Ally would be glad to lend an ear while you unburden yourself. If you feel strong enough, we can walk up to Walt's cabin. It's behind the barn, a hundred yards up an old logging road. It stands on land Walt bought six years ago for two hundred dollars from the state. I'll go in and tell Mother where we're going, if you think you can make it that far."

"I'll try," Ben laughed. "I'm still plenty weak, though. If I play out, you girls will have to carry me back."

"If you play out on us, Ben, we promise to get you back home," Alice assured him, a merry twinkle in her eyes.

"Fair enough," he nodded.

Lynn rushed indoors to tell her mother where they were going. She came back almost at once to say that Mrs. Randall said go ahead, but be on the lookout for snakes. Without further delay, they rose from the porch and started for the cabin.

Chapter 7

*T*he walk to Walt's cabin was a long, slow pull for Ben. He had to stop and rest twice before they made it. Once there, he sank down upon a rustic bench by the front door with a sigh of relief. Alice and Lynn poked fun at him as he panted and wiped sweat from his pale brow, but he only smiled. The bench caught the full force of the heat of the western sun. It was stifling. Glancing around, he spied a maple tree slightly beyond the west corner of the cabin. It looked cool and inviting under its spreading branches, and he suggested that they sit under it. The girls were all for the idea, so with merry laughs, they took Ben by the arms and helped him walk the few steps to the big shade tree.

"Well, now, girls," he began as soon as all three were comfortably settled. "I sure ain't presuming to be nosey, and I have your best interests at heart. Ever since I come to myself here at your home, I've noticed how haggard and worried your father looks. The other day, I asked you, Alice, if anything was troubling your dad, and you told me that he was worrying himself into his grave over a mortgage. I'd like to help you folks, if at all possible. Believe me, because I mean every word of it. First, I have to know exactly what your problem is. Maybe my question will seem nibby, but I can't help that. Take me into your confidence. Trust me. Tell me about the mortgage. I believe I can be of service. All I ask is that you believe in me and share your troubles with me."

Alice and Lynn just looked at each other. To Ben, it seemed as if each sister was waiting for the other to speak. At last, with a shrug of her shoulders, Lynn broke the stillness.

"Sis," she said, "I think we should trust this here seng-digging Ben Waters. Remember what I said the day we found him up in the woods? I have the same hunch I had then. Let's trust him. Tell him our troubles."

"But Lynnie," Alice quavered, "I'm so ashamed of this mess."

"Ashamed, hell," Lynn retorted. "You've done nothing to be ashamed of. Neither have I. We're just victims of circumstance. There's nothing to be ashamed of."

"I'm afraid Ben would find the whole thing amusing," Alice said, a crimson tide sweeping her fair features.

"Girls, I give you my word of honor not to laugh at anything," he said.

Finally, after much arguing, Alice agreed to take Ben into their confidence. Ben was greatly honored by the trust the two girls were placing in him, and deeply touched by the depressed air that clung to them. If it were possible, he would alleviate their troubles. That was the least he could do. Leaning back against the maple tree, he awaited the tale.

Lynn told the story, and she did a complete job of it. She made use of several of her most shocking expressions. Alice sat with bowed head all the while, and though some of her sister's embellishments made her ears burn, she refrained from scolding. Ben vowed anew to help them someway, somehow. For Grant Randall, he felt compassion and a kind of pity. He couldn't say that he admired the man. He was blinded to the real issues of life, and he let himself fall under the influence of a scoundrel.

For Jess Savage, he felt loathing and disgust, and he vowed by all the stars in the sky that the scheming reprobate would never force Alice Randall into a relationship. To strengthen his decision, he had only to recall how she had ministered to him during his convalescence. Her gentle hands and soft voice had soothed him in his delirious hallucinations.

During the month he spent in her home, there had come to him a strange, wonderful emotion unlike anything he had ever experienced, and of late, he had caught himself feasting upon her lovely figure every time she was near. At such times, he cursed the wild life he had led while working on the river. He remembered the passionate sex he had experienced in the arms of beautiful wantons and told himself that he wasn't good enough for Alice Randall. He wasn't worthy of her love, but he couldn't stamp out the fire in his blood.

If this was the fire of love that held him in its burning grasp, then he had to admit that this strange new emotion was the most wondrously devastating passion he had ever experienced. If he let his mind dwell only on Alice, and concentrated on her kindness, her goodness, and her beautiful face and form, he was happy. On the other hand, if he recalled parts of his past that were especially tempestuous, then he would become miserable. To a straight-laced girl like Alice Randall, those escapades would brand him a skirt-chaser, and that was the last thing he wanted. Lynn's good opinion of him didn't matter much either way, he told himself. Lynn Randall had impressed him as a kindred spirit to girls he had had his way with in the past. This fact had been brought home to him more and more as the day had gone by. It was in her eyes, in her talk, her way of walking and rolling her hip. Her challenge to the opposite sex was as much a part of her as any of her physical characteristics. She had been created that way, and this trait of hers would always find a way to express itself. He was as certain as if she had already thrown convention to the winds and stepped forth as the red-hot siren that slumbered in her beautiful body. When that day came and she made a play for his attentions, he hoped he would have the will to resist her charms. A girl like that could make a man's hip pockets dip sand.

When Lynn had finished her narration, she asked Ben what he thought.

"Lynnie," he answered, "that's one of the oldest, lowest tricks that ever a two-legged skunk played. The nerve of the man borders on the insane. He must be one blowed-up specimen of humanity to think he's going to get by with a deal like that while there's still honest, red-blooded men in these hills. Most men of that type never live to a ripe old age. They're too damn rotten and ornery."

"You don't know Jess Savage," Alice said. "He's as hard as rock. A deal like the one he's figuring to pull off is nothing out of the ordinary. There's nothing too low for him. Dad knows all this, but he's letting the weight of his debt blind him. He ain't the father we used to know. He's become a—"

"Does your brother and mother know of all this?" Ben asked.

"Hell, no," Lynn said. "Me'n Allie's been holding the fort alone. Mom's too easily swayed in her judgement, and Walt's temper is about as dependable as a lit firecracker. We've been keeping our lips buttoned, cussing inside, and hoping for a miracle. It's been hell."

"Do you think your brother would trust me?" Ben asked. "Would he throw in with me on a plan to beat Savage at his own game?"

Lynn gave a strange little cry and danced a jig of joy. She rushed over to her older sister and gave her a bear hug and a kiss on the cheek.

"Oh, Allie," she said excitedly. "Did you hear what the man just said? Isn't it wonderful? Didn't I tell you that I had queer hunch about him? I was right. I know I was. Now he thinks he can beat Jess Savage. Ben Waters, you are a godsend from the pearly gates of heaven."

"Alice, what's Lynnie raving about?" Ben inquired. "What's this hunch she's so lathered up over? I don't feel like a godsend. I only want to help you people."

"Well, it's this way," Alice began. "The day we found you up on the Cranberry, I had just finished telling Lynnie. She was the only one I felt I could turn to that would understand my predicament without getting us all in hot water. After I'd unburdened myself, we were feeling pretty low. There's not a soul we can turn to. All our friends are in the same boat financially right now. Three thousand dollars would look like all the money in the world to any of us.

"After we found you, Lynnie got a good long look at your face. When she straightened up, she said that your coming into our lives when we needed a friend was a good omen. She also said that she felt that you were destined to play an important part, and she would be willing to stake her life on it that you would come up with a plan to bust Jess Savage's dirty scheme wide open. If you can outsmart this rat, I'll agree that you really are heaven sent."

"Reckon that's a pretty big order you girls got laid out for me." He grinned. "After this build up, I'll have to make good. If I get your hopes up, and then fail to produce, I'll feel lower than a snake's belly. It's a big order for a well man, girls, let alone an invalid, but I'm willing to try. Even if it doesn't work out, at least we've tried."

"You're a stranger, Ben," Alice said. "We need a fried. You offered us your friendship and help, in exchange for our trust. We do trust you. We don't know why, but we believe you'll be the answer to our prayers."

"I sincerely hope I'll not disappoint you," Ben said earnestly. "What about Walt? Do you think he'll go along with the plan?"

"I guess the only thing we can do is bounce him about it and find out," Lynn replied.

"When will be a good time?" Alice inquired.

"I say the sooner the better," Ben answered. "What I have in mind will call for a heap of walking. I ain't in any condition for that right now, but I will be before too long. Let's see. Tomorrow is Sunday. What say to us three rounding Walt up and fetching him here for another conference?

I'll lay my cards on the table then. I've a hunch I can persuade him to listen to reason when you girls spring Jess Savage's deal on him. It's a chance we have to take."

"I'm not overly hipped on the idea of telling Walt about this mess," Alice said. "Couldn't we put that part of it off for a while?"

"I don't see how," Ben answered. "The success of my plan depends largely on your brother's cooperation. I wouldn't worry about Walt too much, Alice. I've looked him over closely several times lately. I'm willing to lay odds that he'll come through when the chips are down. He's bound to find out sooner or later, so why not take the bull by the horns?"

"I'm for Ben's idea, all the way," Lynn said. "I say let's follow his leadership, but he's getting a little green around the gills. Let's waltz our patient home. He's had enough exercise for one day. No use letting him over do it. Tomorrow is another day. We'll collar Walt before he takes off to see the red-hot piece he's got on the string. I agree with Ben. The quicker we put a plan into action, the better chance we'll have of succeeding."

"Okay," Alice said reluctantly. "I'll go along, but if Walt won't listen to reason and blows his stack, you'll be sorry. He's as bull-headed as a mule, and when he gets mad, he's a lot worse. If we can start something, it'll be far better than just sitting around waiting."

"Well, then, girls," Ben drawled. "We'll bring Walt over here tomorrow and talk this thing out from all directions. Agreed?"

"Agreed," Alice and Lynn chorused. Each of the girls hooked an arm in one of Ben's and stated walking towards home, hope rekindled.

Chapter 8

*T*he following afternoon found them once again under the spreading branches of the maple tree. This time, Walt Randall accompanied them. When approached by his sisters, Ben flatly refused to forego his plans for the afternoon, but when they told him that Ben wanted to talk over something important with him, he had shrugged his wide shoulders and agreed to go along, providing it didn't take more than an hour.

"Now look, Ally and Lynn," he said, "I've got myself a date this afternoon with a sexy little bitch that I've been trying to make for months. She's a hot number, and all the fellows are after her. If I'm late on my very first date, she'll drop me like a hot potato. Flo Bradley ain't the type of girl that'll sit home twiddling her thumbs while waiting for a boyfriend to show up. She don't have to, and she knows it. There's too many two-legged wolves roaming around that'd break a leg to have a chance. No, siree, I don't want to muss it with her on my first trip to the plate."

"If she's that damn finicky, you'll be doing good to drop little Miss Flo Bradley before the romance had a chance to bloom," Lynn quipped. "Walt, what Ben wants to talk to you about is important to all of us—much more important than anything little Miss Hot Pants has to offer."

"Okay, I'll go," Walt agreed, "but if it takes more than an hour, I'll have to postpone the finish till later. It can wait, but Flo won't."

As soon as the four young people had settled themselves comfortably under the big maple, Ben came to the point. "Walt, I know I'm a perfect stranger," he began, "but I'm going to ask you to trust me."

"Sure, Ben," Walt replied, "but I don't understand. You're asking me to trust you. I don't mistrust you, if you know what I mean. I don't know what you're driving at. Explain yourself."

"Be glad to," Ben continued. "It's this way. While I've been at your home recovering, I couldn't help but see how worried your father's been.

He mopes around most of the time, and I've seen him sort of stare into space with eyes that were positively haunted. I wanted to help if I could. So about a week ago, I asked Alice what was worrying your father. She told me about the mortgage that is hanging over your home."

"Sure, there's a mortgage on our home, and Dad's been some worried about it. So have I, for that matter," Walt answered, "but I sure as hell don't consider that any of your business."

"Walt, for heaven's sake," Alice cried. "Ben's only trying to help us. The least you can do is hear him out before blowing your top in all directions."

"Well, I mean it, sis," Walt fumed. "It's no concern of his whether we're in debt or not. That's our business, and I mean to keep it that way."

"Sure, that's our business, Walt Randall," Lynn said in a scathing voice, "and I'm positive Ben Waters would be the last person to want to pry into it. He wants to help, not peek at the family skeletons. He asked you up here to have a serious talk about the debt hanging over our home like a big deadfall. Then the minute he opens his mouth, you bite his head off. That's a real gentlemanly way to treat a man. I'm proud of you."

For a moment, Walt gazed straight ahead, his fine, young face as dark as a thundercloud. Then his anger subsided as quickly as it had risen, and turning to Ben, who was sitting quietly on the maple tree's roots, he thrust out a strong, tanned hand.

"I'm sorry, Ben," he said seriously. "I spoke before I thought. I apologize. Hope you believe me. This lien on our home has been a thorn in Randall flesh ever since Dad borrowed the money. Maybe I'm getting as jumpy and moody as he is. We've been unable to pay a single dollar on our debt since the crash of the markets. If things keep up like they've been for fifteen months longer, chances are we'll lose the homestead—lock, stock, and barrel. This place has been in Randall hands ever since my great-grandfather settled here a hundred years ago. It'd kill my father to be thrown off it. I'm sorry I snapped at you. I'll be happy to hear you out."

Ben looked up and met his outstretched hand with a smile. "Your apology is accepted, Walt," he chuckled. "I don't blame you for the way you combed your hair. I'd have probably done the same thing if the tables were turned."

"No hard feelings?"

"Certainly not. Forget it."

"I sure am glad to hear that. Now, what say we get down to it? My goose is cooked if I'm late for my date this afternoon. It's one-thirty. I got to hit the road by two-thirty."

"Okay, Walt," Ben said in a voice that cracked like a whip. "I'll make it as brief and to the point as I can. About the mortgage on your home— the bank at Richwood doesn't hold it any longer."

"They don't hold it any longer?" Walt spluttered. "What in blazes happened to the mortgage if they don't have it? You're talking way over my head, Ben. Take it easy, and repeat what you just said."

Ben hastened to comply. When he had finished, Walt just looked at him in amazement.

"What happened?" he asked in disbelief.

"The bank sold your mortgage to a private individual," Ben said.

"So that's it, huh?" Walt said from between set teeth. "Sold us out, did they? How do you like that? Isn't that just like a banker to weed out investments he thinks might no more than break even. His business is to run the bank so that it pays off, regardless of whose toes he tromps on. Who is the two-legged rat that bought our mortgage? Someone I know?"

"I'll give you one guess, brother," Alice laughed mirthlessly.

"Come on now, you three. Quit playing hide and seek. Spill it."

"Jess Savage," the two sisters replied.

"Holy jumped-up hell," Walt roared and followed up with a blistering string of oaths that would have done credit to a sailor. "Jess Savage, huh? I'll bet he bought our mortgage so that he can put one of his squeeze plays into operation. That's his style every day of the week. That dirty, low-down, woman-chasing bastard. I don't know what to say. When did the mortgage change hands?"

"About seven weeks ago," Alice said. "Dad told me right after he heard the bad news."

"Well, I'll be damned," Walt roared again, and once more, he swore lustily. "Why in the cat hair didn't Dad come to me with this? I sure appreciate his trust and confidence. Reckon I'll bounce the old man about this little deal. I don't like it a bit. Everybody, even Ben here, knows more than I do. What does Mother say about the turn things have taken?"

"Mother doesn't know a thing about this mess, unless Dad's told her," Alice said. "It was only yesterday that we told Ben, after he'd asked us to trust him with our troubles."

"Even so, all I can say is that this is a fine how-dee-do," Walt growled. "It makes me as mad as a wet hen to be left in the dark this way. I've been a grown man for years, and I think it's about time my father began treating me like one. So that's why he's been dragging around lately looking like a sick calf that's lost its mother. Serves him right to worry for being so close mouthed."

"Walt," Alice said, her eyes full of misery and shame, "Dad would have told you all this before any of us, only he was afraid of your temper."

"Poppycock. Hog wash. I'm as levelheaded as the next person. What the hell? We all have tempers. If we're any good, that is. What harm could it have done, even if I did blow my top after he told me? Is that out of the ordinary for a young fellow when his dander's up?"

"Of course not, Walt," Ben assured him. "However, that wasn't the reason your father didn't confide in you. It goes much deeper than you think. He kept silent for your own protection. I'm certain of that."

"What do you mean, Ben?" Walt asked with a puzzled frown. "Let's quit playing games. Give it to me straight from the shoulder. What say we call a halt to this damn beating around the bush?"

"Okay," Ben replied. "The reason your father kept silent is that the mortgage deal is another of Savage's usual deals. He has a fancy scheme up his sleeve. That's why your father was afraid to tell you, and why he's worrying himself down to skin and bones."

"Now look, Ben," Walt said. "Low-down deals are expected of the man. Everybody knows that. I don't see a particle of difference in it this time."

"But there is," Ben said grimly. Turning to Alice, he said, "Shall I tell him, Alice?"

"Yes," she said, blushing crimson. Her big brown eyes were pools of misery and woe.

"Walt, I'll make it as brief as possible," Ben said. "First, I'd like your word that you won't fly off the handle when you hear Savage's proposition. That two-legged rat would like nothing better than to get the law onto you. I've never met the man, but I know his type. He's one of those yellow-bellied bastards that can dish it out, but whine like a sheep-killing cur when the tables are turned. Do I have your word that you'll take it easy, regardless of what I tell you?"

"You do," Walt promised harshly. "Now let's hear the details of this deal."

"Tell it all, Ben," Lynn said.

"Okay," Ben began. "Hold onto your temper, Walt, and your hat. After Savage bought the mortgage on your home, he told your father that he would tear up the mortgage if your sister Alice became his wife. Wait, boy, before you explode. Hear the rest. Your father ain't been himself, and to make things worse, he's taken to drink. Savage saw to that, damn his dirty hide. Your father sees the old homestead slipping out of his hands, and he's grasping at straws to save it. Don't blame him too much if he's let himself be taken advantage of. The poor man's become blinded to everything but his obsession to save his home. Your father tried to stand up to him. I'll give him credit for that, but he was no match for Savage. Savage told your father that if Alice refused to become his wife before the mortgage came due next year, he'd throw you all out in the road unless you had the money to pay off the lien in full, including interest. That took the wind out of your father's arguments. He folded. Walt, try to understand. Your father wants Alice to marry Jess Savage. Right now, he can see no other way out of the hole. He has his back to the wall, and he's already accepted defeat. Right now, he's willing to go along with Savage's deal. It's his only chance to save the homestead. There you have it. I'm sorry if I was blunt. I know it's a shock. Things like that always are."

"Shock, my ass," Walt spat. "When you spoke of a deal, I suspected the worst. What you've just told me doesn't surprise me. I've been looking for something like this from that rat. I'm not blind. I noticed how he eyes Alice every chance he gets. His damn greedy, desiring eyes are always on her. I knew he was sizing her up for no good. Now what he's had in the back of his mind has come to light. Buying the mortgage on our home fit right into his plan. I reckon the next time I meet up with Mister Savage I'll knock about half of his teeth down his throat, just for luck. That'll be my answer to his proposal. Also, I'll read Dad the riot act for the way he's been screwing around and making us kids ashamed. Right now, all I want to do is to cuss everything and everyone."

"Steady, my boy," Ben cautioned. "If you hop this skunk, you'll be playing right into his hands. My advice would be to let it ride. It wouldn't hurt any to go easy on your father. He's trying to extract himself from the quicksand of debt. So if he kind of bogs down a little at times, I wouldn't worry much about it, or think too badly of him. I'd be willing to lay you kids odds that before this thing is settled your father will come through in a way that will make you real proud of him."

"That's nice of you to say, Ben," Walt said, grim faced and stern. "I hope you are right. I have to be shoving off soon. Is there anything else you wanted to talk about?"

"Yes," Ben answered. "Could you spare me another twenty minutes?"

"Okay. Get to the point quickly, though. Honestly, I'd like to talk all afternoon, but I've got a hot little number waiting to make me forget my troubles, and right now, I could sure use some of that kind of treatment."

"All right, Walt, I'll give you the gist in one big dose," Ben said. "I hope you take kindly to my plan. I believe we can beat Savage at his own game. How would you like to be my partner?"

"Doing what?"

"Hunting seng."

"No soap, Ben," said Walt. "I'd like to, but there just ain't any money in hunting seng in these parts. Dad and I used to hunt some years back. Our efforts fell flat. There's not enough in these woods anymore to pay a person to hunt it. It was all picked clean as a whistle years and years ago."

"Sure, sure, I know," Ben laughed. "It might sound silly, but ginseng will supply the money we need. I hunted it for years back on the Little Kanawha, and I know what I'm talking about. That's why I'm out here. For years, I've thought I'm pretty good woodsman, but these old hills proved me wrong. However, I'm not about to give up. They won the first round. I'll win the second. I'm going to try."

"I'm sorry, Ben," Walt said, with an impatient gesture of his right hand. "This talk of hunting seng to pay off the mortgage is the rankest kind of foolishness. It's chasing rainbows. You've been listening to that old legend they talk about here on the head of the Cranberry."

"What old legend?" Ben asked.

"According the story, about ninety years ago, during the War Between the States, two Confederate soldiers got lost in the woods. As the story has it, during their wanderings, they ran across a huge patch of seng in the center of an immense laurel thicket growing in a natural saddle on the top of a high ridge. The two men were following a game trail through the laurel bed and ran smack-dab into a big grove of black walnut trees. The seng was growing under the walnut trees. Them two old timers claimed later that there was at least two acres standing solid with seng that was waist-high to a tall man. A fortune in ginseng, they said. Anyway, as fate would have it, them fellows was never able to go back to that patch of seng. It was as though that ridge just dropped out of sight. Personally, I say it's just another tall story of the hills."

Chapter 9

As Ben listened to Walt, his heart gave a mighty leap, and his blood began pounding in his ears. Great God above, he whispered to himself. Walt Randall was describing what he had seen. The wild, high ridge with the natural saddle. The big laurel thicket and the game trail through it. That grove of black walnut trees with the treasure of wild ginseng growing beneath their spreading branches. Ben Waters was glad that God had led him across that ridge while he was still able to observe things. As he listened to Walt, he knew that God had directed his feet across that ridge, and the legend was reality. It existed. At that very moment, the mountain ridge with its sea of laurel, black walnuts, and magnificent, wild ginseng was somewhere in the great woodland that stretched across the headwaters of the Gauley River watershed. Ben had seen it with his own eyes, and he knew that ginseng bed would be the salvation of the Randall family.

"Walt," Ben inquired, "how much do you suppose a patch of seng like them soldiers said they seen would be worth on the market today?"

"Oh, I don't rightly know how much," said Walt. "It all depends on the price per pound, how thick it is on the ground, and how big the roots are. What are the buyers paying per pound for clean, dry, seng roots this summer?"

"Eight dollars and better a pound."

"Well, if a two-acre patch of seng was old and well developed, it should yield at least a ton of dry root per acre. The would be two tons of dry root. So at eight dollars per pound, two tons would bring thirty-two thousand dollars. Not bad money for a bunch of weeds in the woods. Ben, if I thought there was even the rarest possibility of you and me being able to strike a fraction of that amount, I'd buddy up with you tighter than a leech to a nigger's naval."

"Do you mean what you're saying?" Ben asked in a voice taut with suppressed emotion.

"I certainly do."

"You'd be willing to be my partner and hunt seng with me if we stood a China man's chance of making good?"

"Yes, Ben Waters, I would," Walt said. "Do you think there's any truth to what them men say they saw?"

Ben feared his account would be considered in the same light as the two soldiers' story had been. He might be considered a crackpot, or touched in the head from being lost in the woods. He had no choice. He had to tell his story. Let them scoff at him. Let them raise their eyebrows and look at one another in pity. The day he produced the ginseng, their tune would change mighty quick. Nothing convinced people as much as proving to them that you were right all along. When that happened, some of your greatest knockers would become your greatest boosters.

"I don't think there's a particle of truth in that old legend," said Walt. "It's just a tall tale. People are funny that way, though. They like old stories. Everybody gets a kick out of them, but they're groundless, as a rule."

"Walt, Alice, Lynn, listen to me," Ben said. "I beg you to believe me. It's the truth, every word of it, so help me God. Those Confederate soldiers were telling the truth about that big patch of seng. It's back there in them woods. I seen it with my own eyes. I, too, crossed a saddle on a wild, high ridge, and in the center of that saddle, I run smack into a laurel bed that was acres and acres wide. It was the biggest laurel thicket I'd encountered, and I was worried about how I'd get through it. I knew I could go around it, but I hadn't the ambition to take a single step out of my way. Fortunately, there was an old trail or game path through the laurel bed. I began following the game trail through the thicket, and I came into a grove of trees at the center of the laurel. I leaned against one of the trees, and when my brain told me that I was leaning against a black walnut tree, I perked up and looked around. Back home, a black walnut tree was a welcome sight to a seng digger. It always seemed like the rankest vegetation grew under black walnuts. Some of the finest seng I ever dug back home I found under an old walnut tree. Even before I looked at the ground, I knew what I would see.

"I was in a grove of black walnut trees. There must have been at least two acres of them. The laurel thicket walled in this grove of trees in every direction like a dense, green jungle. I doubt a rabbit could have crawled through it. When I looked down, I saw a sight for the gods to behold. Waist-high seng covered the floor of that walnut grove. It was dark green and very healthy looking, as thick on the ground as hair on a dog's back. It was like nothing I had ever hoped or dreamed of seeing. A fortune stood before me. Thousands and thousands of dollars of seng roots. Enough to pay off the mortgage on your home ten times over.

"When I finally walked through the walnut trees and seng patch and entered the laurel thicket on the other side, I didn't take a dozen steps before the walnut grove was shut off from view as if it had never existed. Them old hills guard their treasures. That's the truth, folks, as God is my judge. It's in there, Walt. I know it is. I saw it with my own eyes. Will you be my partner and help me find it?"

For a moment, the Randall sisters and brother looked at him in open-mouthed amazement. None of them made a sound for a full minute. Eventually, Walt broke the silence.

"Great God, man," he croaked. "Do you realize what you've just told us?"

"I sure do, Walt."

"You really believe you saw this patch of seng?"

"I'm positive," Ben said emphatically. "I haven't the slightest doubt."

"You're out of your mind," Walt Randall scoffed. "Them woods have given you the willies. You're talking like a drunk. I'm sorry, Ben. You don't know how I'd like to believe you. But I can't, man, I can't. Common sense won't let me. You had a nearly fatal experience back there in them woods. Couldn't a person in your condition imagine all sorts of things? It's been known to happen. I'm sorry, Ben, but I can't buy it."

"I was afraid of how you'd take it," Ben muttered. "Guess I can't blame you, though. I'd feel the same way if the shoe was on the other foot. I told you the gospel truth. I seen that patch of seng with my own two eyes. It's in there, growing big and strong, waiting for the day some lucky seng digger will discover it. My faith is so strong that I'm going back in there, even if I have to find another young fellow to go with me. I'm going just as soon as I regain my health. I want you to go with me, Walt, but I can't force you to go."

"Oh, Ben," Alice cried. "I believe you, even if Walt doesn't. If I was a man, I'd gladly go with you to search for it."

"Me, too," Lynn said. "I also believe you. Please don't take Walt seriously. He's always throwing cold water."

"Thanks a lot, girls," Ben said. "I can't blame Walt. Now look, I've a proposition. Tell me what you think. I'm willing to do this if you'll be my partner and hunt roots with me. Be my partner, and I'll give you all we make if you don't make more with me in the woods than if you were working a regular job. Now ain't that fair? I'd stake my life that you can't lose. Right now, you're only making a dollar a day, when you can get work. With me, you'll be your own boss and make every bit as much. You stand a chance of hitting something really worthwhile. How about it? Won't you change your mind, and come with me?"

"Ben, I have to think this thing through," Walt replied, getting up and dusting off the seat of his trousers. "I can't lose much either way, but before I decide, I'd like to feel that we'd stand a fair to middling chance of succeeding. Guess I'd better be loping along. That Flo'd piss right down her purty legs if I was to stand her up on our first date. I'm going to be a mite late as it is. Reckon I'll have to lie something scandalous to her. She's a prissy little bitch. So long, folks. See y'all later. I'll think it over, Ben, and let you know what I decide."

"So long, Walt," Ben and Alice said together. "Have a good time on your date."

"Bye now, Walter," Lynn sang in a high-pitched falsetto. "Do be careful. A siren like Flo might have all sorts of booby traps set. Don't get your fingers caught in the lace of her black silk panties. That'd be real embarrassing."

"Aw, go to hell," Walt bellowed back over his shoulder as he strode down the old logging road towards the Randall home, Lynn's laugh ringing in his ears. Ben and Alice laughed, but even as she laughed, Alice blushed furiously, scolding her younger sister to watch her language. Lynn grinned impishly and shrugged one of her shapely shoulders.

Soon after Walt's departure, the two sisters began pestering Ben to relate all that had happened to him since he first set foot in the woods. After a bit of coaxing, he told of the ginseng he'd seen. They laughed delightedly and clapped their hands. Ben smiled at their enthusiasm.

"So you really believe, then, that seng would be a good thing for you and Walt to go after?" Alice asked for perhaps the tenth time, her brown eyes fixed on his face.

"Alice," Ben said, "I am as sure of it as if he and I were this very minute digging that big patch."

"Suppose you can't ever find that patch again?" Lynn asked. "Them rebel soldiers never did find that seng again once they'd made their way out of them woods. Them old hills guard their secrets mighty close. They're so confounded big. It's fifty miles through the woods, if it's an inch. A thousand ridges could hide in there, and you would never be any the wiser."

"That's a chance I'm willing to take," Ben said. "Anyways, wouldn't it be better for me and Walt to pitch in than to throw in the sponge and say we're licked before we start? It's there, girls. I seen it with my own eyes. I walked through that patch of seng. I know I was lost when I stumbled onto it, but I know it was no hallucination."

"And you're willing to take our brother on as a full partner?" Lynn asked.

"Yes, indeed," Ben said. "After all, Lynnie, where would I be right now if it wasn't for you good people?"

"But Ben," Alice asked softly. "There might be thousands of dollars' worth of roots in that patch of seng. Does it seem right that you should give half of it away to a fellow that isn't even interested in going with you to look for it?"

"Alice, Lynnie, every dollar that me and Walt make at seng hunting, outside of our expenses, of course, will go towards paying the mortgage on your home. If he'll go with me, that is. Anyhow, that's how it's got to be. I don't want to hear any argument. My mind is made up."

"Even your half of any money you might make?" Lynn inquired.

"That's right," Ben said firmly. "Every red cent will be put towards liquidating that mortgage. That's the least I can do. I owe you good people. I'd be a perfect heel to hold back money that might extract you from the clutches of Jess Savage. I say nix on that."

"Ben Waters," Alice said as she smiled at him in a way that made his heart leap for joy. "You're a prince, a perfect prince."

"I second that," Lynn laughed. "I vote we show our appreciation by each of us giving him a big kiss."

"Maybe our patient doesn't want that kind of gratitude," Alice replied, blushing prettily and dropping her eyes.

"Try me and see," Ben suggested. He couldn't find the strength to say otherwise. Ever since the day he'd come to himself at the Randalls, he had wanted to take her in his arms and kiss her inviting red lips. Now that the opportunity presented itself, he was powerless to fight it. The thought that he was commercializing on the girls' gratitude made him curse himself silently. He was a heel for doing it, but heel or no heel, he wanted very, very much to press his lips to Alice Randall's.

Alice and Lynn laughed merrily and came to stand by his side. When he looked into Alice's eyes, smiled, and wiggled his eyebrows at her, she gave a shaky little laugh. Her beautiful features were crimson and pale by turns as she took hold of his face with her cool hands and cradled it against her bosom. She closed her eyes and covered his mouth with lips as soft as new velvet. Ben reached up and clasped his arms around her, holding her against him tightly.

He smiled and said, "Alice, that kiss was out of this world. Could I be so bold as to ask for one more?"

"Okay," she said hesitantly. "That's all, though. No more kisses until we see that ginseng money rolling in. Next girl."

Lynn was as uninhibited in kissing as she was otherwise. With a grin of pure wickedness, she sat beside him on the maple roots and pulled him across her lap. Bending her head, she claimed his lips with her ruby mouth in a manner that sent tingles through his body. Her lips began to work themselves onto his with a sort of sucking action. Ben could not remember when he had been kissed more completely, or devastatingly. Her red mouth tore him apart. Though he was weakened by his unfortunate experience in woods, he greatly desired the uninhibited girl. She promised him heaven. His blood was a stream of fire. Then, just before she released his lips, he felt the hot lance of her tongue in his mouth.

She had the unrestrained abandon of a siren and the finesse of an artist. He felt as limp as a wet dishrag. With a laugh of feminine triumph, Lynn released him and helped him regain his seat on the maple roots.

"There you are, my good man," she said with pride. "Please accept those kisses as a small token of our appreciation. Hope you didn't mind. We're only a couple of innocent county girls."

Chapter 10

*T*he next week, Walt came to Ben one evening and silently thrust out his lean, brown, right hand. A hard light glinted from deep in his eyes as he spoke.

"Howdy, Ben," he said, "I've made up my mind, and I'm willing to be partners with you. May the good Lord guide our feet to that big patch you seen. You're right. It's our only salvation. I've also decided to take your advice about soft peddling with that skunk when next we meet. I think I'll even keep mum around Dad and let him stew in his own fat, so to speak.

"You and me will join forces as soon as you're physically able to head for the hills. In the meantime, I'll take a little jaunt over to Marlinton and pick up your flivver. Better let your folks know that you'll be staying on here, at least until the snow flies. I'll throw some gear together so's I can be ready to haul ass whenever you think you're in shape to travel. Till that day arrives, we'll just sort of let things drift along. We'll take it easy at first, just short jaunts till you've got your wind and legs back. Here's hoping that we make good. Dad will cuss to high heavens when he hears that I've decided to go seng hunting with you. But what the hell. Let him talk, especially after the way he's been letting Jess Savage lead him around by the nose. Whenever I think about it, I get so mad I could spit. Holy jumped-up hell. Dad sure ain't the father I used to know."

And so a partnership was formed. To one of the young men, it was a chance to pay off a debt. To the other, the partnership represented something different. Young Randall was obsessed with purpose, stemming from a fervent hope that he could save his home and his sister.

During the long days that followed, Ben strove to expedite his recovery. He began to retire as soon as the shadows of night began to creep across the high country. He slept long hours, rising late every morning. He ate strong food and drank plenty of milk and sparkling spring water. As soon as his strength would permit, he began to take daily walks.

Most of the time, Alice and Lynn accompanied him on his walks. On some occasions, however, Lynn went with him alone. Ben soon saw that this would never do. From the very first day that they walked by themselves, Lynn Randall tried every wile known to womanhood to seduce Ben. She was utterly shameless. She was extremely passionate and very beautiful. It was not unusual for her to suddenly and without warning throw herself into his arms and begin to kiss him. Her passion was so pronounced that Ben was hard put to fight her off. Whenever he tried to tell her of his love for her sister Alice, she only laughed at him for being a softheaded sap.

"Look, Ben," she'd say on such occasions, "I know you're gog-eyed over Allie. But what the cat hair has that got to do with what goes on between you and me?"

"Lynnie, Lynnie," Ben would say. "You don't understand. I love your sister. I ain't told her yet, but I will one of these days. When I do tell her, I don't want making love on the sly to her sister on my conscience. Why not get yourself a boyfriend? Give him the works like you've been giving me, and he'll take very good care of your needs if he's half a man and not an idiot. Be a good girl now, and lay off me."

"Nothing doing," she'd laugh. "How you feel about Allie is your own affair. I only want you and me to have a little fun. That's all. What harm could there be in that?"

"Plenty. What if you was to become pregnant?" he asked.

"Nonsense, Bennie-boy," was always her ready reply. "Not a chance. Us backcountry females have homegrown prevention against getting knocked-up against our will. It's foolproof. So calm yourself and let's go to town. We're wasting time, man. I could give you a flouncing that would pass anything them Southern belles you're always raving about could shake up. Honestly, I can't figure you, Ben. Here I am with hot pants every time we're alone together, and all you do is stall me. Don't you have any desire left anymore for the stuff the cats fight over?"

"Damn you, girl, you know I have."

"Then why fight it? As I see it, you ain't got a thing to worry about. Don't be scared to make love to me. I won't drain you so badly. There'll be plenty of you left for Allie. If and when she becomes your wife, she'll never miss what little of yourself you gave to me. Allie need never know anything happened. You ain't got a thing to hold back for. Relax, and let's enjoy ourselves."

"It's like this, Lynnie. I am trying my best to get my strength back so me and Walt can hit the trail. What you're wanting won't hasten my recovery. You know that as well as I do."

"Phooey, Bennie-boy," she would laugh. "What I want won't hurt your recovery. Fact of the matter is it would do you good. Sexual intercourse relaxes those who engage in it. Ask any doctor. He'll tell you as much. And boy, would I enjoy relaxing you in the good old-fashion way that nature intended."

"Lynn Randall, why are you acting this way?" Ben asked Lynn every time they were alone. Her answer was always the same. Even after Lynn gave him a reason for her actions, Ben was as much in the dark as ever. Lynn Randall was at that age when sex dominated her universe. All else was of secondary importance.

"Now, Bennie," she would say in her forthright way. "Try to look at this from my side of the fence. I strongly believe in physical love. My policy is to take love wherever and whenever you find the opportunity. That's the best reason I can give you for my actions. My behavior is part of my makeup. It's the way God put me together. I can't help myself."

"As I said before, Lynnie," Ben patiently pointed out one afternoon as they strolled up the Cranberry, "the solution to your problem is a big, strong, young man. Dig yourself up one. These old hills are full of them. When you find a boyfriend, tell him your trouble. I'll bet money that he'll take the starch out of you. He'll pop your corn in a hurry. I told you this before, but it doesn't seem to register. Maybe it will this time. Stop trying to seduce me. I'm only human, you know. If this keeps up, I may not be able to resist your charms. I'd hate to think I raped you."

"If you did, it would be with my wholehearted consent," she replied, giving him a smile that made his blood race.

"Please be a good girl and find yourself a boyfriend," he pleaded.

"I promise nothing, Ben Waters," she said. "I want you. If you desired me as much as I do you, we could go places and do things, but you don't, or else you're playing hard to get. It's going to take some time to bring you around, but that's all right. I'm still young, and so are you. One of these days, you'll drop your guard. When you do, I'll hit you with everything I've got. You'll think you've been thrown into one of   them

Far East harems. My day will come, friend Waters, and when it does, what a time I'll give you. I can wait. I've the patience of an Indian."

On this particular afternoon, he and Lynn had strolled up the Cranberry to where she and Alice had found him lying in the old game trail. Alice had had a headache and begged off accompanying them. On their way home, they stopped at the fork in the river to rest. They sat on a mossy boulder near a bank on a sandbar. There was a long pool of water that was of goodly depth in places, and Lynn confided that she, Alice, and Walt had often gone swimming there.

No sooner had they comfortably settled on the rock than Lynn jumped up and announced that she was going wading. A calculated, sly smile touched the corners of her mouth. He waved a hand in casual interest and told her to wade to her heart's content. At a call from Lynn a little later, he glanced towards the river and caught his breath. She was standing, delicately poised on her toes, at the very edge of the deepest spot in the water, completely nude. Her clothes lay in a small, rumpled pile at her feet. Looking back, she threw him a smile of joy at being alive, young, and full of zest for living.

"Come in the water with me, Ben, and I'll play you a little game of ping-pong," she said.

"What with?" he asked, straight faced.

"Come on in and find out," she replied.

"Nothing doing," he laughed, but his eyes never left her gorgeously proportioned body. "It would never do. I'm allergic to water and beautiful naked girls with ulterior motives. It's too risky."

"Fraidy-cat," she taunted. Raising her arms above her head, she entered the water in such a way that hardly a stand of her blonde hair got wet.

Ben watched the beautiful, unpredictable temptress cavort the length of the pool sometimes swimming, sometimes wading. Lynn Randall was as much at home in the water as a duck, with her lovely nude body gleaming like polished ivory in the sparkling amber water.

When she quit the pool, she scooped up her clothes under an arm and tripped lightly across the rocky sandbar between the pool and the mossy rock on which she sat. She looked like a mythical wood nymph, with her bare feet and the afternoon sunlight glistening on her as it filtered through the trees, her abundant blonde hair streaming behind her.

Gaining the rock upon which Ben sat, she flung her clothes down with scarcely a glance. She wiped the water from her body with her bare hands, turning this way and that. Her eyes never left his face for an instant. At last, she leaned towards him, and her proud, firmly rounded breasts and their pink, jutting nipples brushed tantalizingly against his right shoulder. It would have put life into a dead man. On pins and needles, he grabbed up her clothes and pushed them into her arms.

"Like what you see, Bennie-boy?" she asked softly.

"For God's sake, girl," he cried hoarsely, as a sweat burst over him. "Have you no shame? Dress yourself before I lose control."

She gave a silvery laugh and flung herself into his arms. He surrendered to his impulses, crushed her naked body to him, and rained kisses upon her half-opened mouth. He fondled her roughly from head to toe. Not a word of protest did she utter. Surprised, he realized that regardless of how rough his hands were, she welcomed his touch, no matter where it was, or how it was administered.

"Let go, Bennie-boy. Please, let go of yourself," she whispered against his lips. "Quit fighting what's bound to happen. I know you're just as hot for me as I am for you. Why keep putting me off? Stop torturing us. When you finally do make love to me, do it the way I want you to. I want my loving cave-man style. I want you to be rough with me. I want you to bust me wide open. Tear me to pieces. Make love to me something awful. I need it. I want it. I've got to have it."

When she began to unbutton his clothes, Ben tore himself loose from her and lurched away from the big rock.

"You she-devil," he said from between clenched teeth. "By the good Lord above, you're asking for it. I'm tired of fighting you off, and it's a waste of breath asking you to be a good girl. Get your clothes on and let's go home. I'll wait for you up the trail. It ain't safe for me to be around you when you're naked as a bird. We both get steamed up too much."

"Okay, Mister Chicken Waters," she said scornfully. "I'll put on my clothes. There wasn't any point in my taking them off in the first place. I've been wasting my time with a man who's as dead as a doornail from the waist down. There ain't no two ways about it. If you wasn't dead sexually, you'd have shown some sign of life below the belt."

"If you keep on thinking that way, I'll be glad," Ben said as a wide grin lit up his face. "Maybe I can have a little peace when we're alone together."

"You'll have peace as far as I'm concerned and to spare," she assured him as she wiggled into her gingham dress. "Listen, Mr. Waters, in the future, please speak softly when you brag about the sexy babes you laid. I think your tales of your many conquests are a crock of you-know-what. You couldn't prove otherwise by me."

"Fine, Fine," he said. "I hope you keep thinking that way. Them tales are true, Lynnie-girl, you can bet your sweet life on it. You're luckier than you know. It's a good thing I've changed since them old days. If I hadn't, you'd have lost your cherry long ago. You are still a virgin, aren't you?"

"Hell, yes," she spat, "and if I depended on the likes of you to change that condition, I'd die of old age and still be as unexplored as ever. What a bright future that'd be. I'll have to start using a sharpened potato on myself."

"Don't you want to stay a virgin until you get married?" Ben asked, as they began walking back down the river trail. Knowing her impulsive nature as he did, he knew what her answer would be. She did not disappoint him.

"Definitely not," she replied. "What profit is there in that? How much fun can a girl have by keeping her legs crossed every time she's out with a boyfriend? There ain't no percentage in that. Why stay a virgin? There ain't one man out of a thousand who does. Why should us girls keep ourselves untouched for some man who's probably laying every female he can get his hands on? In the long run, we're never loved any better by our husbands, anyway. Live for today, I say. Tomorrow will take care of itself."

"What about your wedding night?" Ben asked.

"To hell with my wedding night," she said. "That's one night I sure ain't building any air castles about. Why should I? I'm not worrying about it. Suppose I'm not a virgin when I get married. So what? I don't expect my husband to be. There's one thing I'll guarantee you, though. On my wedding night, I won't be flinching all over the bed, trying to get away from the stiff dilly my husband is dying to acquaint me with. I'll give him a wedding night he'll never forget."

"Good girl." Ben grinned at her. "I wish you luck."

"Damn your hide, anyhow, Ben Waters," she cried in a ringing voice, followed by hair curling curses.

He listened in open-mouthed amazement and envy. He'd known few men who could let off steam like that, let alone a winsome, eighteen-year-old girl. She flabbergasted him. She was a never-ending source of wonder and delight, with as many moods as the weather. One minute sunshine. The next tempest. Beautiful to behold. Lovely to look upon. Secretive, mysterious, incomprehensible. In short, a woman.

"I see through your little game," she continued. She delivered an open-handed slap on the back that nearly sent him sprawling in his face. "I'm telling you, my fine, feathered friend that it won't work. You ain't fooling me a bit. One of these days, I'll slip past your guard, and when I do, I'll ask payment in full for the way you're putting me off, and you'll pay up. Never fear, Bennie-boy."

Chapter 11

*F*rom that day forward, Ben made an effort never to be alone with Lynn Randall. She knew he was dodging her company, and she smiled in a superior sort of way and was nice as pie to him. Ben knew that there would come a day they would clash again, and his chances of having the stronger will were getting slimmer all the time. From experience, he knew that he couldn't alter what was to be, so he decided to let the future take care of itself, and not cross any emotional bridges until he came to them.

Maybe Lynn would find herself a boyfriend. If she snagged one, he wanted him to be the sort of fellow who would knock the edge off her desires in double time. She would forget all about pestering him, and he would have plenty of time to win Alice's heart and hand. But where he found Lynn willing and waiting anxiously for his love, Alice was altogether confusing. It was not that she was indifferent to his advances. Far from it. She enjoyed his company, but every time he broached the subject of romance, she retreated inside herself. It was as if something was holding her back, and she was unable to break loose.

At last, Ben could stand her mysterious martyrdom no longer and demanded to know the reason for her freeze every time he mentioned love to her. Alice burst into tears and her dilemma came gushing out like the floodwaters from a busted dam. Ben listened to her story with murder in his heart.

"Damn his dirt soul to hell," he said at last. "It'd be a shame to waste ammunition on that rat, but if he was here right this minute, and I had a gun, I don't think I'd object to little target practice. Honestly, I don't."

"Please don't talk that way," she entreated. "If you was to do a thing like that, you'd be a murderer. The law would be after you. It's bad enough now. Please don't do anything to make it worse."

"Alice, why not throw off all this and let me court you like I want to do?"

"I can't."

"But in heaven's name, why? You're a free woman, if only you'd forget all this and exert your God-given rights. Throw off this yoke that's holding you like a bound boy."

"You don't understand," she whispered.

"I most damn certainly don't," he roared with fire in his eyes. "You ain't in exactly what I'd call a hurry to explain."

"I'll tell you now."

"I'm waiting."

"It's like this," she began, tears running down her face. "My life is not my own these days. At least, that's the way I've got it figured. My parents are counting on me to save their home, even if it costs me my happiness. It's a hard thing to say about one's parents, but it's true.

To save the Randall homestead, I'll have to become the wife of a man I loathe, a man who embraces everything sinful and lusting, but I must carry on. I'm duty bound to my parents to help them. I think you're wonderful, Ben. I wish with all my heart that I could welcome your courtship, but I can't. I can't."

"Alice," he said. "I love you. I love you. You saved my life. I believe that in time you will come to love me as I love you now. It would kill me outright to see you made Jess Savage's bride. I believe I would kill that bastard if it come down to brass tacks and he claimed you in exchange for the mortgage on your home. I would fix his clock."

"Hush, Ben," she said as she wiped her tears away with shaking hands. "For god's sake, take it easy. I'm still a single girl. There's many a slip, as the old saying goes. Who can say? Maybe by the time the mortgage is due, he'll be six feet under. Until I know for sure which way the cards are going to fall, I'll not commit myself. Now please be good. Don't make my burden more difficult to bear. A person can endure just so much, you know."

Ben's answer was a blistering curse as he stalked away. Talking Alice out of her martyrdom was hopeless.

During his recuperative period, he had his first meeting with Jess Savage. On numerous occasions, he gotten glimpses of the man as he drove Grant Randall home from town, but he had never come in close contact with him. One evening in early August, Ben, together with most of the Randall household, was sitting on the front porch of the rambling homestead. The only exception in the family gathering was the master of the house.

Grant Randall had left for Richwood early that morning, and he was late getting home. It was twilight. The day had been hot and humid, with heavy clouds drifting across the skies. The promise of rain did not materialize. At sunset, the clouds parted and the sun shone forth in blazing glory as it slowly sank into the western sky. Just as it slipped below a lofty ridge far down the Cranberry, the entire sky woke to pay homage to its celestial supremacy.

Ben watched the gradually changing sunset with an appreciative eye. He loved that time of the day best of all. The hurly-burly of the noon hour was long past and nighttime crept over the land. Regardless of the trials of the day, twilight always seemed to look forward to tomorrow with hope and faith in better things.

"Reckon Pa'll come dragging in about dark, plastered to the gills as usual," Walt was saying in disgust from his seat at the top of the porch steps. Alice and Lynn nodded, their faces resigned. Mrs. Randall rocked in silence in the ancient rocking chair. Not a word passed her set lips. Her faded eyes were fixed meditatively upon the soaring mountain ridges that stepped down the Cranberry. Maybe she drew a measure of strength from those lofty ramparts.

Ben wisely refrained from commenting on the elder Randall's absence. What could he say? Every hospitality had been shown to him. He had been taken in and nursed back to health. He was lonely wanderer of the woods, with no occupation or means of livelihood, except as a ginseng hunter, which was a carefree, irresponsible vocation. To a very few was it profitable. If one were an experienced seng digger, he knew the most likely places to search for the elusive plant. To the inexperienced, all the woods looked alike. Ben was an experienced ginseng hunter, regardless of his recent misstep. He hoped that he never had an experience like that again.

Many topics were discussed, pro and con. Eventually, Ben and Walt's partnership came up for its share of criticism. Mrs. Randall made some pointed remarks that made her disapproval clear. Alice and Lynn exchanged knowing glances with Walt and Ben. The two young men looked at each other. They wouldn't soon forget the storm that had crashed down upon their heads the day Walt announced his intentions to partner with Ben to hunt ginseng. Grant Randall and his wife had thrown their hands in the air in disgust. To them, it was the rankest foolishness to quit working for the farmers and become a seng digger. The idea was preposterous.

"Son," his father boomed in righteous wrath. "Give up this hair-brained idea. You're kidding yourself. Maybe there are sizeable patches of seng in there, but God only knows where they are. The hills never give up their secrets. You're old enough to know that. If it's there, it's so well hidden that you'd search a lifetime for it. It'd be an accident if you happened to stumble onto the right spot. Take my advice, son, and give it up. It's like chasing rainbows. If you persist, it's against my better judgement. If that kind of seng was to be found in there, I'd be the first to go after it. I know it ain't there. You're wasting your time and making yourself look ridiculous."

With the tenacity of bulldogs, Walt and Ben kept their own council and went ahead with their plans. Ben tried to tell them of the big patch of ginseng, but his efforts were worse than wasted. They laughed at him, and told him that his tale was a figment of his imagination, induced, no doubt, by being lost in the woods. They even cast sympathetic glances at him.

Ben stopped trying to convince them of what he had seen. Until he could prove himself, he would hold his silence, but he, Walt, and the girls held their own councils quite frequently up at Walt's cabin, discussing their problems from every angle. As the long summer days passed, their respect and appreciation of each other's ideas and suggestions grew.

A low, distant hum caused Ben and the others to stiffen and exchange glances. The hum became a roar, and a motor car swept around the bend a half mile or so down river. It approached in a whirl of yellow dust. The dust behind the car rose in the motionless air and drifted up the wooded slope, across the narrow mountain valley. The car roared on until it reached the knoll upon which the Randall residence stood. The driver changed gears with a high-pitched, grating squeal.

"Here comes Pa. Got his chauffeur along again, I see," Walt growled. He spat on the ground before him. "Now I'll have another trip after his horse in town at the livery stable. Pa lately grips me all to hell."

"Walter," his mother chided. "Have patience with your father. These are bad days for all of us, and especially for him. Be careful of your temper. I imagine he's been drinking again, and the least said is easiest mended. Don't start anything that you'll be sorry for later. Promise me."

"All right, Ma," Walt muttered. "I'll keep my lip buttoned,   though I'd like to blow my top, but I'm telling you the gospel truth. One of these days, that low-down rat is going to haul Pa home, and I'm   going to explode like a stick of dynamite. I'd bet my last dollar that he eggs Pa on. It's his way. I'll wager he even—"

Just then, the car roared into the front yard and came to an abrupt stop. The dust swirled for a moment, shrouding it from view. Mrs. Randall held up a hand, and Walt was silent.

The automobile was expensive. Big, long, and low it was. If it had been clean, it would have been shiny black, but it was generously coated with dust and splattered with mud from bumper to bumper. Killing the motor, the driver opened his door and stepped out. With a mocking smile, he nodded to those upon the porch, slammed shut the door, and leaned against it. Ben recognized him from Alice's description as Jess Savage, and his body jerked violently in white-hot anger.

"That's him," Walt said, nudging Ben with his knee.

Ben looked into a pair of eyes that were as cold and unfriendly as a rattler's. Ben's contempt for the man rose. Great God, Ben breathed. He would rather die than see Alice forced into marriage to this loathsome creature. His features were a dead giveaway to his soul. They shouted of Savage's love of power. The man's face was stamped with lust, greed, and cruelty.

When Jess saw Ben on the porch, he looked him over with a sharp and disapproving eye. Grant Randall lurched out of the car from the other side, and on rubbery legs unsteadily made his way around the car to where Savage stood. He was intoxicated.

"Ho, Grant," Savage said. "Who's this bird roosting on your front porch? You never said anything about having company. Introduce me."

Grant Randall lifted an unsteady hand and motioned from one man to the other, making introductions. Savage demanded to know where Ben was from and what he was doing in that part of the country. When he was informed that Ben was a hunter of wild ginseng, and that Alice and Lynn had found him lost in the woods and nursed him back to health, he snorted like an angry bull.

"A seng digger, eh?" he sneered. "Feller, that's just another name for a bum. How long you been here?"

"A month, at least," Ben replied, fighting to keep his temper.

"What?" Savage asked. "You've been here all that time with Alice and Lynn waiting on you?"

"Every day."

"Are you ever alone with the girls?" Savage inquired. It wasn't hard to figure out what he was worried about.

Let him think what he wants, damn him, Ben thought gleefully. "I sure have been, buddy." He grinned. "Sometimes me and the girls go for walks in the woods."

"Yeah?"

"Naturally. Oh, we're real chummy. Found out we had a lot in common. These girls are tops with me in any man's language."

Savage's face turned livid. "You bastard," he said, furious. "For two cents, I'd drag your ass off that porch and kick your damn guts out. I'd do it for free if I thought there was a single word of truth in what you're hinting."

"What am I hinting at, Mister Savage?" Ben asked. "Did I upset you?"

"You're damn right you did," Savage snarled. "You insinuated that you've been having your way with these two innocents."

"Jess Savage, you're a rotten, foul-mouthed liar," Walt Randall said softly. He rose from his seat on the porch steps and stepped down to the ground. Though he appeared singularly unconcerned, his father, even in his drunken state, sensed that violence was impending.

"Hold your horses, Walt," Grant said. "And you, Jess Savage, can keep a civil tongue in that fat head of yours. This is still my home, even if you do hold the mortgage. I ain't sunk so low yet that I'll cotton to that kind of talk. Especially when it concerns my family."

Walt stalked out of the yard and up the old logging road that ran up to his cabin. Not once did he look back.

"See here, Grant," Savage growled, looking from Alice's flushed face to Ben's cold, contemptuous eyes. "I have to ask you to show this bird the road. I don't like what's been going on here since this galoot crawled out of the woods. It's a pity you didn't let him starve. If this keeps up, don't be surprised if you wake up one of these fine days and find a knocked-up daughter on your hands, maybe two of them. I say show him the road, while things are still in hand. I don't want him hanging around here anymore. I've a considerable investment tied up in this place, as well as one of its inhabitants. I ain't aiming to have it jeopardized by you dragging home every hobo you meet."

"Well, well," Ben spat, a cutting edge to his voice. "Mister, I'm right happy to have met you. I wouldn't have missed this for the world." He got up from the porch steps, strolled over to Savage, and looked him squarely in the eye. He tapped him a couple of times on his chest with hard knuckles. "Jess Savage," he drawled, "it's been my lot in life to meet up with plenty of low downs, but for genuine lowdown-ness, my puffed-up friend, you take the cake. During the past six weeks, I've heard scads of things about you that were anything but complimentary. Now that I've met you, I know that everything I've heard is true. You've got brass. These good people saved my life. I'm trying to regain my health so that I can pay them for what they done for me. Sure, I hunt seng. A lot of people do. It's common back where I come from. I'm a seng digger, but I'll make it very clear right now to you, Mister Loud Mouth, that I'm no bum. Hit the road back to Richwood while you're still able to navigate under your own steam. You're about as welcome here as a case of smallpox."

"You damn, weak-kneed sponger," Savage roared. His beefy face was mottled with rage. "Don't threaten me. For two cents, I'd have Sheriff Craig on your ass so quick it would make you head swim. I think I'll tip the sheriff off anyway. Might not be a bad idea to investigate you. It's a long ways from here to Parkersburg. One can't be too careful. You might be on the dodge. If the law was to ask me about you, I'd have to be truthful. I don't like your looks."

"No, Savage, it's not my looks that get you worried," Ben said quietly. "What you're het up about is my being in the Randall home. You're scared I'll throw a monkey-wrench into your plans. Upset your apple cart. Well, listen to me, feller, and listen to me closely. That's what I'm going to do, or bust a gut trying."

"What are you talking about, Waters?" Savage asked narrowing his eyes. Savage was as cunning as he was bullying. He played for keeps, but only when the cards were stacked to his advantage.

Ben laughed. "You'll have to figure it out for yourself. I will say this, though. You'll remember what I told you when the right time comes."

"Look, seng-digger, don't get smart with me. I could have you picked up by the law on suspicion, and don't think I wouldn't do it, either. My word carries weight in these parts, and the law is always interested in investigating shady characters. Waters, you fit that bill to a tee."

"Investigate and be damned," Ben said. He noticed with satisfaction that a crimson wave was creeping up Savage's neck. "Investigate me to your heart's content. I've nothing to hide, but I'm willing to lay you five to one that there's plenty about yourself that you wish to remain hidden. Your type always has shady deals in their past. It never fails. Excuse me, my friend. Reckon I'll take a bit of a stroll up by Walt's cabin. Want to go along, girls? I'm sure Mister Savage will excuse us. I have a weak stomach at times, and this has all the earmarks of being one of those times. See you later, friend Savage. I can't say it's been a pleasure, so I'll just chalk it up to experience. Something tells me we ain't seen the last of each other."

"Get out of this country, Waters, or you'll be looking real trouble in the face," said Savage as Ben and the sisters strode out of the yard and started up the old logging road towards Walt's cabin.

"And as for you, Grant Randall," Savage snarled, casting baleful eyes on the old mountaineer, "I'll hold you responsible if anything happens to my plans for Alice and me because of this Waters feller."

"What are you driving at, Jess?" asked Grant. He was a sorry spectacle sitting there, his head hanging low on his chest and his iron-grey hair straggling over his eyes.

"You know damn good and well what I mean."

"Can't say that I do," said Grant. "Put it in words a person can understand."

"What I seen of this wood bum convinced me that he could talk the pants off any girl anytime. I think Alice is took with this bird already. I saw the way she kept looking at him. I know calf eyes when I see them. Get wise to what's going on right under your nose, old man."

"Is that what got you pissed off, Jess?"

"It sure is."

"Forget it," Grant said. Lifting his head, he combed the hair out of his eyes with a shaking hand. "It's not unusual for two young people to be attracted to each other. That's life. Stuff like that makes this old world go around."

"You drunken idiot. Have you forgotten our agreement?" snarled Savage.

"Don't reckon I'll ever able to forget that. You know that's against my will."

"To hell with your will," Savage roared. "I'm boss here, and I intend for things to stay that way. Now get this straight. I ain't wanting to find Alice running around here one of these days with a possum in her belly.

When she does have a brat swelling her ass all out of shape, I want to be the man who did the plowing and planted the seed."

"You foul-mouthed bastard," Grant Randall snarled. "You're every bit as black as you've been painted. I wish I had the nerve to get a gun and blow your rotten, scheming brains out. Maybe then, I'd be able to sleep nights. I hate myself for getting sucked into your plans. If I was half the man that I was thirty years ago, I'd tell you to take this place and go plumb straight to hell with it. It ain't right. No, siree, it ain't right."

"Just keep your end of the bargain, friend, and show this Waters the gate, like I told you."

"I won't order Ben away," Randall said. "I wouldn't do it on your orders, even if I wanted to, which I don't. That would make me a laughing stock. As far as I'm concerned, the young man stays. Anything different wouldn't be the hospitality of the hills."

Up the road towards the little cabin, Ben and the girls were slowly walking along. Alice, as had been her way of late, was silent. Not so Lynn, however. She was in a beautiful rage and voluble in her denouncement of Jesse Savage and all that he represented, using many shocking expressions from her amazing vocabulary.

Chapter 12

*E*ventually, the day came when Ben Waters was once again physically fit. This time, however, he was not alone. Walt Randall strode by his side. Their first day out together, they didn't range far from home. Ben had to build his strength and endurance up gradually. Take it easy at first. That was the ticket. Soon he would be as tireless as he had always been. That was the program for recovery he had outlined for himself, and he meant to stick by it.

The partners' first hunt netted them exactly a dozen small roots of ginseng. When Walt's parents asked about their success, the young men laid out the pitiful pile they had found, and Randall threw back his shaggy head and roared with laughter.

"Boys, I ain't ever been one to say I told you so, but I reckon that expression sums it up. It's hopeless, lads. The seng was cleaned out years back. It's gone. Persisting in this foolishness is like looking up a dead horse's ass. I knew when you boys went out this morning that you could carry all you found in one pocket and have room to spare. My advice, my son, is to forget these wild dreams and go back to work for the farmers between here and Richwood. Take Ben with you. He can scare up a farm job, too. That way, when evening comes, you'll know you've earned yourself a buck. It's foolproof. This other depends on luck. I tell you, boys, it ain't worth the risk."

Walt laughed and said that he thought it only fair that he and Ben be given a chance to see whether ginseng hunting would pay off in the end or not. When his father again urged him to dissolve his partnership with Ben, he only smiled and shook his head. Grant strode to the ancient rocking chair on the front porch, sat down, and began to rock slowly, looking moodily at the soaring, timbered ridges stepping down the Cranberry. Walt looked at Ben, and a wide grin split his somber features.

The next day, Walt broached the subject while they were the woods. He told Ben that he intended to stick with him until Ben himself suggested they fold up and call it quits. Ben kept his own council, and refrained from comment. Time, he knew, would decide the issue.

As the bright clear days of early September came into being, Ben and Walt began to range deeper and deeper into the vast woodlands. At first, Ben was nervous. Every day and night, he wrestled with the horrifying thought that he might get lost again. The feeling was pure hell, but he gritted his teeth and fought it with every ounce of will he could summon. In time, he began to lose his uncertainty and fear.

As time passed and they ranged farther and farther, his old confidence returned. Never again would he plunge recklessly into the fastness as he had the June before. He had learned a hard lesson, which had almost cost him his life. Henceforth, he employed as systematic a method for his forays as he could. Whenever possible, he and Walt hunted up a watershed. To be safe, and not get turned around, all they had to do was cross over and work back down on the other side of the stream. It was as simple as that. Work up one side, and down the other. The method was foolproof.

Ben began to realize that if he and Walt were ever going to find that wild, high ridge with the immense patch of ginseng, they would have to hunt more high ground, and therein lay great danger. Crossing a dividing ridge in unfamiliar terrain is very foolish. It could be a death sentence. All too often, the watershed on the opposite side of dividing ridge brought an unwary hunter out of the woods miles from where he expected, so completely turned around that he might never find his way back. As he and Walt delved deeper into the remote recesses of the woods, Ben pictured the bleached bones of a human skeleton lying white and ghostly in any one of a thousand lonely spots.

As September slowly passed, Ben regained his strength and endurance. He could roam from sunup till sunset, over as rocky a country as one would care to see, and return home in the evening as fresh as when he started out. He became as tough and wiry as seasoned hickory. His nervousness and fear left him, and he came to a deep respect for West Virginia's vast forests.

As summer merged into fall, Ben and Walt began to appreciate the magnitude of the task they had set for themselves. There were a tremendous number of ridges, slopes, spurs, and coves incorporated in a fifty-mile square of mountain wilderness. The figure was staggering. Every watercourse, regardless of its size, was flanked on either side by a branch ridge or spur off the main ridge. Any one of these spurs or branch ridges could house the patch of ginseng. The two hunters looked at each other with grim smiles, clenched their belts another notch, and shook their fists at the soaring ridges.

A voiceless challenge was flung down at them from those mighty ramparts. Grimly, Ben Waters and Walter Randall accepted that challenge. During the third week of September, the hunters found their biggest patch of ginseng to date. They were out on a three-day hike, working out a cove on the headwaters of the branch of Cranberry that Alice and Lynn had found Ben on. It was a Friday. The day before, they had packed food and equipment and headed up the Cranberry to hunt every nook and cranny at the head of the right-hand fork. Of late, they had been finding considerable ginseng, but not the legendary patch.

On the first day out on their three-day hunt, their luck began looking up. That night, they camped on a little flat area close by a spring of amber-colored water that gushed out of the side of a rocky slope ten miles from the Randall homestead. That evening, Walt called Ben's attention to the tracks of enormous cat in the sandbar of a little stream they were working up.

"Hey, Ben," he called. "See those tracks in the sand? Them tracks were made by a cat. A big one, too. You can bet your sweet life it wasn't a house cat that made them."

"What kind of cat tracks are they?" Ben asked. After he walked down to where Walt was standing, he knew that they had been made by a large animal. With a rippling thrill, the thought came to him that they might be panther tracks.

"Panther tracks," Walt said. "If I know anything about tracks, I'd say that the cat that made them tracks is one right fair-sized kitty."

"Do you think he or she is still around here?" Ben asked.

"I wouldn't doubt it for a minute," Walt answered pointing to the rocky, rugged slope to his left.

Rocks were scattered all up the slope, from ones the size of a man to huge blocks of stone as big as a small dwelling. Far up the mountain were the dim outlines of a ledge outcropping running parallel along the crest of the first steep slope. Weeds grew rank, green, and tangled. The soil was a black, sandy loam. All along the stream, the hunters had been finding some nice ginseng with beautiful roots. Each of them carried a strong cloth sack. By evening, they had a pleasing amount of roots, the largest roots to date. Luck seemed to be swinging in their favor.

Ben cast an apprehensive eye up the rocky slope. With a thrill, he recalled the terrifying serenade he listened to on his first night in these woods. Smiling, he shared his experience with Walt, who gave a deep roll of laughter. He seemed to think Ben was stretching things.

"Reckon that would scare the pants off a fellow," he said, laughing. "I've never heard one of them big cats sing yet. No doubt, two panthers put on a show for you. Was you scared, Ben?"

"Was I scared? Walt, I was petrified. The cats, if that's what they was, didn't come anywhere near my camp, but they sure gave me a bad time. That was the worst scare I ever had in all my life. That may sound cowardly, but I admit it."

"Pa always did say them big cats can make the hair stand straight up on your head when they want to," Walt drawled. "Could be we might hear one sing tonight. I ain't craving to hear one of them old boys let off steam, understand, but if he does, I'll listen. Can't do much else, I guess."

"Partner," Ben laughed. "If you hear one of them big cats scream, you'll swear on your family Bible that it's the most God-awful sound you ever heard. If it's possible, it sounds worse than a woman does when she's having a baby without anything to deaden the pain. That's one sound I can do without."

Before night wrapped the forest in darkness, the partners gathered dry wood for a fire. As they cooked and ate their evening meal, they heard nothing unusual. Afterwards, the hunters sat and talked for an hour before retiring for the night. They lay on half of their light, waterproof tarpaulin, and the other half they threw across their blanket-shrouded forms. It was excellent protection against creeping dampness and rain, should it fall during the night. After a long, hard day in the woods, a man needed a dry, warm bed, even though that bed was sometimes hard and rocky. Dryness and warmth were the most important virtues a bed could possess. Buoyancy mattered little.

Soon Walt's deep, even breathing told Ben plainer than words that he had fallen asleep. For an hour or so longer, Ben lay awake, his ears keenly attuned to every night sound. He heard the weird cry of the screech owl, the lonely call of the big hoot owl, the haunting song of the whippoorwill, and a medley of insect and night bird cries. Though he listened long and intensely, everything was as it should be. The late summer night was calm, serene, and uneventful.

Hours later, he was rudely awakened by a vigorous shaking from a heavy hand. With a weary groan of protest, he turned to face his problem. Walt was sitting up with his blanket clasped about his shoulders Indian-fashion. He gave a low "Hssst" and gripped his friend's arm with fingers of steel, his hand shaking violently.

"What's wrong?" Ben asked.

"Just listen and you'll find out," Walt said.

A chill had crept into the night air, and there was a strong hint of frost. Their fire had burned down to a pale glow and a few embers. Leaning forward, Walt carefully laid some small branches of dry wood on the live coals, and fanned it with his hat, hoping that their campfire would rekindle. He settled back and adjusted his blanket more snugly. He was as tense as a strung wire.

Raising himself on an elbow, Ben probed the night shadows around their camp with searching eyes. All he could see were ghostly shafts of pale moonlight slanting through the trees. A full moon swung low in the southwest sky. The light was weak and unreal. After listening for several moments, Ben noticed the conspicuous absence of night sounds. The forest was as silent as the grave. It was as though all other forms of life were waiting, listening, and holding its breath. Ben began trembling. He looked at Walt, who nodded. He'd been awakened by a panther's scream, and if he called once, he would do so again. They were in for a hair-raising experience, a savage serenade that would freeze the narrow of their bones. All they could do was lay there, listen to it, and shake.

Eventually, the cry came. It cut through the stillness, horrible to hear. Ben's body became as rigid as ice. For a moment, he couldn't move. When he did, he looked at his partner and saw his friend's hair standing straight up on his head. Walt sat as though turned to stone. Only his hoarse, uneven breath could be heard. Otherwise, not a sound or move did he make.

Again and again, that horrible cry smote their aching eardrums. Sometimes they were so close together that it sounded like a legion of demons was invading the woodland. At other times, the screaming ceased and a terrifying new sound was heard—a low, long, drawn-out mewl.

The sounds came from high up the rocky slope. As he lay wrapped in his blanket and shook, Ben swore that he would not have ascended that mountain spur for a thousand dollars. He freely admitted his fear. It was there, as big as life, gripping him while icy tremors chased each other up and down his spine. In that moment, Ben felt himself to be a coward, but there wasn't a thing in the whole world that he could do about it. He was completely unnerved, and he knew it.

Grey daylight was creeping over the mountain when the serenade ended. It faded into silence, and it was heard no more. More than an hour later, Walt shook the blanket from his shoulders and pulled on his heavy leather boots. He had slept with all of his clothes on, except his footwear. Kicking the fire into life, he stood over it and peered into every shadow near their camp. Ben smiled. In spite of his bravado, and even though the last scream had been more than an hour before, he was still plenty shaky. In years to come, perhaps he would tell his grandchildren of the night he and Ben slept in the woods and heard the panther scream. Maybe he would even brag a little about how brave he had been. Right at the moment, however, Walter Randall was in no bragging mood. He was pale and grimly silent as he began to cook breakfast.

Chapter 13

*T*he morning sunlight had slanted through the trees and into the lonely cover by the time the hunters had eaten their breakfast. For perhaps the dozenth time, Walt shook his head. Under any other circumstances, Ben would have laughed at his friend's demeanor. In the clear light of day, it seemed almost impossible for any denizen of the forest to so unnerve him. It was preposterous, but true. He just couldn't believe that it had actually happened.

"Ben," he growled. "How did all that screeching, mewing, raving, and crying strike you last night?"

"Not so hot," Ben replied, grinning broadly. "It was quite a show. Did you enjoy it?"

"God almighty. No. I never was so scared in all my life. Them screams seemed to tear the hair right off my head."

"Same here," Ben answered. "I was petrified. I make no bones of admitting it, either. If I told you I wasn't afraid, I'd be a bald-faced liar. When that singing was going on, I wouldn't have climbed that slope for a thousand dollars' worth of the long green. If there'd been a hole handy, I think I would have crawled into it."

"Well, partner," Walt said, "my old man was right. That big cat really rocked me. If I live to be a hundred, I'll never forget how awful he sounded."

Ben nodded as they prepared for the day's hunt.

In the early afternoon, they chanced upon a patch of ginseng unlike anything they had found before. It was in the center of a small cove, a good two miles above where they spent the night. Ben spotted it from fifty yards away. Practically all of the ginseng plants had turned bright, golden yellow, and most of them had ripe, red seed clumps sticking out of the center of the prongs. The patch covered approximately thirty square feet. Most of it stood waist high.

When Ben first saw the patch, his heart gave a great leap for joy. Quickening his steps until he was practically running, he rushed up to the patch of ginseng with his heart in his mouth, beating like a trip-hammer. Now he could lay to rest the doubts that had assailed his partner. Walt hadn't said so, but Ben could tell that he had begun to feel that he made an unwise decision when he threw in with him, but was too much of a man to fold on an agreement. Walt would stick. Of that, Ben was positive. The beautiful patch of ginseng before him represented a considerable amount of money. He believed it would yield more than a dozen pounds of dry root. At least a hundred dollars' worth.

Raising his voice, he bellowed for his partner, who was working the woods a good two hundred feet up the slope.

"Hey, Walt," he yelled. "Come here." His voice was tight with the excitement of his find. At last, he could produce the goods to justify his faith in what he had seen. "Come down here, Walt. Here at last stands the kind of seng I've been telling you about. Partner, just feast your eyes on that patch of Chinese herb. Ain't that one of the prettiest sights you ever did see? We've got it made for this trip, and I don't mean maybe."

"Great day in the morning," Walt said as he strode down to where Ben stood and took one look at the patch of ginseng. "Ben, old man, you sure hit a mare's nest this time. Boy, oh, boy. Put her there. Congratulations." Smiling broadly, a glad light in his eyes, Walt thrust out his strong right hand. Ben met that hand with an iron grip. They shook.

"Thanks for the kind words, Walt," he returned. "Glad you like what you see."

"Like it? I think it's a humdinger of a strike. It's restored my faith in the possibilities of seng hunting."

"I don't follow you, Walt," Ben said.

"Well, it's this way, Ben," Walt began. "I've little confession to make. Don't think too badly of me when I unburden myself. Maybe you've noticed that my interest in our partnership has sort of waned. Maybe it's because our luck has been on the stinking side most of time. I don't know. But I do know that I didn't ever mean to lose interest. It just sort of crept up on me, and you know how my pa kept after me to quit you. I'm very sorry Ben, old man, but doubts creep in. We ain't done too good up to now, but this patch makes up for all the long, hard treks we've had. It'll make Pa laugh out of the other side of his mouth for a change. It'll do him good. After all, he seems to have taken a special delight in heckling us. Maybe that was brought on when I went against his wishes. What the hell, though? I'm old enough to know my own mind, but he don't think so. It's high time Pa got over his bossy ways. After the way he's let Jess Savage wrap him around his little finger, I think he'd be too ashamed to boss me, Allie, and Lynnie around. I'm past twenty, Ben. Maybe I've been too easy-going with my father. I know if a boy or girl lets his or her parents dominate them, it cramps their decisions, even after they come of age. That's gospel truth, Ben, old man. See what it's done to me? I almost failed you. I sure never meant that to happen."

With an easy laugh, Ben thrust out his right hand once more, and Walt was quick to meet it. Ben slapped his partner on the shoulder. Walt had told him nothing that he hadn't divined already. His partner's loss of interest was expected. It was typical. Ben had known many young fellows who begged him to take them on as a partner. Succumbing to the natural desire for human companionship, Ben had, on several occasions, taken different fellows with him on long treks. However, for various reasons, these partnerships were short lived.

He could still hear the excuses. He knew them by heart. They were all the same. Too much walking. Ginseng hunting was harder than they had expected. It was too demanding, too rigorous. The returns of so much effort were often unsatisfactory. However, the dominant reason for their reluctance to continue had more to do with prestige. The long, tiresome, grueling tramps in the woods they could take. Doing without water on the long trails, fighting off mosquitoes, the constant threat of the elements, and the uncertainty of returns from their efforts could likewise be endured. The thought that they had lowered themselves in the estimation of their fellow man was the deathblow to all the partnerships Ben had entered into, except one. His father's estimation of other people's opinions always brought a smile to his lips. It was short, sweet, and to the point.

"To hell with what the other fellow says, son. Long as it's honest work, forget the wagging tongues. Do what you like best and let the rest of the world go by. Do what you like, and you'll be a much happier man." That had been his father's philosophy, and Ben had found it to be a good one.

As he smiled at his present partner, he realized that perhaps Walt felt had also suffered an eclipse in prestige since joining up with him. It took real nerve to become the partner of a wandering nomad, a lowly seng-digger, but though he had wavered, Walt had come through with flying colors. Ben suspected that henceforth, his loyalty was assured. He hoped so. Momentous things depended upon their working together.

"Walt," he said, "I'm not condemning you. It's a common ailment when things are rough. I've been guilty of it plenty of times."

"You mean you ain't mad?"

"Of course not. I would like to know if you still feel you should ditch me."

"I certainly don't."

"You still want to go hunting with me? No matter what anybody says or what kind of luck we have?"

"Yes. I want to keep hunting with you, now more than ever. I'm not saying that solely because of this fine patch of seng we just found, either."

"Then why are you saying it?" Ben asked.

"It's mainly because I've woken up, I guess. I'd hate to think I failed you if I folded up now. No man could be proud of such a thing."

"Walt, I'm sure glad to hear you say that. I've the feeling that our partnership is more solid than ever. We have to stick together, man. Alice depends on us. The Randall homestead is in grave danger. We need to stick together."

"You're absolutely right, partner," Walt replied.

"And you're sure you ain't feeling badly towards me?"

"Forget it. It's a common human ailment."

"Thanks a million, Ben," Walt grinned. "Now, if I ain't too presumptuous, how much of the long green do you think this patch will bring us?"

"That's hard to say right off," Ben replied. "I don't want to sound as though I'm exaggerating, but if this stuff is as old and well developed as I think it'll be, I feel safe saying that it'll yield at least a hundred dollars' worth of dry root. I may be wrong, but I don't think so. I'll be able to give you a more accurate estimation after we have it above ground. What say we hit it? Time is wasting."

"Right-o," Walt boomed. "You're positive there're no hard feelings?"

"None whatsoever." Ben grinned. "I'm human, too. Them long hauls would try anybody's patience. I hope this patch here drives the doubts from your mind. It's in these hills, Walt. Right here stands the proof. All we have to do is keep our faith and keep searching till we hit that patch in the laurel thicket."

"After looking at this seng, I can't help but believe you seen what you said you did," Walt said slowly. "Take this stuff here. I never seen such big stalks of seng in all my born days. I'll bet there's roots in this patch that'll look like sweet potatoes."

Two hours later, the patch of ginseng was dug out. A pile of roots three feet high lay in the center of the dug-up space. Walt's prediction had come true. Many of the big white roots looked not unlike sweet potatoes. Several of the larger roots were as thick as a grown man's wrist and more than a foot in length. While digging the patch, the hunters had found nearly as many roots with no tops on them. The big pile of roots completely filled their heavy cloth sacks.

As soon as they got the big patch of ginseng dug, they headed home. Each carried a heavy sack of roots. That, together with their packs, made a considerable burden. They hunted no more on the steep slopes as they worked their way downstream. They kept to level ground as much as possible. Camp that night was made miles below where they had camped the night before. The night passed uneventfully, unless Ben and Walt slept through the panther's cries, exhausted.

Chapter 14

*T*he following afternoon, at sundown, they arrived home. It was Saturday, and for some reason, Grant Randall had not gone to Richmond. When Ben and Walt strode up to front porch and poured out the two sacks of root, Randall rose from the ancient steer-hide rocking chair and strode to the edge of the porch. He looked surprised. He did not utter a word as he came down the steps and examined several of the larger roots. When he straightened up, his eyes held a strange glint. Ben and Walt grinned and waited for him to speak.

"Holy Moses," he said. "That's quite a pile of seng roots, and big ones, at that. Did you find that patch Ben's been raving about?"

"No, Pa, not yet," Walt replied, "but what do you think of that for a nice bunch of roots?"

"Son, that's the most seng roots I've seen at one time since I was a kid. You boys sure hit a mare's nest this trip. Wherever did you find it?"

"At the very head of the right-hand branch of the Cranberry," Ben said.

"Mister Randall, after seeing what we hit on this trip, do you still want Walt to quit?"

"Ben, that's a hard question," Randall answered. "I believe you're broadminded enough to know to know that anything I said was said solely for Walt's benefit. It wasn't that I've anything against you personally, boy. Far from it. I like you. I thought Walt would be wasting his time out looking for something that isn't there, but now that you boys have really brought in the bacon, I reckon I better keep my big mouth shut. You were right. He is making out far better with you than he would if he was kissing the farmers' asses between here and Richmond. You boys have sort of got me over a barrel. What I can I say, except good luck on your future hunts. How much do you think you'll have in the pile?"

"Ben says we've got well over hundred dollars' worth," Walt replied proudly. "At least, that's what he thinks. We'll know more after we've cleaned and weighed them. Honest Injun, Pa, no more digs and jabs against me and Ben? No more complaining?"

"No more, Walt," his father assured him. "I was wrong. You boys proved it to me. I've no reason to object further. My reasons against hunting seng for profit won't hold water any longer. I'd like nothing better than to take a little seng hunt with you boys myself, only I'm afraid I'd play out in the woods. My strength ain't anything like it was years back. In the last three years, I went downhill fast. I've shot my wad, and I know it. Tell me all about your trip. That's the least you fellows can do after bringing in the bacon."

Ben and Walt narrated the events of the three-day hike. When they told him about the panther tracks and the terrifying screams they heard the following night, Grant Randall threw back his head and roared with laughter.

"Boys, your fears were groundless," he said. "It would've taken wild horses to drag that old cat down to your camp. His screams were just his way of telling you boys that he scented you. He's free and wild. Mankind means capture and death. If you'd gone up there where he was raising all that hell, he would have sneaked off in the woods without a sound, his tail between his legs. The only time them big cats are dangerous is when you have them cornered, or when they are starved for food in the dead of winter. Other than that, you can tramp through them mountains all your life and never catch a glimpse of one. They're very shy."

"But Pa, how can you say a panther's harmless?" Walt asked. "That cat scared me out of a year's growth. I never heard such screams in all my born days. They crucified me. They was positively awful."

"Naturally," chuckled his father, sitting on the porch steps. "Even if he did scare the pants off you boys, he hadn't the slightest intention of coming down and raiding your camp. Scaring his enemies half out of their wits is half of the panther's defenses. He'd much rather run than fight. The next time you boys hear one singing, remember that. Just roll over and go back to sleep. As far as the cat's concerned, you haven't a thing to worry about."

Ben and Walt laughed with the elder Randall. Just then, Alice and Lynn came up from the barn, where they had been doing the evening milking. At sight of Ben and Walt, each waved a cheery hand. When they saw the pile of ginseng roots on the flagstones, they squealed with joy and hurried into the house with their milk pails. Then they came rushing out, their mother trailing along behind. They dropped down on their knees beside the pile of roots and examined several of the larger ones in wonderment.

Mrs. Randall stepped up to Ben and Walt, an embarrassed smile on her face.

"Boys," she said, "I don't know what Pa said to you two before I came out, so I'll speak for myself. As you know, me and him have been dead set against this seng digging. We couldn't believe that you would find enough to pay off. Maybe you two ain't done real well before now, but you really brought home the bacon. You was right all along, Ben. I guess all it takes to find it is sticking with it till you hit the right spot. I want to apologize to both of you boys for the way I acted. Me and Pa was wrong. From now on, I guess me and him had better sit tight, keep our mouths shut, and let you boys alone. You're doing all right without our advice. That's an awful big pile of seng roots. How much do you think there'll be when it's dry?"

"Hard to say, Mrs. Randall," Ben replied. "We'll know more after we wash the roots and dry them. Walt and I accept your apology. We found a nice bunch of roots this trip, but who knows what we'll hit the next time out. Let's hope we do good. I think this haul will net Walt and me over a hundred dollars. Outside of that big patch of seng I stumbled across in the laurel thicket last summer, the patch I found yesterday was the finest I've ever seen."

"I'm real happy you boys hit it," Mrs. Randall said. "What are you going to do with all that money? I wouldn't be surprised if Walt blowed his on some moon-eyed girl. How about you, Ben?"

"What money Walt and I make hunting roots is already spoken for," Ben replied.

"I don't understand."

"I'll explain someday," he said. "Believe me when I say it'll be spent for a good cause."

"Son, I sure hope you and Walt ain't entertaining the idea of going into the moonshine business," Grant Randall said. "Still costs plenty of money, and them revenue agents have real long noses. Seems like them fellers can see right through a stone wall. They're smart as all hell, with noses like ferrets. You boys would be foolish to get yourself mixed up in that."

"Not a chance," Ben laughed. "Everything is perfectly legal and above board. I can't tell you right now, but you'll know one of these days."

"It's okay, son. Spend whatever you make any way you see fit," she said quietly. "You boys will earn every penny you make tramping over these mountains."

"I wholeheartedly endorse what you just said, Ma," Grant boomed in good humor. "Anyway, boys, good luck to you both."

"Oh, Ben," Alice said in a tremulous voice as she rose. She smiled up at him in a way that made his heart leap. "I'm so happy for you and Walt. You boys hit it, as I felt sure you would all along. I never doubted that you fellows would make good. What do you think, Lynnie?"

"I say it's scrumptious," Lynn replied, rising. With a devilish gleam in her eye, she surveyed the hunters. "There's one thing, however, that I'm a little scared of."

"And what's that, sis?" Walt inquired.

"Well, you know," she answered, a big smile flashing across her features like a ray of sunlight, "this sudden good fortune might turn your heads. You boys might get this right. Such things happen every day, you know."

"Aw, hell, sis," her brother growled. "Calm your fears. Ben and me definitely ain't going to get puffed up over a few toad-skins. Money never did go to my head. I never had enough of it at any one time to draw a long breath over. Sis, you're worrying needlessly."

"Lynnie, please," Alice said. "Cut your silly kidding."

"Let her have her fun," Ben said, studying the younger sister speculatively. As always, Lynn was a delight to behold. She was vibrantly alive from the tip of her shiny blonde head right down to the end of her pink little toes. She sensed Ben's eyes on her and gave him a look that promised him her luscious young body. The message was there, as plain as day, for him to see.

"Come and take me. Come and take me as I want you to. Stop putting me off. Let us enjoy that which nature has given us. It's what I need. It's what I want so badly. It's what we both need. Why torture yourself and me, you foolish man?"

The promise of heaven and hell was in her eyes. Looking at her soft body, Ben wished he could do as she so shamelessly pleaded with him to do. As if she read his thoughts, Lynn looked at him again and winked. His blood began to race, and he groaned. Oh, Lordy, he sighed. Oh, Lordy.

"That's right, Bennie-boy," Lynn said with a merry, tinkling laugh. "You know me. I got to have my fun. If possible, I mean."

Grant Randall and his wife smiled broadly. They had thrown off the yoke of worry and anxiety and were enjoying themselves. They seemed to have forgotten the shadow hovering over their heads. Ben was happy to see them enjoying some levity. This light mood was the best medicine they could take. He hoped to see more smiles in the future, and he hoped to be instrumental in putting them there. He longed to lighten their burden. It was a herculean task he had set for himself, but he welcomed the challenge. By bringing deliverance to this worthy family, he would be doing himself a service, as well, paying a debt of gratitude and winning the heart and hand of a wonderful girl.

Alice Randall was worth any effort he might make. His great fear was that he might not be worthy of her love. Her younger sister Lynn was using every wile to seduce him. She was a natural siren, if ever he saw one, capable of turning any man's head against his better judgement and will. She possessed in abundance that feminine appeal to which all men are susceptible.

"Yes, folks," Walt said, pointing to the ginseng roots on the flagstone. "That's one nice little pile of the good root. Me'n Ben hit it good this trip. Hope we can do as well a time or so again this fall, but time's running out on us. Could frost any night now. When that comes, we'll have to wait for next May to dig seng again. I hope we can hit it this fall. I'll bet two to one that our friend Mr. Savage would bust a gut if he knew me'n old Ben had brought in the bacon."

Everybody nodded. Then all fell silent. It was as though a blight had fallen upon Grant and Beatrice Randall. Randall's features resumed their harried look. Ben cursed under his breath. Walt fell silent as he bent to gather the ginseng roots. Ben helped. They always washed clean every root they brought out of the woods. This time, Alice and Lynn volunteered to help.

Randall and his wife got up and disappeared into the rambling old dwelling. The mere mention of Jess Savage's name had a cast a shadow over them. Even Lynn had no witty remarks or quips as she and Alice went to prepare water to wash the roots in. Alice was miserably silent and preoccupied. Realizing it was Saturday night, Ben offered Walt the use of his ancient touring car to go and see his girlfriend Flo. With a wide grin, Walt accepted the offer and threw off his depression. They plunged into eager discussions of their plans for hunting ginseng that fall. Ben was glad to talk and plan with him.

Hours later, Ben and the two sisters were sitting on a low bench under the spreading branches of an oak tree that stood at one end of their front yard. The late September night was balmy and soft. Overhead, the stars twinkled and blazed. To the southeast, a pinkish glow marked the spot where the round harvest moon would soon appear. The punkies were in full force, but the three young people ignored the ravenous gnats as best they could and talked about how their parents had brightened at the sight of the roots Ben and Walt brought home.

As usual, Ben and Lynn monopolized the conversation, but Alice seemed content to sit and listen. She always replied when spoken to, but immediately drifted back into her detached state. Once Ben slipped an arm around her waist and squeezed her closer to him on the bench. With a low apology, Alice removed his arm from her waist and placed it by his side. Ben was shocked and hurt by her resistance. She had forsaken happiness and embraced martyrdom on behalf of her family. Nothing Ben could say or do seemed to penetrate the shell she had placed around her heart. Joshing her out of it was as futile as beating one's head against a wall. Ben decided to wait until she was in a more receptive mood. He loved Alice Randall, and he would fight the devil before giving her up.

Soon after Alice had removed his arm from around her waist, she rose from the bench and announced her intention to retire for the night.

"Coming, sis?" she asked.

"Not yet, Ally," said Lynn. "I'll be in after a little. It's hot tonight, and I want to pester Ben a while longer."

Ben knew why Lynn wanted to be alone with him in the warm, velvety darkness. She was planning to try to seduce him again. Of that, he was as certain as life itself. She did not disappoint him.

No sooner had her sister crossed the yard and entered the house than Lynn, with a low, throaty laugh, and no preliminaries, threw her young body into his arms. Flinging her arms around his neck, she began to kiss him and press her quivering breasts against his chest. Her nipples were as hard as ripe cherries, and as hot as live coals. Her breath came thick and hot. She trembled from head to foot as she worked her luscious, ruby lips onto his. Ben was quite overcome by her behavior. For several moments, he was at a loss for what to do.

When he recovered, he reached up and unclasped her arms from around his neck. This was no easy task. Lynn Randall possessed amazing strength. She was as strong and wiry as a boy, and she wriggled all over him and the bench during the struggle. When at last he had her under control, he chided her strongly for her actions. His half-angry words never fazed her. Turning her head, she put her lips against his cheek.

"Lynn, for God's sake," he growled. "What in the hell is the meaning of this?"

"Can't you guess, Bennie-boy?" she asked.

"I've a pretty good idea what you've got up your sleeve, young woman, but you tell me."

"You don't know why I threw myself into your arms?"

"I didn't say that."

"You leave that impression," she said.

"All right, all right," he said from between set teeth. "Enough. Come clean at once, or I'll turn you over my knee and spank you so hard that you won't be able to sit down for a week."

She laughed merrily. "I dare you to lay one single finger on my body, Ben Waters," she taunted. "You're scared stiff that once you get started working on that part of my anatomy, you won't be able to stop. I know what you're thinking. You can't fool me."

"Poppy-cock, Lynnie," he growled, giving her a shake. "Now quit stalling and tell me why you jumped me. That ain't a bit becoming of a lady, you know."

"Fiddle sticks, Bennie-boy," she laughed. "Who gives a damn about acting like a lady? I don't. My reasons are quite simple. I need some loving."

"What's that got to do with me?" he asked, but he knew what her answer would be.

"Plenty, Ben Waters," she said. "I need some loving. I need my corn popped. Get my drift?"

"Lynnie," Ben cried, aghast.

"I need some loving, or I need my corn popped. Say it anyway you want, but that's what it adds up to. And you, my good man, need your cob shucked the worst way. That's our condition in a nutshell. So what say you and I rectify the situation? It's nice and warm outside tonight, and we're all alone and in no danger of being disturbed. The grass is soft and deep here by the bench. I am in your arms, in the mood for you to possess all of me—Oh, so utterly. What better setup could anyone   ask for? It's made to order. Quit wasting time and go to town."

"Hush, girl," Ben whispered. "What you're asking for must never be. I happen to love that foolish older sister of yours, and I hope with all my heart that she'll snap out of her self-sacrificial role before she's lost to me forever. That's how it is, Lynnie. I want to be worthy of her if she does change her mind. What kind of fellow would I be if I satisfied my sexual desires with her sister? To do a thing like that, I'd have to be lower than a snake."

"I don't agree," Lynn said. "I'd say that you was behaving as any man would, or should, who is tired of being strung along."

"Maybe so," he agreed, "but that would only get me in hot water. No, Lynnie. My best bet is to keep my nose clean until I know either way."

"Ben Waters, you're crazy," she said. "We could have so much fun if you'd wake up to the facts. I love my sister, but get your loving while you've got the chance, and let tomorrow take care of itself. Right now, she won't give you a tumble for love, money, or good looks. You and I know why. Allie is bowed down with an oversized sense of duty. You've tried to get her to see things your way, but it's no soap so far. If she keeps turning the cold shoulder to your romancing, I'd say you're wasting your time. Here's another thing. Some other fellow might turn up, and Allie could become interested in him and drop you and Jess Savage like a pair of hot potatoes. Don't laugh. I'm not kidding. Such things happen every day. And if it should happen, I bet you'd be one sorry fellow that you threw over your shoulder what I'm so anxious for you to sample. Think it over, Bennie-boy. You know I'm right."

"I have thought it over, Lynnie," he replied. "You're right. It could happen, but the odds are against it. I'll just wait it out and see which way the cards fall before I get involved with an amorous little charmer like you. After all, there's more sensible things for me to do than stick my long neck out."

"Imbecile," she hissed. She even stomped her feet.

Ben shook with silent laughter, but he didn't realize she still had the ability to turn the tables to her own advantage. Twisting her supple body sideways, catching him off-guard, his hold on her was broken. As a quick as flash, she leaned forward and gave him a violent shove backwards. Before he could regain his balance, he tumbled off the bench and onto the grass. Quick as a cat, Lynn flung herself upon his prostrate body,   using her outstretched hands to break her fall. With a low laugh, she wrapped her arms around his neck and pressed her body close to his on the mat of dewy grass. Her eager mouth found his with long, passionate kisses. Her vibrant young body began shouting her desire. Waves of response coursed through his veins. His will power suffered. He had to flee or all would be lost. All he could think of was that he must be true to his love for Alice at all costs, so he fought free of her arms, her hypnotizing lips, and her body, and he plunged away into the gloom.

Chapter 15

For the remainder of September and the early part of October, Ben and Walt roamed the wilderness in their quest for ginseng. In some sections of the forest, their luck was very rewarding, while in other parts, they couldn't find as much as a single stalk. The two hunters had grown more compatible as the weeks went by until they were able to take the good days with the bad without protest or praise either way. It was all just part of the day's work. Gradually, Walt became a seasoned hunter. It gladdened Ben's heart to witness the transformation, because he knew they would have to have and exercise patience if ever they were to find that elusive ridge. It was there. It would take a world of hunting to find it, but find it they would. Find it they must. Failure was not an option.

In mid-October, they realized that they would have to wait for May before they could dig ginseng again. The season was over. When they estimated the value of the roots, Ben said that they had at least three hundred dollars' worth of dry root. They were well pleased with what they found, though they hated falling short of their goal. They comforted themselves with the knowledge that come spring, they would haunt the hills until they found success.

The week following the end of the root season, Ben went home to visit his folks for a few days. Walt and Lynn accompanied him. He tried to talk to Alice into going, but she retreated into her shell of self-sacrifice and refused. No amount of entreaty would change her mind, so he gave up in a huff and left without her.

The trip was uneventful, and they arrived at his parents' home just at sundown. They were received with open arms. As he shook hands with his father, and gave his stepmother a hug and a kiss, he remarked that it was good to be home again, but that the old place looked different. When they asked in what way, he grinned and shrugged.

"Oh, I don't know," he replied. "More open ground than I've seen for a while, and neighbors that weren't here last June. It's the same old hills, but they look low to me now. Enough gabbing. I want you to meet two very good friends of mine. This is Walt Randall and his sister Lynn. Walt and Lynn, this is my father and stepmother, and that woman standing to one side with the baby in her arms is my oldest sister. Her husband is there in the doorway. This bunch ain't much for looks, I know, but I reckon I got to own them. Haw, haw."

"We sure are glad to meet you young folks," Moses Waters said, shaking hands with Walt and Lynn. "Come right on in and make yourselves at home. This ain't no country mansion, but you're as welcome as the flowers in May. We've had our supper, but Ma and Effie'll soon scare you all up plenty to nibble on. Dog gone it, if we'd known you was coming today, we'd've been loaded with fancy grub and waiting for you to show up, but as it is, you'll have to take potluck. It's the best we can do on short notice."

"Shucks now, Pa," Mrs. Waters said. "Take Ben and his friends on into the living room and take it easy. Don't make it sound like we've ate up all the victuals. There's plenty left. You folks just sit, talk, and rest up a bit. Me'n Effie'll call you when it's ready."

Walt and Lynn liked Ben's parents, and as they retired to the living room, they told them not to go to any bother in preparing supper for them. Just set out anything at all, they said, and they would eat it and be happy. An hour later, Ben and his friends were well fed and back in the living room. Outside, night was dropping fast. A chill had crept into the air, announcing winter not too far in the future.

Ben's father asked him to talk about being lost in the woods the June before, and as he related the frightening experience, they all listened intently. To people of rural districts, there is probably nothing more horrifying than being hopelessly lost. Ben's folks were no exception, but they listened with awe to his narration about stumbling across the huge patch of ginseng.

"Great day in the morning," his father boomed. "Well, hang me for a horse thief. Son, that matches a tale I heard more than thirty years ago. I didn't believe it then, but reckon I do now. That would be some patch of seng. Boys, I'm putting in my bid to help you fellows dig that patch. How about it? Will you humor an old man and let me in at the finish?"

They immediately promised he could. Midnight had come and gone before Amos Waters let his son and friends retire. The grizzled farmer was wound up like a phonograph, and he just wouldn't run down. Eventually, however, he caught Ben dozing in his chair, apologized for his poor manners, and shooed them off to bed.

On the fourth day of Ben's visit, Amos collared Ben for a long man-to-man talk. They retired to the barn for their talk. Men of their ilk spoke more freely and easily in their own element. As soon they were comfortably seated on bales of hay, Amos turned to his son and began.

"Boy, oh, boy," he chortled. "Son, we'll talk of more serious things later, but right now, I want to let off a bit of steam. I'm ashamed to carry on this way, but that gal you brought home is about the hottest looking piece I've seen in many a long day. What looks! What a shape! What wicked eyes and rolling hips! Wow. Take it from me, son, she's got it, and I don't mean maybe. I used to meet up with that kind in dance halls and such years back, but not lately. I ain't saying any harm about this gal, or even hinting at any. I just can't keep these old eyes off her. Tell me about her. What's she like?"

"Now look, Dad. You ain't trying to say Lynnie is a girl with loose morals, are you?" Ben asked.

"Hell, no," Amos said. "It ain't that at all. It's only that she's different from the ordinary run of girls, if you know what I mean."

"In what way?"

"That's sort of hard to explain. Maybe if I was good at words, I could put my meaning better."

"You could try," Ben said. He wanted to hear his father's view. He never had before, but now he did.

Amos looked at him. "That little gal ain't a bad one. I can see that, but heaven only knows what she would turn out to be if conditions thrust her into the wrong environment. She's as high spirited as a thoroughbred, and I'd stake my last cent that she would make love as wildly, passionately, and completely as any gal could make it. I may be wrong, son, but that's how I've got that little lady pegged."

"You're not far wrong, Dad," Ben replied, as a smile played at the corners of his mouth. Thoughtfully, he wondered what his father would say if he confessed the many times and devious ways that Lynn Randall had tried to seduce him.

"What do you mean, Ben?" the older man asked.

Ben's answer was noncommittal. Perhaps he should confide in his father. After all, he reasoned, sometimes the advice of an older person was all that was needed to set a fellow straight. For months, he beat his head against a stone wall trying to talk to Lynn out of her foolishness. Maybe his father could give him pointers on how to handle her. At the thought, he grinned to himself. It was worth a try.

However, before unburdening himself, they quit the barn and strolled up a wooded ravine that sloped down from the ridge behind the structure. Coming to a small bench about halfway up the ridge, they found a comfortable seat on the trunk of a dead chestnut tree. Ben sat down and leaned against the trunk of a sapling. Before seating himself, his father knocked the ashes out of his pipe, took a twist of homegrown tobacco from his pocket, and proceeded to shave enough tobacco to fill his pipe. After he had his pipe going like a smokestack, he looked at his son.

"Okay, son," he said. "I've got the impression there's something on your mind. If there is, spill it. Anything you tell me will be held in the strictest confidence. Besides, there ain't a soul around to listen to your story except you and me. These trees standing ain't got no ears to hear with and that bright October sunlight will only make your story easier. Your friends took Mom into Parkersburg this afternoon, and your sister and family are up at Grantsville visiting her husband's folks. We ain't likely to be disturbed, so if there's anything you'd like to talk over, I'd be happy to lend an ear and help iron out any rough spots. Don't reckon we could have picked a better time and place."

"Yeah, Dad, I know," Ben answered as he gazed at the far off ridges across the Little Kanawha River. The wooded ridges brought back memories of the ginseng roots he had gathered there. Those hills and coves were the scene of many long hikes in the woods. He would have liked to go back to those days. However, the mere thought of the serenity of the past brought back the present's mental chaos.

"Dad, remember those babes I used to brag about laying when I worked on the river?" he asked.

"Sure do, son, and I don't mind telling you again that I have the same opinion of your tall tales now that I had when you first told them."

"Still think I was pulling your leg? Still think I was spreading it a bit thick?"

"That's right."

"I can't say as I blame you. But honest Injun, Dad, everything I ever told you was gospel truth. If anything, I didn't tell you half of what some of them sexy babes actually did when they got lathered up. You'd have to experience that sort of thing to believe it, I guess."

"All right, all right," his father said. Though he claimed to believe Ben's stories, doubt lingered in every word, look, and action.

"I've something more I'd like very much to confide in you," Ben said. "This ain't about an affair I've had, but I can't for the life of me see that it differs much. All it lacks is action on my part. Want to hear about it?"

"Naturally. I'm only human. All people love to hear a story of sex. Get it off your chest, son. Maybe you'll feel better."

"I hope you won't think me an utter fool," Ben said as a wave of crimson washed over his features.

"Has this got to do with this split-tail you brought home with you?"

"Yes."

"Shoot the works, then," Amos Waters drawled as he blew out a huge cloud of smoke. "Where a woman is concerned, anything can happen and usually does. From what I've seen of this filly, I'd say she's capable of kicking up one hell of a storm in any man's pasture. If you went off the deep end over her, you're not the first man to make a fool of himself over some skirt, and you sure won't be the last."

"Look, Dad, you don't understand."

"Maybe not, but I know a few things about women. I ain't lived more than three score of years for nothing. Are you in love with this girl?"

"No."

"Have you been so in the past?"

"No."

"Then what in the cat hair has got you on the fence? I don't understand."

"Be patient and you will. First, though, have I your word that you'll keep everything I tell you under your hat?"

"Sure, son. Haven't I always? I can be as close mouthed as an Indian when I want to. I don't get the deal with you and that gal. If you're not in love with her, I can't see where she figures in your trouble. You know what she needs, don't you?"

"I most certainly do."

"Then why don't you give it to her? Afraid she'll like it? Or have you lost your manhood? Is that what's holding you back?"

"Hell, no," Ben roared.

"Well, what is your trouble then?"

"I'm in love with her sister," Ben replied miserably, dropping his head.

"Aw, balls," his father grunted. He spat on the ground. "You let that stay your hand. You're not the son I used to know."

"You're right. I'm not," Ben agreed without rancor. "Listen to my story, and then maybe you'll understand why I tried to put my old life behind me. Why I've wanted to turn a new leaf where girls were concerned, and why I'm now sort of between a rock and a hard place. It won't be easy to tell it as it happened, but I'll do my best."

"Proceed," his father said with a gleam in his eyes. "I doubt I'll understand it, son. Especially if it involves that hip and tit shaking little filly. Go ahead and talk. I'll just sit here and listen. Maybe you can convert me. I ain't guaranteeing results."

Smiling, Ben began. As Ben talked, his father listened attentively, but made no comments. For this, Ben was grateful. He told of his love for Alice Randall, of its gradual birth during his convalescence, and of its eventual maturity.

When he related Jesse Savage's scheme to enslave Alice to his lustful desires, his father awoke with a thundering curse. Then he lapsed again into silence, but his eyes spoke volumes. Ben told him of the girl he loved, who loved him, but because of her imagined duty to her parents had shut their love out of her heart, and his father again cursed roundly, and then caustically denounced Jesse Savage as an unprincipled cad. Then Ben paused, at a loss for words. He didn't want his father to think him an absolute ninny.

"Get with it, Ben," Amos guffawed. "Stop beating around the bush. You ain't told me nothing yet that a blind man wouldn't know after being around her for just an hour. I have a feeling I know what you're trying to tell me. Go ahead. Just state the facts. That's all I want to hear."

Finally, under his father's prompting, Ben disclosed how she had repeatedly tried her feminine wiles to seduce him and hung his head in embarrassment.

"You say she stripped off all her clothes when you took her for a walk up the Cranberry?" he asked.

"That's right."

"All of them?"

"As naked as a bird."

"Did she make a pass at you then?"

"And how!" Ben laughed.

"I'll wager that you rolled her good in the leaves right then and there."

"No, I didn't."

"What?"

"Dad, I know you can't believe me when I say this, but Lynn Randall is still a virgin. If she's lost her cherry, it ain't my fault."

"How come, for crying out loud? This ain't like you at all. Especially after she throwed it in your face and rubbed it on you. I'm getting more balled up by the minute. Son of a bitch. What in heaven's name has come over you out there, Ben?

"It's this way, Dad," Ben explained. "After the girls found me in the woods, took me home, and nursed me back to health, I resolved to put that wild streak behind me. I fell in love with Alice, and I'm very fond of Lynn. I've tried to persuade Alice to respond to my feelings. So far, it's been hopeless. She persists in holding me at arm's length. She says that if she must marry this Savage to save her parent's home, she'll do it. Marry him, and he'll tear up the mortgage. Refuse him, and unless they have every last red cent on the day it's due, he'll throw them all right out in the road, bag and baggage. Until she knows one way or the other, there can be nothing between us. That's my problem in a nutshell. Alice is in a trance, and Lynn is throwing herself at me every time she has the opportunity.

"And I take it that you've let her get away with it so far, right?"

"That's about it."

"But why, for heaven's sake?" Amos asked.

"The only explanation I can give is that I'm hopelessly in love with Alice. If she does finally throw off this yoke, I want to feel worthy of her love. Sounds foolish, I know, but that's how I feel."

"In the meantime, I suppose you're going to keep letting this hot little bitch rub it all over you?"

"That's about the size of it," Ben acknowledged, red-faced. "I don't see what else I can do. If she'd latch on to a boyfriend, maybe she'd concentrate on him and lay off me. I'm hoping that'll happen."

"I'll be damned," Amos Waters said in disgust. "Son, do you want my advice?"

"I reckon I do," Ben replied slowly, though he knew beforehand what his father's diagnosis would be before he had spoken a single word.

Amos Waters was an old school man. He firmly believed in an eye for an eye, a tooth for a tooth, and calling a spade a spade. Toe the line, and let the chips fall where they would. That was his code, and he lived by it.

"Son," he said. "There's only one solution to your problem. You have to exert your manhood before any kind of peace can be yours. As far as Alice is concerned, you're beating your head against a wall. Stop worrying, and let time work this thing out. I don't see how you can do otherwise. In the meantime, stand up and be a man. Let no hot-crotched little bitch put anything over on you, regardless of whose sister she may be. It's the only way. Before that trouble out there is over, you'll have to do with Lynn Randall what I'd have done long ago. It's unavoidable. Mark my words."

Chapter 16

*F*our days later, Ben was back on the Cranberry. He took leave of his folks with relief. He had grown apart from them during his journey to the Gauley River country. He couldn't explain why, but he felt that his place was there in the shadow of those soaring ridges and domes, waging a battle against terrific obstacles for Alice's heart and hand. In reality, the explanation was quite simple, but Ben didn't ponder why he felt as he did. He only knew that that was how it was and humbly accepted this phase of his life. Biological experts could have given him a reason for his newfound convictions, but that truth had not revealed itself to him. Nature could have told him that home is where the heart is.

His parents bade him God speed and wisely refrained from comment when he informed them of his intention to spend the winter with the Randalls. He told them that he and Walt had decided to run a trap-line on the upper Gauley River watershed. Maybe while the leaves were off the trees, they would find that elusive ridge. Once they found it, they could tell Jesse Savage to go straight to hell and take all of his rotten schemes with him.

Grant Randall and his wife received him with their customary hospitality upon his return, and he was shocked to see how hollow and haunted their eyes were. Save for a few questions as to the pleasantness of his trip and the reunion with his family, they lapsed into brooding and scarcely uttered a word thereafter, except when spoken to.

For once, Alice acted glad to see him. As he rattled up into the front yard in his automobile, she ran out of the house with outstretched arms and a wild cry. Straight into his arms she flew, like a frightened bird seeking refuge. He clasped the trembling girl close to his breast, speechless. His heart was overflowing. Wordlessly, he bent his head and kissed her upturned lips.

When he raised his head, he looked into her parents' eyes. They knew she loved him. They came down the steps and out across the yard to greet him. Their welcome was genuine, and he was glad. There was no false front with these good people, just simple, openhearted hospitality.

However, Alice immediately withdrew into her preoccupied state, and quietly voiced her intention to go back inside and begin supper. Ben marveled at her control. In a moment's time, she had become as calm and unruffled as though he had not been away from her at all. Alice reentered the house, and with a wink, raised eyebrows, and a shrug, Lynn followed her older sister. Ben remembered his father's words. To apply them, he would have to forsake that for which he had so valiantly fought. Maybe there was another way to bring Lynn's emotions under control without becoming intimately involved. He fervently hoped so, anyway. With a disgusted shake of his head, Ben swung on his heel and began helping to unload the car.

Later that evening, he persuaded Alice into going for a car ride with him. With knowing looks, Walt and Lynn begged to be excused, pleading fatigue after the long ride home from the Ohio River Valley. Gratefully, Ben accepted their excuses. Bundling Alice into his drafty old car, he started off with a rattle, a wheeze, a chuckle, and a roar, resolved to make the most of his opportunity. He decided to keep her out with him until midnight or later, if possible, and headed towards Richwood, a good thirty miles to the southwest.

As the miles sped by, Alice looked at him, wondering at their destination. Ben looked neither right nor left, but grimly ahead, and said nothing about where he was taking her. He just wanted to get her a goodly distance from home. Maybe by the time he returned, he would have talked her into giving up her martyrdom.

At last, Alice's curiosity could contain itself no longer. "Where are we going, Ben?" she asked.

"Oh, for little ride in the moonlight."

"Little ride, my foot," she scoffed. "We've already come further than that. You can turn around right here and take me home."

"No."

"What's wrong?" she asked. "Why are you acting this way? You lied to me, Ben Waters. You said this was going to be a short ride. I don't like being lied to. Not a bit. The least you can do is tell me where you are taking me. I deserve to know that much and I'm cold. This antique you call an automobile is as drafty and cold as a barn."

"All right," Ben answered. "We're headed for Richwood."

"What?" she gasped. "Why are we going there, for heaven's sake? Richwood must be another twenty miles up the road, if it's an inch. It'd be ten-thirty by the time you coaxed this limousine that far."

"So what?" he said. "Is that such a late hour for a justice of the peace to be dragged out of bed?"

"What did you say?" she asked in disbelief.

"You heard what I said," he growled.

For a moment, she stared straight ahead. After a while, she began to mumble under her breath.

"Rushing to Richwood," she mumbled, "in the middle of the night. Just him and me. Dragging a justice of the peace out of bed. Why do that? What use could we have for his services? What am I saying? What I am thinking? He's dragging me away from home in the middle of the night to force me to marry him. Stop this car at once, Ben Waters."

"Why?" he asked, driving right on as though she had not spoken. If anything, he increased the speed of the car.

"Ben, have you lost your mind?"

"I don't think so. I feel perfectly normal."

"You're trying to force me to marry you against my will."

"Did I say I was?"

"No. Not in as many words, but ain't that what you've got up your sleeve?"

"Is that what you think I'm up to?"

"What else can I think?" she quavered. "What other reason would two young people have for visiting a justice of the peace?"

"Oh, there's scads of reasons. Justices of the peace have other duties."

"Then you're not taking me to Richwood to force me into marrying you?"

"Never," Ben thundered.

"And you don't love me or want to marry me?"

"Girl, you're plumb dotty," he groaned. "I love you, just as you love me. Do you think I don't know why you flew into my arms this afternoon?"

"I don't know why I did it. I don't want to ask myself that question."

"Alice, quit denying your heart. You love me, yet you're so blinded by duty that you'll marry another."

"Ben, you're heartless," she cried out. "I'm tortured enough without you adding to my suffering. I'm doing what I feel I must."

"Girl, admit it. Tell the truth for once."

"I can't. I can't."

"Liar, cheat, two-faced, deceiving female!"

"Oh, terrible, terrible," she gasped. "Now I know that you don't love me. You couldn't. No man ever loved a girl and talked to her as you do to me."

"Good God, Alice Randall," he cried. "Do you think I'm made of stone? I love you more than I can put into words. Oh, you foolish, blind imbecile of a darling. I'd give my right arm to make you my wife. Now get this straight. Before I'd marry you against your will, I'd die a bachelor. Forget my hot words. Forget anything I said about a justice of the peace. I wanted to see what you'd do and say. If I frightened you, I'm sorry. I think it is a wonderful idea, this getting married, I mean, but calm your fears. If you ever become my wife, it'll be because you're willing, not because you're forced into it."

She sat as though turned to stone for several moments. If it had been daylight, however, he would have needed one glance to see that her heart was in her eyes. For the second time that day, she uttered a wild, heart-broken cry, a cry known only those to who are desperately, hopelessly in love. Covering her face with shaking hands, she burst into sobs. Ben pulled to the side of the road, halted the car, and shut off the motor. He gathered Alice close, and she did not protest. It was as though he represented peace and security.

With gentle hands, he tilted her face and bent with hungry lips to claim hers. She responded to his kiss as though she was trying to drink him down. Eventually, reluctantly, she released his lips, but her trembling hands only clutched him harder. He covered the pale oval of her face with kisses, savoring the salty sweetness of her tears shed for love of him. He remembered the many months he had longed to hold her, only to be denied, so he felt justified in glorying in her tears. Perhaps this outburst meant that she had come to her senses and would return his love. He fervently hoped so.

Finally, her tears subsided. With a few remaining sniffs, she withdrew and began to dab at her eyes with a white, lace-trimmed handkerchief. Ben silently waited for her to speak. She rapidly drew back into her impenetrable shell. It was in the stiffening of her drooping shoulders, the prolonged silence. Ben ground his teeth in hopeless rage and held his tongue with difficulty.

"I'm sorry, Ben, for being such a cry-baby, but I can't help it," she murmured.

"That's all right, Alice," he replied. "Now, if I'm not being presumptive, tell me why you cried at all. Or are you afraid to answer that question?"

"Ben, don't speak so to me," she pleaded. "If I told you why I broke down, it would only kindle hope in your heart for something that may never be. It wouldn't be fair to you."

"Girl, quit hedging," he cried hoarsely. He grabbed her by the shoulders and shook her roughly. When he released her, she fell against him. He once more folded her in his arms. "You know as well as I do that you love me. That's why you go around looking like a sleepwalker. You're a young, single woman who's free, white, and old enough to make up her own mind. It's the only way you'll ever find happiness. The sooner you recognize this, Alice Randall, the better it'll be for you and me."

"Ben, I can't lie to you," she said quietly, pulling away. "I do love you. I can't hide what's in my heart. I'm the most miserable girl alive. This life is hell. What can I do? My parents depend on me to save their home. If I fail them, they'll spend their old age in the poor house. I can't let them down, Ben. I can't. I know it means sacrificing any happiness you and I might have shared, but I can't help it. You're young yet, Ben. Put me out of your mind. Forget me, darling, and look for love elsewhere. You'll find another girl. Then you'll laugh when you recall the silly girl who put duty ahead of her heart's desire. What can I say, Ben? What else can I do?"

"Marry me," he roared. "That's what you can do. Let the hide go with the tallow as far as the homestead is concerned. Let Jess Savage have it. Your folks can come and stay with us after we're married. They'll always be welcome. I'd treat them right."

"I'd do what you suggest in a minute if it was that simple," she replied wearily. "But it ain't. Mother might be all right, but it'd break Dad's heart to have to give up his home. It's a part of him, and from the way he's acting these days, I'd say it's a big part. That place has been the Randall home for a hundred years. To lose it now would kill my father."

"But what of you and me?" he persisted.

"Forget our happiness, Ben," she answered with a break in her voice. "Maybe life has good things in store for us later. Let's wait and hope. Remember what it says in the Bible about honoring our parents? That's me, exactly. I may be crazy and blind, but I'm going to do for them what I can and try not to remember our sacrifice too keenly."

"Dear heart, waiting and hoping can be a dangerous thing between two people in love," he muttered, remembering her sister Lynn. He recalled his father's advice and predictions. Oh, lordy, he groaned. If she only knew, she was driving him straight into her younger sister's eager, waiting arms.

He wondered how long a man's love could be denied. Things could not go on as they were indefinitely. Some kind of a break was bound to come. Her sad voice recalled him from his brooding thoughts.

"You're absolutely right," she was saying. "Uncertainty between two lovers is dynamite. It can't be helped. Ben, why don't you play up to Lynnie? She likes you a lot, and it'd do you both good to have a few dates and go to dances. You know how tomboyish she is. She'd get a kick out of showing an older man off to the girls her own age. What do you say? At least that way, you wouldn't be sitting around brooding about us all the time."

"Good lord, Alice," Ben cried. "You don't know what you're saying."

Her words had come as a terrific shock. If only she knew how her younger sister longed for such an opportunity. She would make   every effort to take advantage of the situation.

"Alice, you're out of your mind," he said firmly. "That would be very unfair to Lynnie. She's practically a child."

"Oh, Ben, please," she half-laughed. "Don't be foolish. Lynnie's past eighteen. A child my foot. She's as much a woman now as she'll ever be. In body, I mean. That little sister of mine will make some man a very interesting wife someday. I know what I'm talking about. We share the same room and bed, you know. There's been plenty of times I've seen her get hotter than a firecracker. Oh, don't laugh. I know what I'm talking about. She's got as well developed a body as any girl could ask for. There's any number of girls who are married and have babies that ain't a single day older than Lynnie. So if you was to change your mind and take my sister to a dance, don't think that you'd be robbing the cradle. Far from it. She's plenty old enough to go out with a   boyfriend.

Here's another thing. If she was out with you, I'd know she'd be in good hands."

Ben shook his head. Good hands, she said. Good hands, indeed. Oh, brother. Here was temptation if ever he saw it. In years gone by, he would have jumped to take advantage of the possibilities, but now he was fighting a fight that he was not at all certain that he would win. He had wanted to laugh when Alice spoke of how well developed Lynn was. As if he didn't already know. Would he ever forget her loveliness that afternoon up the Cranberry? And would he ever forget how her lusciously curved young body had clung to his as though she had been tailored to fit? No, he would never forget, not in a lifetime. His mind swung to other occasions when Lynn had thrown conventions and good behavior to the winds and employed every trick to attain her sensual desires. Months ago, he could avoid it. In the past, flight had been his surest escape.

Such an arrangement would be ruinous. No man alive could associate for long with the beauteous temptress and successfully resist her. At least, no strong, healthy, red-blooded man could. He told Alice he couldn't consider her proposal, double-checking every word he uttered. Just one little word at the wrong time, in the wrong way, would disclose his most carefully guarded secret. A woman could find more ways to pry things out of a man than an octopus has legs, and he was in no mood for long explanations.

After a while, Alice stopped trying to convince him that her suggestion was good. She explained that she was trying to make the waiting and uncertainty more bearable for him. Ben gathered her into his arms again and soundly kissed her against her half-hearted protests. Before releasing her, he thanked her for the consideration. Alice, he knew, believed that his only reason for refusing to take Lynn out was loyalty for the love he bore her. The more he thought on the subject, the more he was convinced that the less said would be the easiest mended.

"Did Mister Savage call while I was visiting my folks?" Ben asked casually. At the mere mention of the man, an intense animosity towards Jess Savage rose up, as big as life.

"Yes, he did," she replied in practically a whisper.

"When?"

"Two evenings ago."

"Did he see you?"

"Yes."

"How was he? As revolting as ever?"

"Even more so, if that is possible," she answered bitterly.

"In what way, darling? Please, tell me. I must know. Surely, there's a limit to the extent he will go. I knew something happened while I was gone by the way you flew into my arms when I got back. Don't be afraid. I promise I won't hunt him down and shoot him as I would a rabid dog. It's what he deserves, but I won't jeopardize any future happiness we might have by gunning him down. Now tell me everything, little girl. I might cuss a bit, but don't mind that."

"All right," Alice said reluctantly. "I'll tell you all about Mister Savage's latest visit. He was his usual obnoxious self. Dad surprised me, though, by standing up to him when he got snotty."

"Was that part about me?" Ben asked.

"It was."

"And your father stood up for me? Well, pardon my saying this, honey, but I'm pleasantly surprised. I'd say it's a good sign."

"I hope so," she said. "During the argument, he seemed for a while like the dad I used to know. I was proud of him. The way my father stood up to that bullying skunk made me more determined than ever not to let him and Mother down."

"Well, I'll be doggonned," Ben said. "I've been thinking all along that your dad was as weak as a kitten where Jess Savage is concerned. Forgive me, Alice. Keep on with your story, dear. I'll try and not interrupt again."

"As usual, Dad had gone to Richwood. Savage drove him home. Father was quite tipsy, but not as much as I have seen him during the past six months. No sooner had they gotten back than Savage sailed into Dad and asked if you was still hanging around. When Dad replied that you was, Savage blew up like a firecracker. He ranted, raved, and used the most awful language a person ever heard. He was practically shouting. Eventually, he told Dad if you wasn't off the place damn soon, there'd be holy hell to pay. Dad let him pop off to his heart's content, as cool as a cucumber. It sure stumped me. Then Dad up and tells him that you was welcome to call our home your home for as long as you pleased, and to hell with anything Savage had to say about it.

"I nearly fell over. Savage actually turned green with rage. The instant he saw me, he began raising hell all over again. This time, all of his spleen was directed at me. He accused you and me of carrying on a love affair under my parents' noses and told Dad that I was probably carrying your kid in my belly. I didn't wait to hear what Dad had to say. I thumbed my nose at him and went down to the barn to start the evening milking. He followed me to the barn."

"What?" Ben cried. "Alice, did that specimen make a pass at you?"

"It was nothing, Ben," she replied.

"I want the truth, darling. Please tell me. I am certain that he tried something by the way you're acting."

"Ben, promise me you won't do anything that'll get you in trouble," she said. She clutched him with shaking hands.

Life was really hell at times.

"I promise not to kill him out right, girl, but I won't promise not to call him to an accounting the next time he tries his crap. Now tell me."

"He tried to embrace me," she faltered.

"You mean kiss you?"

"Yes."

"What happened?"

"It was this way," she said hurriedly. "I no sooner got down in the pasture by the barn, than here he comes. Right off the reel, he began telling me that I'd better get off my high horse with him if I knew what was good and proper. When I got up, he grabbed me. I spilled all the milk I had in the bucket, but managed to slap his ugly face good and hard. When he seen that he couldn't make me give in to his attentions, he released me and left. I was scared, Ben. No telling what he might have tried if he'd dragged me into the barn. I'm still shaking."

"Did he kiss you?" Ben asked.

"No, but next time he might."

"Alice, don't worry about the next time," he said. "If he ever starts anything again, I'll knock half his teeth down his throat. It's unthinkable for you to marry such a beast. I'd kill him with my bare hands before I let it happen."

"Oh, please, Ben," she pleaded. "Don't talk like that. It'd mean prison for you. Then where would we be?"

"It's more than right. We love each other. We belong together."

"I know. I know," she faltered. "It's horrible, but I've my duty to uphold. The Bible will justify me. Forget about me, and the sacrifice I must make. You'd be better off in the long run. Your life is ahead of you yet. You're still a young man. You'll find another girl who'll love you, one that won't be duty bound."

"Bah!" he roared. "Alice, for God's sake, snap out of this. You hold the key to our happiness in the palm of your hand. Use that key. To be the wife of a man like Jess Savage would kill you and ruin me. Do you think I want to look on your grave?"

"Oh, no. Oh, no," she moaned, covering her face with shaking hands. "It's the only way I know to save the homestead. I have to do it. I can't fail Mother and Dad. We'll—"

He waited to hear no more. With a strident curse, he jumped out of the car, cranked the motor back to life, and got back in. Turning around in the wide place in the road, he started back the way they had come, murder in his heart.

Chapter 17

A fortnight later, Jess Savage showed the cloven foot again. It was the week of Halloween, and preparations were being made for the annual dance at the schoolhouse. It was a gala affair for the inhabitants of the surrounding countryside. They looked forward to the get-together, the cider, doughnuts, music, square dancing, gossip, and romancing. A fiddle in the hands of a professional could cast a spell over all within hearing distance. At country dances, everyone sat and lounged and talked until the musicians began tuning up. The instant the fiddle began to wail, moan, cry, chuckle, and laugh with a banjo to rat-a-tat-tat in accompaniment, all those within hearing would lose interest in everything else. As though an unspoken signal had flashed, they would begin to sway, clap their hands, and stamp their feet in time with the music, from the oldest down to the toddling children.

When the caller shouted for all present to choose partners for a quadrille, bedlam broke loose for a few minutes. Every man and boy that could shake a leg made a mad, bold scramble to get his hands on a desirable female. Married men generally looked upon this as an opportunity to flirt with and hug the local beauties. The young married women behaved in much the same manner. This was their night to howl also, and they wasted no time in getting started.

With many a giggle, blush, and sly, hopeful smile, they rushed headlong into the hungry arms of burly mountaineers and were whirled around the floor, tromped on, pawed, hugged, propositioned, and flirted with until the quadrille ended. All of the participants seemed to enjoy it tremendously. Once the dance ended, should an overly flirtatious man persist in his unwelcome advances, violence was sure to follow. Dances were often the scene of bitter fights, places to work out differences and create new ones. Be that as it may, hill folk would no more think of dispensing with their square dances than they would give up their parson. To them, dancing, drinking homemade liquor, flirting, fighting, lovemaking, preaching, and praying made up the better side of their colorless lives. These diversions were essential. They made their lives bearable.

On Wednesday evening, Ben was, as usual, down at the barn helping Walt do the chores for the night. The day had been clear and brisk, with a bite in the gusty air. The partners had driven down to Charleston that day and sold their ginseng roots to the local dealer. They were jubilant. Their root hunting had netted them far more money than they had dared hope. Most of the roots were of outstanding size and quality, and the dealer had upped the price by seventy-five cents per pound. For forty pounds of dry, wild ginseng roots, he gave them three hundred and fifty dollars. As they breezed towards home in Ben's ancient "flivver," Walt marveled.

"Dog gone," he said repeatedly. "This is the most money I ever made. If I wasn't convinced before about the possibilities of this Chinese herb, I am now. My only regret is that tomorrow isn't the first of May. The six months till then is a helluva long time to wait till we can dig again. Oh, well, what's the use to dream? We gotta do it, hey, partner?"

"Right-o," Ben laughingly agreed, as the rumble of an automobile was heard.

Going to the barn door and looking down the Cranberry Valley, Walt swore lustily. Stepping back inside, he spat at a manure pile outside one of the stalls. "That car coming up the road belongs to our friend Mister Savage."

"Is your father with him?" Ben asked, conscious of waves of blind, unreasoning rage washing over him. The veins on his forehead and neck stood out like ropes, and his body was bathed in sweat. "Perhaps Alice didn't tell you, but the last time Savage was out here, he made a complete ass of himself. He raised hell all over the place because I was still here, accused Alice and me of having a love affair, then followed her down here to the barn and made her spill all of old Bossy's milk. He grabbed her and tried to kiss her. What do you think of that for brass?"

"Well, I'll be a lop-eared son-of-a-bitch," Walt exploded. "I'll lay odds that it happened while you, me, and Lynnie was visiting your folks, right?"

"Correct."

"When did you find all this out?"

"The same day we got back from the Ohio Valley. Remember I took Alice for a car ride that evening? She told me then."

"How come you and her never told me anything? Ain't I to be trusted with things like that anymore, especially where it concerns my own sister?"

"Easy, Walt, old man. Easy," Ben said, laying a long arm across his shoulders. "Look, pard, I'm the one to blame for her not telling anyone about what happened."

"But why, Ben?" Walt asked. "We're partners, ain't we? Reckon that ought to entitle me to your confidence. Don't you think so?"

"Sure it does," Ben said. "I'm not trying to hold out on you. It was different this time, that's all."

"I don't follow."

"I'll have to lay it on the line then," Ben muttered as he removed his battered felt hat and wiped his brow with an unsteady hand.

"Come clean with me, pard," Walt insisted. "What held your tongue?"

"I love Alice," Ben said.

Walt cussed long and low at the hell in his friend's eyes. "Holy Moses," he whispered. "I might have known. That explains why you ain't ever been interested in going on my girl chasin sprees. Ben, old pard, put 'er there. Alice couldn't be loved by a better man, but that must be hell. Especially when the one you love is mixed up with a rat like Savage. Can I do anything to make your cross easier to bear? Can I help you in some way? You know I'm on your side, one hundred percent."

"It's this way," Ben explained. "I'm in love with your sister. I have been from the very first day I saw her last June. I've been pestering her to throw off this yoke of duty and marry me. So far, it's been no dice. Walt, that pretty sister of yours is as stubborn as a mule. She says she loves me, but she'll have to marry Jess Savage to save the homestead. Trying to get her to look at this differently is like pulling sound teeth. When she broke down and told me what he did while we was away, I asked her not tell anyone else about it. The next time he pulls some stunt, I'm knocking his block off. I was afraid that if Alice told you, you would beat me to him. As it is, I'll probably land in jail, but jail or no jail, I don't give a damn. He's been getting away with murder. It's high time he was tripped up. Now you know why I didn't want you told."

"Yes, Ben, I reckon I do," Walt answered with a grim smile. He grasped his friend's hand. "I'd feel the same way if it was Flo, bless her cute little hot pants."

"Okay, then. Glad it's settled," Ben said. "I may get my chance this very evening. I'd appreciate it if you'd let me carry the ball. Right now, he's up at the house, probably making an ass of himself. Alice promised to tell me at once if he stepped over the traces again. I ain't saying he will, but he might. If he does, I'm going to just naturally kick the living hell out of Mister Savage."

With a grim laugh, Walt clasped his friend's hand, assuring Ben that he need fear no interference. Turning away, Walt busied himself with the evening chores. It was growing dusky. Nighttime was not far distant. Submerged in bitter reflections, Ben stepped outside the barn door. The evening air was crisp and cool, and the sky was void of clouds, with only a faint tinge of pink lingering on the western horizon. In a few minutes, a huge, round, silvery moon would sail into the heavens.

The mountains thrust their proud heads into the sky. They looked so close Ben could throw a rock at them. However, they were miles distant. The air was deceptive when it came to distances. Suddenly, he heard loud voices, followed by a bellowed oath, from the Randall residence. A door slammed, and in another instant, he heard running footsteps approaching the barn. Walt stepped outside and listened. Two figures materialized out of the evening gloom. Alice and Lynn rushed up to the partners, and without an explanation, Alice walked into Ben's waiting arms. Wordlessly, he folded her close. She was trembling. He looked at Lynn, and she jerked her head toward the house.

"That no-good, son of a bitch is kicking up a storm again."

"What about Dad?" Walt grated.

"Drunk again, and right now dead to the world," she said. "Dad's asleep in the big armchair in front of the fireplace. He no more than got home before he folded up. Forgive me, Ben," she said, blushing furiously. "Seems like I'm always running for the shelter of your arms. I don't know why, but I feel safe there."

"Alice, what happened up at the house just now?" Ben asked.

"Jess Savage brought Dad home about half an hour ago," she answered. "We all wanted him to go to Charleston with you today to sell your roots, but he can't seem to break away from the booze lately. He left for Richmond this morning, right after you boys left for Charleston.

Now he's back home and soaked to the gills. It's just horrible, that's all there is to it."

"But what's the trouble if Dad's asleep?" Walt inquired. "Why is Savage acting up? What's he trying to pull?"

Lynn sighed. "Dad said that he would sit down by the fire and rest a while before starting home. As soon as he hit the chair, Dad fell asleep. After a few minutes, Savage mentioned the Halloween dance coming up this Saturday night. Then, right out of a clear blue sky, he up and asks Allie what time she would like him to call for her that evening. Sis was struck dumb, and so was I. She quietly, but firmly, informed him that she was going to that dance with her family and you. That did it. Like a flash, our dear friend had a tantrum. He yelled that Allie would be smart to go with him, if she knew which side her bread was buttered on. He said he was getting damn well fed-up with her standoffish attitude, and that she would be smart to loosen up a hell of a lot in her relationship towards her future husband. Otherwise, he said, us Randalls would be in for one fair-sized lump of trouble. Ben, he cussed you out something scandalous. My ears are still burning."

"That dirty bum," Ben growled from between set teeth. "Then what happened, girls?"

"He grabbed me again," Alice quavered, bursting into tears. "Oh, Ben. How am I going to marry that beast and hold my sanity? I fought him off as best I could. When I finally did get loose, I kicked his shins good and hard and hit him over the head with a stick of stove wood. That almost floored him. Before he could get himself pulled together, I was out of the house like a flash and on my way down here, Lynnie right at my heels. I'm sorry to dump my grief in your lap all the time. It ain't right. But I got no one else to turn to."

"You did perfectly right coming to me," he assured her. "If you were in trouble and didn't come to me, I'd feel slighted. Now about this louse—me and Walt agree it's high time he was taught a lesson. This heavy-handed way of his has to stop. I'm going up there this minute and demanding an apology. If he refuses, I'll call him outside and beat the pink outta him. You girls stay down here with Walt till I get this behind me."

"Not on your tin-type," they all said. "Forget it. If there are going to be any fireworks, we all want to see them. Let's go."

"Hsst," Lynn said. "If I'm not mistaken, someone is coming down the path from the house. Maybe our boy is coming to take his medicine like a man." She looked out the door. "By heavens, it's him all right. Get set for action. Here he comes."

Jess Savage strode out of the twilight, into the full view of the four people standing in the barn. He peered this way and that, as if he was looking for someone. Upon seeing Ben, Walt, and the two girls standing together, an obscene expression fell from his lips. He ignored everyone except Alice. As he drew near, she involuntarily shuddered and pressed close to Ben. His right arm went around her trembling   shoulders.

"So here's where you flew to," he snarled. "Right into the arms of your lover."

Alice shrunk away, but not a word passed her pale lips. Not so with Lynn, however. She stepped out and met his onslaught with scorn and fury.

"You low-down skunk," she hissed. "For the last time, lay off my sister. She wants no part of you. If she marries you, it'll be to save our home. That's it. So until then, lay off. If you don't, I won't be responsible for what I might do to your ugly face."

"Get out of my face, you man-hungry little bitch," Savage roared, "or I might be tempted to slap that big mouth of yours. My business this evening don't concern you, so I'll thank you to keep your two cents' worth out of it. The same goes for anyone else thinking of interfering in my affairs."

Out of the corner of his eye, Ben stole a look at Walt. One look assured him that Mister Jesse Savage was in for a bad time very shortly. If not from him, then from Walt Randall.

Walt's face was as dark as a thundercloud, and he was muttering to himself. His big hands were clenched into fists, which swung menacingly. It was time to start the ball to rolling. He was itching to get his hands on Savage.

"Hold, Savage," he bellowed. His adversary froze in his tracks. "I don't like the way you've been riding roughshod over Alice lately. I demand that you apologize to her."

"Apologize, my fanny," Savage retorted, purple faced. "What mix is this of yours? I'll treat this little lady in any manner I prefer. After all, she is my promised wife, and that's good enough for me. I'll thank you to get your filthy arms from around her. If she needs protecting, I'll do it. Right now, all this filly needs is to be handled with a firm hand and shown who's boss. After we're married, I'll be occupied with more important things for a spell, especially at night."

"Savage," Ben said quietly. "Do you love this girl?"

"Love? Hell," Savage sneered. "Who said anything about love? You amaze me, Boy Scout."

"Answer my question. Do you love her?"

"I never want in for that mush and milk stuff."

"If that's the way you feel, why are you forcing her to marry you?"

"That's my business. I'm under no obligation to answer any questions. You're trying my patience to the breaking point. Step aside now, and let me have it out with this clinging vine."

"Feller," Ben said coldly. "Let me put you straight. Alice ain't about to go any place with you. Not even to a dogfight. If you crave company for the Halloween dance, bring one of your other females. One of those painted hussies from the sporting houses in Richmond would make you an ideal dance partner. You'll feel at home with her. In your own element, so to speak, if she ain't too particular. If she kicks on your company, a ten spot will save the evening. Get the drift, brother Savage?"

Jess Savage raised a heavy hand and clawed at the collar of his shirt as if it had begun to choke him. A gasping, gurgling sound came from his half-open mouth. For a few moments, he appeared incapable of speech. When he could, his voice was so thick with fury that it was difficult at first to make out.

"You lousy, long-nosed sponger," he cried. "So that's your game. I told her parents weeks ago that you two were having an affair. Now I'm positive of it. Belittle me to her, will you? Grind your axe at my expense, you sneaking snake? Well, listen to this, lover boy. I hold the whip hand, and she'll dance to my tune when the time comes. Then she'll pay the hard way for the embarrassment you're causing me."

Ben was hard pressed to keep his hands off Savage's throat. "Alice Randall is as pure and untouched as the morning dew, as far as I'm concerned, but that ain't letting you off the hook. Not by a long shot. I love Alice, and she loves me. Do you hear that, Savage? Are you capable of understanding that? She loves me as much as she loathes you. See her in my arms? Ask yourself why she is here. Do you know the answer? She loves me. See my arms around her? See my lips meeting hers. Do you see her protesting? Never. Take a good look, Savage. That's where you stand with her. I know you're trying to trap her into becoming your wife, but it's not because you have affection for her. Hell, no. You merely want to satisfy your ego. She's your rag to use, then kick aside. What a bright future for her to look forward to. Have you no pride? Would you force a girl that hated you to marry you? Is that how you operate? Is that the code you live by?"

"How I live and do things is my own affair," Savage shouted. "My mind is set on Alice Randall, and by Satan, I'll have her or know the reason why. Waters, get out of this country while the getting is good. You've interfered in my affairs long enough. Make tracks, you back woods hobo, or you'll wish you had. Don't harp to me about love and being a gentleman. I never did go for that crap, and I never will."

"Then why are you forcing Alice into becoming your wife?"

"That's my business."

"But she hates you."

"So what? Let her hate to her heart's content. So much the better. Let her fight to the last minute. Do you think that'll alter my desire? If anything, it'll only make me keener. Look, hillbilly, get wise. Surely, you're not that dumb. It's better when you have to fight for it. The harder it is to get, the bigger thrill I have when a split-tail finally does give in, sheds her panties, and throws her dress tail over head. Then I can really go to town. I never obligate myself to a female, but in this case, I'm willing to go all the way. I hope it's worth it. I hope she'll turn out to be good in bed."

"Man, you'd gag a dog off a gut wagon," Ben said in disgust. "It's no use talking to you. You're not a man at all. You wear the face and form of a man, but that's as far as it goes. You've the soul of an ape. Even your name gives you away. Jesse Savage. It should be Savage Jesse."

"See here, rube, don't insult me," Savage snapped.

"That would be impossible," Lynn said in a scathing voice. "Ben, what's staying your hand? Slap the tar out of this foul-mouthed bastard. Don't make me ashamed of you. He's insulted Allie all over the place. You say you love her, well, prove it. Don't tell me you're going to stand there like a ninny and let him get away with this smart crap."

"I'm not," Ben said. "Savage, I'm giving you ten seconds to apologize to Alice. If you don't, I'll beat it out of you or die trying. Make up your mind. Which will it be? Fight or apologize?"

Jess Savage looked at the people standing before him. Not a shred of mercy showed in those faces, but the only emotion he felt was indifference. To hell with them all. Who did these hillbillies think they were, anyway? Just let that seng digger start something. He had the ways and means to put an upstart backwoodsman in his place.

"Waters," he snarled, "I'll see you in hell with your lazy backs broke before I eat one single word I said about this pale-faced little bitch, or any other hot crotch like her. That's my answer. Keep your dirty hooks off me. I know my rights. If you muss a single hair on my head, and I'll have your ass clapped in jail so fast it'll make your head swim. Now make up your mind, wise guy, or button your stupid lip. You've interfered in my plans already. Play it smart. Hit the road while you're a free man. They have a nice strong jail in Richwood. You're fairly begging to get into it."

"Is that your last word, Savage?" Ben asked quietly.

"It is."

"No apology to the girl you're forcing to become your wife? Nothing to show you're sorry that you treated her so badly?"

"Nothing. It's not my way," Savage said. Turning on his heel, he began walking away. "To hell with you. I'm going home."

With a firm, but gentle hand, Ben put Alice out of his arms. With a roar like an enraged lion, he leaped upon Savage. With one sweeping blow, he knocked his enemy sprawling. No sooner had Savage hit the ground than he bounced up like a rubber ball. He charged in with both huge fists flying in all directions. A cry of rage escaped his bleeding mouth. Ben met the terrific blows and shrugged them off. His strength was insurmountable. Walt yelled his encouragement. Lynn screamed her delight as she danced around the fighters. But Alice stood mutely by and looked on the carnage. She gave no encouragement to the man who championed her. Only her hands moved, like fluttering birds.

The fight raged on. Sometimes it looked as though Ben was winning, while at other moments, the tide of battle appeared to be swinging towards Savage. Though Savage lived a soft life, he possessed the strength of two ordinary men. Ben was hard put to hold his own but he fought violently and watched for the opening he knew would come. When it came, he moved to take advantage. The blow sent Savage crashing backwards to the ground, bleeding at the mouth and nose. Jess Savage had lost half a dozen front teeth. He was beaten so badly that even his closest acquaintances would not have recognized him. Wiping his brow, Ben stood over his fallen foe and demanded an apology to Alice. He stepped back and gloried in what he had accomplished. His only regret was that he had not slapped Savage down months earlier.

While Walt and Lynn crowded around Ben with words of praise, Alice began walking up the path towards the house. She hadn't thanked him or cast a glance of gratitude upon him. With a great, rasping sigh, Ben shook his head. He would never understand Alice Randall.

Moments later, Jess Savage picked himself up and turned towards his automobile. All the arrogance and cockiness had been knocked out. He looked as if he had been run through a threshing machine and run over by a steamroller.

"You'll pay plenty for the night's work, Ben Waters," he gasped. "I'll see to that if it costs me my last red cent. You better haul your ass outta this county tonight. Come morning, I'm sending Sheriff Craig after you." His wheezing voice died away as he turned back around and got into his automobile with agonized slowness. As soon as the motor roared into life, he gunned it and roared away.

For once, the tables had been turned upon Jesse Savage. He was quitting the field in humiliation. That was as bitter a pill to swallow as the sting of death.

Chapter 18

*T*he next day, Jesse Savage made good his promise. It was mid-afternoon and Walt, Ben, and Lynn were out in the wood yard, sawing and splitting firewood, when Sherriff Craig from Richwood drove up in a battered coupe.

Lynn was piling up the wood in a neat, even pile as the two young men cut and split it. At the sight of the tall, raw-boned peace officer, she abandoned the wood, rushed over to Ben, and clasped him with shaky hands. Ben grinned and gave her a bear hug. "Thanks, Lynnie, but don't look so downcast. All he can do is jail me for a while. I ain't going to hang. Not yet, anyways."

"Don't jest, Ben," she whispered. "Take this any way you want, but I got plans for us. I'll have to chuck them overboard if you're in jail."

"What plans, baby?" he asked, but he knew what she meant.

"Bed plans, Bennie-boy," she whispered shamelessly. "If that son-of-a-bitch causes them to miscarry, I'll feel like shooting Sheriff Craig with his own gun. Good luck, lover of mine to-be. I'll put my two cents' worth in for you if I get any opening."

Climbing out if his dilapidated vehicle, the sheriff strolled over to the three young people. Seeing Lynn rush to Ben's side, the veteran peace officer put two and two together. That's my man, he mused. I'd bet a month's pay. That eyeful clinging to him is one of them two girls. I haven't seen them in a coon's age, but unless my memory fails, the older one has dark hair. This one's a blonde, and what a blonde. God, what a shape this little lady is carrying around. I'd give ten years off my life to be twenty years young and have her to bed down with for a few nights. She'd wring a man as dry as a bone in jig time. Her kind always does. He slowly walked over. I'm a married man, by cracky, but I ain't too old to know a good piece when I spot one.

His thoughts concealed behind a broad smile, the sheriff lifted a long, lean hand in friendly greeting. A holstered police thirty-eight-caliber revolver bumped and swung from his right hip. A pair of cold, gleaming handcuffs dangled from his wide leather belt.

"Howdy, folks," he drawled. "Sure is a jim dandy day for sawing and splitting wood. Reckon it'll come in handy soon. Winter is just around the corner."

"Hello, sheriff," Walt said dryly. Lynn nodded curtly and sat on the wood she had just piled, looking at the law officer with a decidedly unfriendly eye.

"What brings you out this way today, sheriff?" Walt asked, seeing no point in beating around the bush.

"Well, now, Walt," came the guarded reply. "I'm out here looking for a feller by the name of Ben Waters. He is charged with beating the pink dog-water out of Jess Savage last evening. Know any feller by that name?" The sheriff looked at Ben.

Ben stepped forward, thrust out his right hand, and looked in the sheriff's eyes as he introduced himself. "If ever a man needed what he got, Jess Savage is that man."

"I'm powerful glad to make your acquaintance, son," the grizzled law officer said as he met Ben's hand with an iron grip. "My name's Craig. I'm sheriff of Nicholas County. Let me sit down. Then, if you don't mind, I'd like to hear what happened last night. That's better. This woodpile ain't no feather cushion to sit on, but it'll beat standing hollow. Now one of you three loosen up and tell me about it. My big ears are wide open."

"I'll tell you, sheriff," Lynn said, jumping up from the woodpile. "I can tell you everything you want to know, cause I seen it all. Walt and Ben have no objections, I'm sure."

"Fire away, Lynnie," Ben grinned. "Tell the sheriff why I put the bee on Jesse Savage."

Sheriff Craig laughed. "I take it Savage ain't no great shakes of a man in your book. Am I correct?"

"Right as rain, sheriff," Ben replied. "That bird would never win   a popularity contest around here."

"I gathered as much," Craig said dryly as he removed a corncob pipe from his shirt pocket, filled it with tobacco, and lit it. As soon as he had his pipe going like a smoke stack, he turned to Lynn and grinned at   her through the smoke. "I beg your pardon, little gal," he drawled lazily, "but I saw the way you hugged this here Ben Waters. I know I'm as old as the hills and my eyes are poor, but I'd say you're considerable interested in this gent yourself. Right?"

"That, Sheriff Craig, is none of your damn business," Lynn snapped.

Ben and Walt threw back their heads and laughed heartily. The sheriff joined in.

"Well, well. Seems like I struck fire. I apologize if I offended you. Which of the Randall gals are you? If I remember right, the oldest had dark hair. Could it be that you're Lynn, the youngest?"

"I am, you old busybody," Lynn replied testily with the hint of a smile tugging at the corners of her wide mouth. "I don't see that how I feel about Ben here is anybody's business but my own. And I resent any remarks either way."

"My mistake, Lynn," the sheriff grinned. However, his eyes spoke volumes. Lordy, she would be one enjoyable little wildcat. Craig, you old dog, get down to business. This kind of drooling can get you in trouble. Even so, she's the type I'd give a pretty penny to try my hand at taming. Be well worth getting tuckered out over.

"Okay, folks," he said. "Tell me the story from beginning to end, little firecracker. Excuse this old smudge pot. It stinks like fury, I know, but I think better when it's going full blast. When you tell the story, start at the beginning. We'll get a better idea of what brought this on and know whether it was justified or not. I'll just sit here, listen, and smoke."

Lynn took a long breath, looked at her brother and Ben, winked at them, and then plunged into the narration. She got straight to the point of it at the start, and there were times she became caustic. She mentioned Savage's acquisition of the mortgage on their home and the man's diabolical scheme to ensnare her older sister. She didn't spare her father for the way he had fallen from grace in the past years, either.

Lynn told the sheriff that she and Alice had found Ben in the woods and nursed him back to health. As Lynn told Sheriff Craig of Ben's almost miraculous arrival, a smile replaced the frown she had worn since the beginning of her story. Obviously, she was thankful for Ben Waters. The sheriff smiled knowingly and nodded his silvery head. She told of the partnership between Walt and Ben and of their decision to hunt ginseng, Ben's love for her older sister, and Alice's sense of duty.

"So there you have it, Sheriff Craig," she said. "From the very first time Jess Savage saw Ben here, he's raised nothing but holy hell about it. He's jealous, I know, but I'm of the opinion that stupidity and a puffed-up feeling of importance is the main reason for his actions. He's also afraid that Ben will figure out a way to upset his applecart. He called Ben every mean name he could—bum, tramp, hobo, no-good loafer, seng-digger, hayseed, rube, country hick. Since he first met Ben, he's never passed up an opportunity to run him down, and he's come to look on my sister Alice as his personal property. To tell you the gospel truth, if it'd been me, I'd have knocked that bastard's block off months ago.

"Now he's beginning to force his attention on Alice. He seems to think that since she promised to marry him to save our parents' home, it gives him the right to do with her as he pleases. Two weeks ago, while me and Walt was with Ben visiting his folks in the Ohio Valley, Savage brought Dad home one evening and showed his rear proper. He followed Alice down to the barn and tried to kiss her. When we got home, Alice told Ben about Mister Savage's actions, and Ben promised that if he ever stepped out of line again, he would knock half his teeth down his throat. That's what happened last night. He brought Dad home and asked Alice to go to the Halloween dance with him this Saturday night. When she turned him down, he blew his top all over the place. Dad was asleep before the fire by then, and Mother was out in the kitchen.

"When he got rambunctious, Allie conked him on the head with a stick of stove wood, and we went down to the barn where Ben and Walt were finishing up evening chores. We thought he would go on home, but he followed us to barn and continued his hell raising. Ben demanded he apologize to Alice for the crummy way he'd been treating her. Savage swelled up like a poisoned pup and said that he'd see the lot of us in hell with our backs broke before he'd swallow a single word of what he'd said or apologize for anything he had done. That did it. Ben gave him two seconds to change his mind before he beat the living hell outta him. Ben and him argued and argued, but at last, Savage turned on his heel and began walking towards his car. If he'd gone on and kept his big mouth shut, perhaps nothing would have happened. But he didn't. When he was about half a dozen paces away, he turned back around, told Ben to go to hell, and called him a son of a bitch. That was the straw that broke the camel's back. Ben hopped him. They had a terrible fight. In the end, Ben literally mopped the ground with him. That's the story, Sheriff Craig. I don't know what kind of cock and bull story he fed you, but I've told you the straight of it, so help me God."

"Well, well," chuckled the sheriff. "That's quite a story, young woman. I ain't doubting a word of what you told me, but Jess told me an entirely different version." He studied the chips of wood at his feet for moment then looked up again. "Young man," he said suddenly, focusing on Ben. "Are you in love with this girl's older sister?"

"Yes, sheriff, I am." Ben's face became crimson and pale by turns.

"Does she return your love?" the sheriff asked.

"Well, yes and no."

"What kind of an answer is that? It should be definite one way or the other. None of this on the fence stuff. I don't get it."

"Alice loves me, but she won't commit herself. Right now, all that poor girl can see is blind duty. She's going to marry that skunk to save the homestead from being foreclosed on. That was Savage's proposition, and she's going to meet it."

"Ah-ha. Did Lynn tell me the straight of all this?"

"Every last word she told you was gospel truth."

"How come you never acted before last night?"

"Always before, I let Alice talk me out of going after him. She was more concerned about my safety than she was about herself. She knew that he would never take his licking like a man. He'd holler his head off then sic the law on me to get revenge, and he'd swear to anything. Take that story he told you last night. He isn't to be trusted. Have you a warrant for my arrest?"

"Reckon I have." The sheriff pulled a legal paper from an inside pocket and scrutinized it.

"Are you going to serve that warrant?" Walt inquired.

"Son, I don't know," Craig replied as he turned the warrant over. "I find myself in an embarrassing position. I'm thinking to hell with the letter of the law and duty to my office. I'm inclined to listen to my heart. Maybe I oughtn't, but I kind of like what my old ticker is telling me."

"What do you mean?" Lynn asked.

Craig smiled. She was so clearly infatuated with Ben. The man's an idiot if he doesn't play ball with her, he mused. I sure would if I was in his shoes. She could give him more thrills in a month than another girl could give him in a lifetime.

"It's like this," he said as he replaced the warrant in his pocket and knocked the ashes out of his pipe against a block of wood. "I got no love for Jess Savage. I don't know anybody in these parts who has. This deal he's figgering to pull on you folks is typical of him. Your story rings true, and I believe it. He swore to me over the phone that you, Waters, had attacked him, unprovoked. He said he believed that you meant to kill him. I know Savage far too well to take his word on anything of importance. When I began questioning him, he gave me a snippy answer or two and, after informing me that he would be at my office this morning to swear out the warrant, hung up. This morning it was the same thing over again. He refused to answer any of my questions. All he really wanted was to see Ben in jail."

"How did his ugly mug look this morning?" Lynn asked with a laugh. "Did he look a bit worked over?"

"Haw, haw," roared Sheriff Craig as he recalled Jess Savage that morning. He gave his knee a resounding slap. "Yes, he did," he chuckled. "Savage was a sight to see. His eyes were as black as coal and almost swelled shut. His face was covered with red lumps and scabs. Six of his front teeth are missing. When he talked with me, his breath whistled through the gap in his teeth. I almost laughed in his face. Ben Waters, reckon I strike you as one hell of a sheriff. Here's the rub. Jesse Savage ain't a native son of West Virginia. He's one of them stuck-up, over-bearing ginks from down Louisiana way. He's the only child of extremely wealthy parents. They came north about twenty years ago. His father was sharp in his business deals. Before he passed on, he made a lot of money in timber and coal. A year after his death, his wife died of pneumonia. Folks tell me she was a good woman, but she was treated worse than a servant by her rotten son and husband, Judson Savage. Reckon Jess come honest to his dishonesty and low-down meanness, and he's not tried changing his ways. He never married, but he has had any number of housekeepers. Mostly he engages a widow woman with a teen-age daughter. Rumor has it that more than one widow left his employ with a daughter in the family way. These women and their pregnant daughters just fade out of sight, and no one knows where they came from or where they went.

"If ever a man deserved a working over, Jess Savage is our boy. It'll take time and plenty of dental work before he looks natural again, if ever. Yes, indeed, my boy, you really put the bee on Mister Savage. He'll carry the marks of the drubbing you gave him for many a long day. I've a teen-age daughter, and when she gets a little older, I'd like to feel that there's a man like you around to champion her if she ever needs a friend. Son, here's my hand."

"Sheriff Craig, I tried real hard to lay off that man, but it was no go," Ben said with a slow smile and a shake of his head. He met the sheriff's hand with an iron grip. He liked this loquacious, amicable peace officer. Craig was not like the elected officials he'd known back in the Ohio Valley. He was not bound by the shackles of influence that bound so many politicians. Jess Savage represented the long pocketbook, wealth, and position. He was used to his wishes being granted. On the other hand, Sheriff Craig was a man who knew justice when he saw it. He was the type of man Ben had always admired. He would never forget this day, not if he lived to be a hundred. He had seen the designs of wealth and prestige shunted aside, and the needs of the common man served.

"Yes, folks," Sheriff Craig drawled. "Reckon I'll just tear up this warrant and mosey on back to town. It's not procedure, but I've got my reasons. Savage will blow his stack when I don't show up with Ben in tow, but I've an idea that will take the wind out of his sails in a hurry. I'll tell our friend that I was out here and talked with you folks. Then I'll inform him that if he presses charges against Ben Waters, all of you are prepared to swear in court that Ben was defending Alice's honor.

"I'd lay money that he'll turn tail and run like a scared rabbit—black eyes, bruised face, knocked-out teeth, injured dignity, and all. I know his kind. Met plenty of them in my day. The last thing they want is the truth coming out. I better quit batting the breeze, crank up my tin lizzy, and head back to town. I'll probably be out this way again tomorrow to let you know how I make out with Savage. Don't worry, Waters. I think it's in the bag."

After shaking hands with all present, the lanky, old-fashioned sheriff cranked up his automobile and drove down the Randall driveway.

The next day, shortly after noon, he came wheezing and rattling up the driveway again. It was another fine fall day, and the entire Randall household, except Mrs. Randall, was out in the chip-yard, hard at work on the winter woodpile. Ben and Walt were sawing, Grant Randall was splitting, and the two sisters were piling it up.

Ben had told Grant Randall, his wife, and Alice of the sheriff's visit and its outcome. Grant Randall had stalked about and thundered at the humiliation of his position. Then he turned to Ben and thrust out his right hand.

"Shake, boy," he'd said. "It humbles me something awful to face what's come to us Randalls. I blame only myself. If I hadn't been so shortsighted a few years ago, we wouldn't have our backs to the wall now, but there ain't no need crying over spilled milk. My hands are tied. It's hell to admit that, but it's true. Ben, I'm very pleased at the way you tanned Jess Savage's britches. Maybe that'll take some of that meanness out of him, but I doubt it. He's not the kind to learn anything useful through experience. Had his own way too long. I want to apologize for being drunk when one of my daughters needed me. I am turning out to be a mighty poor excuse for a father. Anyways, if Sheriff Craig shows up tomorrow, I want to be on the scene. Hard to tell what he thinks of me anymore, but I ain't letting that hold me back. If he tries serving a warrant on you, he'll have to have it out with me first. I'm expecting some kind of lowdown trick from Savage before he lets you off the hook. He's capable of anything. He won't take a licking such as you gave him lying down. Sheriff and me used to be good friends some years back. I'd like a man-to-man talk with him. It may be a bad practice to lose your temper and kick hell outta people, but I'm right glad you did. Guess that's all I have to say. I'm tuckered out, so I'll be turning in. See you tomorrow. Goodnight."

When Sheriff Craig approached the woodcutters, he had a big smile on his leathery face. He raised his right hand and hailed the group then shook hands with Randall and put the farmer at ease.

"Well, well, Grant, old hoss," he boomed. "Long time no see. How've you been?"

"No damn good, Craig, as you well know," said Randall, "but it's good to see you again. Reckon I know what brings you out, so let's not waste time. Give it to us from the shoulder. What is that bastard Savage up to?"

"Easy, Grant, old friend," said the sheriff. "Relax and get hold of yourself. Ain't no need to get lathered up. Things are going to work out all right for this boy. Easy does it."

"Easy, my rear end. Look here, Craig," Randall said. "What is that louse up to? You know him as well as I do, and I know he's up to some kind of skullduggery. Is he going to press charges against Ben? If he is, we're going to slap a few on him. What did you find out?"

"I'm coming to all that, only I'd like to tell it in my own way."

"Okay, but get on with it. This not knowing is plumb hell."

"All right, folks, but first, let me sit down on one of these blocks of wood. It tuned out just as we figured it would. When I told him that I wasn't arresting Ben Waters on an assault with intent to kill charge, he cussed and raved like a mad man. He was fit to be tied, and I couldn't get a word in edgewise. He couldn't seem to get his words out, so at first, he just roared. Finally, when I did get to talking, he began to listen. At first, he was out for Ben's hide at all costs. When I pointed out the loopholes in his demands, he began to lose some of his cock-sureness. Eventually, he wasn't half as sure of himself as he had been at first. He began to hem and haw and I kept picking away at him like a woodpecker after a worm. Finally, we reached an agreement. He agreed that if Ben packed up and got off the Randall estate, he would drop the charges. If Ben refused, he would prosecute to the fullest extent of the law. Well, there it is, boy. It's up to you now. What do you say?"

"Sheriff Craig, can I talk to you?" Ben asked.

"Hell, yes, boy. Just fire away anytime you're ready. I'm all ears, and I have all the time there is a-going. What's on your mind?"

"Did that rat say that I was to get clear out of the county when he demanded I leave the Randall home?"

"No, he didn't."

"Then if I just pack a few things and get off Grant Randall's property, I'll be complying with his request. Right?"

"That's right as rain," the sheriff replied with a twinkle in his eyes. "Have you got something figured out to pull his teeth with?"

"I sure have," Ben answered. "Walt has a perfectly good cabin up that old logging road behind the barn. I'll move all my stuff up there. It's as simple as taking candy from a baby. I'll keep my promise and still be as close to these good people as ever. I owe the Randalls a tremendous debt. They saved my life last summer. For their services, I'd gladly fight a dozen Jess Savages."

"Well, I'll be dog-gonned," said Craig with a hearty laugh. "That will work. I'll bet Walt's cabin never entered his mind. Probably plum forgot it. Is it on the farm here?"

"No, sheriff, it isn't," Grant Randall said. "Walt owns the cabin and that land free and clear. He bought it from the state a few years ago. I didn't think it much of a buy, but now I reckon I'm glad that he hooked into it. But what difference would it make?"

"Lot of differences, Grant, old friend," said Craig. "Savage agrees to drop all charges against Ben providing he gets off your property. If Ben moved up to Walt's cabin, and it was on your property, then he'd have reason to squawk, but if his only demand is that Ben pack up and get out, then you've got him both coming and going."

"Look now, Craig," Grant Randall said. "For the sake of old times, do your best to out-wit this weasel. He's causing me more grief than I care to admit. I'd take a gun to him, but I hate to think of spending my last few days on earth behind bars. I'm old and weak-kneed, I guess."

"I'll do my best with Savage and let you know how I make out," said the sheriff. "Keep your chin up. The last chip in this game ain't been dropped. It's no more than right for a feller like Savage to get his just dessert eventually. His luck can't hold out forever. Bye, now. See you tomorrow."

That evening, Ben took a stroll, and at his suggestion, Grant Randall went along. At first, the mountaineer was reluctant to leave the warmth of the blazing log fire, but he grumblingly consented to go along. As soon as they were clear of the yard, Ben started.

"Mister Randall, please bear with me."

"Ben," the elderly farmer grumbled, "get it off your chest, pronto. It's colder than a witch's butt out here. I'd be lots more comfortable inside the house."

"It's about Alice and me," Ben said.

"What about Alice and you?"

"We love each other, that's what."

"Son, that's unfortunate. I ain't been exactly blind to what's been going to these past few months. How can I help you? What do you want of me?"

"Free Alice from that bargain you made with Savage."

"Ben, if she turns back from her duty to her parents, I won't try to prevent it. However, if she don't turn back of her own free will, I won't ask her to."

"But why? For God's sake, why?"

"I'm an old man, boy, that's why," the mountaineer answered. "You are a young man. There will be plenty of girls for you to fall in love with. If I muff this up because of two love-sick youngsters, me and Ma might spend our last days in the poor house."

"Grant Randall, I owe you a great debt, but you talk like a mad man. Think what a marriage like that would do to Alice. It would kill her, sure as shooting."

"Boy," the big man rumbled, "I've news for you. These tender looking little ladies can take a heap of killing when it comes to flouncing and rough treatment. However, whether Alice lives with Savage after they're married is entirely up to her. What puts me in the clear is that she becomes his wife. Nothing more or less."

"Mister Randall, I beg you," Ben implored. "Be a man. Better to spend your last days in the poorhouse, than to break one of your children's hearts. Don't do this. Don't let yourself sink so low. Your entire family will be ashamed of you to your dying day."

"Enough of the quibble-quabble," thundered Randall. "I won't lift a hand to stop this marriage, and you'd better not interfere, either. If you can come up with three thousand dollars before October 16 next year, Alice is yours with my blessing. Try praying to the powers on high to guide your steps to that big patch of seng you claim you saw last summer. That's the kind of miracle us Randalls need. Fine words, good intentions, and golden dreams won't do it. Try to see my side. I'm not unfeeling, but I got to think of Ma and me. We're in a tight spot, and no mistake. Try to understand. I'm going in now. Go to bed, boy, and get your rest. Good night."

"Wait, wait," Ben cried desperately, for naught.

Grant Randall was as immovable as a rock and dumb to the situation into which he had put his eldest daughter. Nothing Ben said moved him. Ben gave up and returned to the house, but sleep eluded him. For hours, he tossed to and fro, wrestling with his problem. Time was still in his favor, and for that, he was deeply grateful.

The next day, at ten o'clock in the morning, Ben moved all his belongings into the little cabin up the old logging road. He would reside there during the long winter months. The following weekend, the annual Halloween dance was held in the one-room schoolhouse at Holcomb. As usual, the building was full to overflowing with hill folk. Alice and Lynn went with Ben in his ancient automobile, and Walt took his best girl, Flo. Before he left to go to Flo's house, Walt came up to the cabin to visit Ben for a few minutes, as full of joyful expectations as a schoolboy.

"Boy, oh, boy," he chortled. "Will I ever give little Flo a roll in the grass tonight. That gal's a hell-cat when it comes to loving, but it's heaven on earth to partake of her charms, if you know what I mean, pard."

Ben laughingly assured his young friend that he did as he waved him away.

Jess Savage did not appear at the dance. Word drifted out from Richwood that he was trying to heal the lacing he had received and get his features back to a reasonable facsimile of their former appearance. He had yet to have the dental work done which Sheriff Craig had said he so badly needed.

Chapter 19

Winter settled over the mountains of West Virginia early that fall. During the first week of November, the first snow fell. It was a two-inch-deep, wet, slushy, dabby affair that melted off the ground within twenty-four hours. On the sixth day of the month, Ben and Walt took the long-eared hounds and went bear hunting. The snowfall was rapidly disappearing, but enough of it remained in the dense woods to show the tracks of any large animal that might have passed that way.

Walt supervised the hunt, heading for a great hogback ridge five miles to the east. Laurel grew atop this mighty rampart in tangled profusion. As the hunters trudged through the soggy woods, Walt explained that a bear loved a dense laurel thicket to hole up in during winter. During the first week of their partnership, they had explored this ridge thoroughly, as well as any spurs they could find. Any ridge where laurel grew in abundance might well be the one they were looking for. They had tramped this ridge from one end to the other, cutting their way through the laurel beds.

Minutes after arriving, the two hunters were gazing at the huge tracks of bears. The tracks led into and around the evergreen jungle in all directions. Upon close inspection, Walt called Ben's attention to some of the tracks that were fresher than the rest. The laurel there had not reached the ground. Instead, the long greenish leaves were matted together overhead.

Walt pointed to several big black holes that led back under this particularly dense spot.

"See them big, round holes, pard?" he asked.

"Sure do," Ben said. "Is that where the old bears are hiding?"

"That's the place. They've got these laurel beds honeycombed with holes. The only way a feller can get a bear outta a place like this is to send in a dog or two and let them rout him. That's what we'll do today. We'll send the hounds in, and while they're ferreting out where old Mister Bear is snoozing, we'll look for a tree to climb, just in case. Them old boys are hell on wheels once they're roused. When that happens, the best thing to do is shoot fast and straight, climb a tree, pray, or run like hell itself was after you. It's every man for himself and heaven help the hindmost. Haw, haw."

Ben agreed with his friend, though dubiously. If any bears came charging out of the laurel bed, he hoped he would conduct himself in a manner that he would not be ashamed to recall later. Bear hunting was new him, and it promised to be very exciting. Dangerously so. Nevertheless, Ben thrilled to the challenge. He hoped that he would be able to measure up to Walt's expectations.

Eventually, after much speculation, Walt sent the hounds into the laurel bed. At a low word from him, they dashed into two big, round holes, and disappeared from view. Walt and Ben chose positions from which to watch for results. Five minutes went by. Then one of the hounds began baying from somewhere near the center of the laurel bed. The sound was deep and muffled. Soon the other hound joined in. Walt gave low whistle to attract Ben's attention.

Glancing in his friend's direction, Ben laughed to see his partner perched on top of a flat rock that jutted up out of the mountaintop near the edge of the laurel bed. The rock stood a hundred feet to Ben's left, and reared up at one end a good hundred feet or more.

"Get set for action," Walt bellowed across the distance.

Ben waved in reply, clutching the high-powered rifle he had borrowed from a neighbor tightly, surveying the terrain. He looked in vain. There was nothing big enough for him to climb onto and feel a measure of security. If a bear should come charging out of the laurels, he'd have to face it on foot and take his chances or shame himself by climbing onto the same rock with Walt, which he had no intentions of doing. However, before many minutes had passed, he wished desperately that he had swallowed his foolish pride.

A sound jerked him to attention. A hoarse roar of rage rang out on the still air. More snarls were heard, each more vicious than the last. The hounds set up a terrible clamor. The sounds of a fight were heard, and as time passed, the sounds got closer to the edge of the laurel bed.

Ben set himself for action and cocked the thirty-thirty. A terrific thrashing and snarling was heard in the laurels. Then, not a hundred feet distant, a huge round, black, furry ball erupted from the roots of the evergreens. In an instant, that ball of fur transformed into a raging black bear, great slavering jaws agape, and little pig eyes blazing with insane rage.

For just a moment, the bear stood up on his hind legs and faced the hunters, flinging a spine-chilling roar of hate into the faces of the two men. Ben shook all over. He would have turned and ran, but his feet seemed rooted to the spot.

Dropping to all fours, the bear burrowed out of sight. Immediately, the hounds gave chase again. In less than a half a minute, the bear dashed out of one of the round, black holes in front of Ben, the two hounds snapping at his heels. The cumbersome-looking beast turned, and with two swipes of his front paws, he knocked the hounds end over end. Whirling around, he charged at Ben.

Ben began pumping lead into that charging black fury. Dimly, he heard Walt yelling. He realized afterward that he heard rifle shots other than his own. In that moment of stress, the report of a six-inch cannon wouldn't have registered. He was desperately trying to kill the bear before it reached him and tore him to shreds.

Four times, he leveled his rifle and shot. When the raging animal finally did fall, he was less than a score of feet in front of Ben. As he began to breathe again and looked at the fallen forest monarch, lying so close, Ben's legs suddenly were as weak as water. He leaned against a hemlock tree to keep them from buckling. As he gulped the cold air, he felt his heart settle back down.

Walt dashed over to where he stood, his eyes as big as saucers, and his face was white clear up to the hairline. Coming up to Ben, he clasped him by the shoulder with a shaky hand and peered anxiously into his face.

"Wow-ee, pard," he gasped, "but that was close. You all right?"

"I think so." Ben grinned weakly. "But I sure feel like a bowl of jelly inside."

"Son-of-a-bitch, but that black bastard gave me a scare," Walt swore as he mopped the cold sweat from his brow. "For a minute, I thought it was all up with you. I nearly died when he made for you. The big boy meant business. A half minute more, I might have had to hunt seng next summer all by my lonesome. Brother, that was too close for comfort. Are you sure you're okay?"

"Hell's bells, yes," Ben replied. "I'm in one piece yet, thank god. I'm only scared half to death."

Walt once more peered intently into his face. Something must have allayed his fears, because he threw back his head and roared with laughter that was half amusement and half relief. His laughter was contagious. Ben joined in, and the two friends slapped each other's backs while their laughter drove the fear out of their hearts. After their mirth had subsided, they turned to the slain bear and drove the dogs off the carcass.

Within an hour, they had the bear skinned out and as much of the meat cut off the carcass as they wanted to keep. Then the long trek back home began. Night was falling by the time they arrived.

Lynn gave Walt a dig in the ribs at sight of the rolled-up bearskin, and turned her eyes on Ben with all the promise of heaven in their mysterious depths. With a trilling laugh, she linked arms with him and deliberately snuggled up to him as they marched into the front room.

"Here are the hunters, folks, home from the hills," she cried gaily to her parents and Alice, who were sitting before a blazing log fire. "They've brought home the bacon, hair and all."

Grant Randall and his wife congratulated them for the success of their hunt. Alice just rocked in silence. She had no interest in the black bear. She had a meditative air. One look at her pale, set face, and Ben turned away. Would she ever wake up and exert her rights as a free, red-blooded woman born to know the love of a man of her own choice? Ben fervently hoped Alice would come to his arms and share his love and dreams, but until she did, his hands were tied.

An hour or so later, as the hunters narrated their hunt to an appreciative group of listeners, the mouth-watering aroma of frying bear steak wafted out of the kitchen and into the living room. Ben looked at Walt and grinned broadly as he pointed his nose towards the ceiling like a hunting dog.

"Partner," he laughed, "do you smell them hunks of bear meat frying out there in the kitchen? I reckon they'll offset the danger we run to get them. What say?"

"Righto," Walt agreed. "The danger was great, I'll allow, but the steaks off a bear's ass make mighty good eating. We'll have to go again before they hole in for the long sleep."

The partners did go bear hunting again that fall. In fact, they went four more times. Twice on their own imitative, and twice upon the request of a neighbor who raised sheep. He lived five miles down the Cranberry, and he had been losing sheep to predatory animals.

The first three of these hunts produced game, but the fourth time out, the hunters came home empty-handed, with the two long-eared hounds showing signs of battle. Ben and Walt had decided to hunt for bear at the head of the right-hand branch of the Cranberry, where they'd heard the panther's screams the summer before. They hoped to kill two birds with one stone. They might get lucky and bag a bear, as well as get a line on where that big cat had his lair.

There was another light snow on the ground, which deepened as they gained elevation. By mid-afternoon, they reached that rocky slope that slanted back to the craggy heights above. There were no bear tracks in the snow down in the ravines, but the tracks of a huge cat were plain to see where the end of a rugged spur sloped down to intersect with the ravine. The cat tracks came down the sloping crest of the spur, turned left, and continued on up the ravine. At the sight of the tracks, Walt stopped walking.

"Ho, ho," he said heartily, but his face had grown a shade less tanned, and he looked apprehensively at the formidable terrain.

"There she blows, pard," he said briskly. "Take a good squint at the size of that kitty's feet."

"Wow," Ben said with a thrill of excitement at the thought of bagging the owner of those tracks. "Walt, that's probably the cat that gave us such a rough night up here last summer. The tracks are fairly fresh. Are we going to trail him?"

"Indeed, we are, but I don't mind saying that I'm scared stiff at the thought of meeting up with that four-legged devil. Call the dogs. He came down off the ridge and turned up this hollow. We'll hit this trail. He might stick to low ground, but I doubt it. He'll probably head for high ground again soon. Judging from the fresh look of these tracks, I'd say our boy ain't more'n an hour head of us. Here are the dogs. Let's be on our way."

They set off up the ravine with the hounds loping ahead, keen on the scent of the big cat. For a half mile or more, the panther kept to low ground. Suddenly, the tracks took a sharp turn to the left and began to ascend the slope. On two occasions, they came to where fallen   trees stretched across the path nearly twenty feet apart. At both of these places, the great cat had leaped from one tree trunk to the other, without touching a single flake of the snow that lay between.

"God almighty," Walt gasped. "Ben, old boy, we're trailing a bird, not animal. Look at the distance between them logs. It's twenty feet if it's an inch, and I'll bet he skimmed over it without as much as a grunt. I don't know if we're smart trailing this panther. I'd wager he's big enough and strong enough to kill both of our dogs in gig-time if they come to grips with him. What do you think, Ben? Think we ought to go on or give it up before we lose a dog, or both?"

"You're the boss of that, Walt," Ben replied as he studied the forbidding country around them. This section had been plenty difficult to travel, even in summer, but now that it was locked in the grip of winter, it was doubly hazardous to traverse. Even so, Ben was reluctant to call it quits without even getting within shooting distance of the panther. "You're the boss of whether we turn back. I'd hate awful bad to lose one of them hounds trying to bag an animal we may never get our eyes on, much less get a shot at, but this big cat presents a challenge. If we turn back now, without even getting a decent crack at him, we'll feel like kicking ourselves all winter. You're the boss, but I feel like giving Mister Kitty something to remember us by, if we can do so safely."

With a shake of his head, Walt opened his mouth to protest, but closed it without a word. At that moment, they heard the deep baying of the hounds ahead of them and to the left. With a ringing yell, Walt Randall called encouragement to the dogs. Swinging around, he looked at Ben with fire in his eyes. All doubt and indecision had been swept away, and he was aquiver in his concern for the safety of the dogs.

"Let's shake a leg, pard," he roared. "Too late to turn back now. Them fool hounds have jumped that cat. He'll run for a while then maybe go up a tree. But if they press him, we just might have two dead dogs on our hands. Come on. A cat that size is dynamite when he's in a tight spot. It's goodbye dogs if they crowd him."

The partners began following the tracks of the panther and dogs. For a few minutes, the tracks held to the ravine then they swung to the left and began an ascent of the rocky slope, where the traveling was doubly difficult. Great slabs of rocks lay scattered about, expertly camouflaged by the deep snow. Slipping and sliding, and cursing the treacherous footing that held them back, they slowly scaled the mountain slope. Far above, the hounds had settled down to a steady baying, which signified that for the present, the big cat had taken to a tree.

After an age of climbing, they reached an uneven line of jumbled blocks and shafts of rock that crowned the crest of the bulging slope for as far as their limited vision would permit. The tracks in the snow cut between two great slabs of rock and then continued up the slope. Here the terrain became less formidable, and the traveling less strenuous. A hundred yards ahead, a stand of virgin hemlock trees came into view. As the hunters hurried into their midst, Ben found himself studying the stand of timber. Some of the trees were fifteen inches or more at the butt and as straight as gin barrels. Owing to the altitude and rocky setting, their growth had been very slow. They that were doubtless centuries old, but they were still comparatively small. Ben estimated that centuries more would be needed before these trees reached the growth their brothers had attained on a lower level.

The baying of the hounds came to them from directly ahead. The slope here was more even and free of underbrush. They could see a considerable distance in all directions. Soon they saw the hounds leaping around one of the largest hemlock trees. It had forked about twenty feet above the ground. A solitary rock lay near the base that from a distance looked to be six or eight feet thick. The instant they spotted the hounds, Walt held up a hand and stopped dead in his tracks.

"By heavens, they've treed him," he whispered hoarsely as he smiled wryly at Ben.

"What do we do now?" Ben asked, keeping his voice low, but his heart was pounding like a trip-hammer.

"Creep as close as possible and try to get a good shot at that long-clawed devil," said Walt. "He's up there in that tree with the big fork in it, but you can bet your bottom dollar that if we go running up there, hell-bent, he'll jump out, claw hell outta the dogs, and be off again before you can say beans. We gotta move slow now, pard. Get set for some straight and fancy shooting, and please don't forget the dogs when you shoot. He may jump before we're ready, but we'll have to chance it. Come on."

They worked their way up the slope, foot by foot. When they were a hundred yards from the dogs, they got their first look at their quarry. A great, greyish blob untangled itself, stepped out on the right-hand fork of the tree, and looked down upon the frenzied hounds with a snarling mouth, switching tail, and flattened ears. He kept changing his position. First he faced this way, then that way, but more often, his attention seemed centered upon the dogs below, more often than all else his attention seemed centered upon the dogs below. The great cat was a bundle of nerves, snarling his hatred and fear, and constantly moving.

Slowly, cautiously, the hunters picked their way closer, studying the footing ahead, not the quarry. Fifty yards from the treed cat, they were frozen in their tracks by a piercing scream. Their eyes darted to the tree. The big cat was facing them, standing like a carved statue. Jerking their rifles to their shoulders, Ben and Walt snapped two quick shots at the snarling cat, but just as they pulled their triggers, the panther dropped lightly to the top of the big rock. Then with another hair-raising scream, he leaped squarely upon the raging hounds. All hell broke loose. Screams, snarls, and growls of rage split the air as the three animals became a huge whirling ball of hounds and cat. Suddenly, the panther freed himself. He reared back on his haunches and prepared to defend himself. Without hesitation, the hounds rushed him. The ensuing fight was over in the twinkle of an eye. The panther flung the two dogs to one side, bleeding, and torn in a dozen places from his razor-sharp claws then he disappeared up the timbered slope, his long tail flipping high in the air behind him.

That night, the hunters camped in the lee of a great, over-hanging rock miles down the ravine. The two hounds were badly mauled and weak from loss of blood. After the evening meal, as the hunters applied salve to the canines' wounds, they resolved to have another try at the big cat later in the winter.

Chapter 20

*T*rapping season opened officially on the fifteenth of November, and during the first week of the season, Ben and Walt blazed out their trap line and set their traps in a tremendous circle that covered at least thirty miles—fifteen out and fifteen back. A stout, snug shelter was built at the extreme end of the line where it swung back towards the Randall homestead. The partners stocked it with such provisions as they deemed necessary.

The weeks slipped by, and each day, their stock of pelts grew. At Christmas, they had more than a hundred skins ready for market, and a week of the trapping season remained. January saw the close of season on most fur-bearing animals, but the hunters felt that they had a score to settle with the panther. Their pride was in the hunt, and they went after the big cat with grim determination.

The hunt consumed three days. It was a grueling chase, over one hogback ridge after another, covering miles and miles of territory that neither hunter had ever been in before. At last, after having treed the big cat unsuccessfully five times, they struck upon plan. Always before, the panther jumped out of the tree just when the hunters were almost within shooting distance. The sixth time the dogs barked treed, Ben and Walt held a conference. Luckily, they were on the top of a ridge, and the land here was comparatively level. After much speculation, they decided to separate and approach the tree from opposite directions. Their plan was simple. Creep in as close as they felt was safe, then dash in, yelling at the top of their lungs and beating against the trees with clubs.

The hunters separated with a low "good luck," and in a moment were lost to view of one another. The only sounds were the barking of the dogs and the snarls of the panther. Ten minutes passed. Ben had chosen the opposite side of the ridge. He crept in until he could see the hounds jumping around the base of an oak tree. He waited yet another five minutes, but heard nothing from Walt. Just when he had decided to whistle to let Walt know he was in position, his partner's low whistle floated to him on the still, cold air. Smiling grimly, he answered it in such a way that Walt would know he was ready for action. Another low whistle sounded on the motionless air. That was the signal he had been waiting for. Leaping up, he made mad dash for the tree, yelling and beating as he went. He heard Walt approaching from the opposite side with fiendish yells, whacking every tree and bush in his path.

When Ben was within a hundred feet or so of the tree, he glanced up. He was gratified to see a huge, grayish-brown cat climbing into the top-most branches. Just as he reached the base of the oak tree, Walt came rushing up, puffing and blowing like a steam engine.

"He's up there, partner," Ben cried, pointing with a shaking hand. "We fooled him this time."

"Right-o, Ben," said Walt. "Look now, Ben, let's not stand around and chew the fat. Let's plug the big devil before he scoots down the trees and decides to jump. He's scared right now, but our surprise might wear off real quick. Let's rustle our humps while we still have him up there. Back off and get a bead on him just behind his shoulders. I'll shoot first then you shoot quick as you can right afterwards. We want to fix his clock before he hits the ground. If we only wing him, he'll come tearing outta there like a house-a-fire and maybe kill both of the dogs before we can finish him off. That's a risk we can't afford. Get set. We ain't got a minute to lose."

Backing away from the base of the trees a few feet, Ben raised his eyes and studied the actions of the big cat. The panther appeared very nervous as he clung to his precarious perch and snarled his hatred and fear. Ben raised his rifle, and sighting up its barrel, found the target.

At a low, hissing sound from Walt, the whip-like crack of a rifle shot rang out. The great cat momentarily stiffened. Taking careful aim, Ben pulled the trigger. Another sharp report followed. At the second shot, a shudder ran the length of the panther's body, and he went limp. His claws lost their hold on the branches, and he tumbled end over end to the snow-covered leaves. For a few moments, the hunters let the dogs worry the carcass, to be certain that no spark of life yet remained. With just one stroke of a powerful paw, the great cat could disfigure a man for life. Finally, they drove the dogs to one side and stretched out the body. Taking a steel tape from his pocket, Walt ran a quick measurement.

Stretched out, the panther measured seven feet, six inches, from the end of his nose to the tip of his hind legs.

With the closing of the trapping season, Ben and Walt took stock of the furs they had taken and found that they had done much better than they had anticipated. All told, they accumulated slightly more than one hundred and fifty pelts from the smaller animals, as well as five bearskins and one panther pelt. Furs were selling cheap that winter. Nevertheless, after numerous inquiries from different fur houses, they packed up their catch and headed to Charleston, West Virginia. After much bickering and dickering with the dealer who had bought their ginseng roots the fall before, they sold him their entire lot of furs. The pelts netted them well over two hundred dollars.

The long winter months dragged by. For a few weeks after the trapping season closed, the partners made long hikes into the wilderness beyond the area they had trapped in the hope that by a miraculous stroke of luck, they might happen onto the ridge Ben had stumbled across the June before. However, after many fruitless and hazardous trips, they bowed to fate and decided to discontinue searching until winter had loosened his hold on the land. As the winter season advanced, traveling became more and more difficult. All of the ridges were heavily mantled with snow. Crossing them had become a herculean task, and a very dangerous one. Under their cloak of white, they all looked alike as Walt and Ben toiled up one slope after another, only to make an even more precarious descent on the other side. Often, they struggled through snow that was waist deep, where it hadn't drifted well over their heads.

After many days in perilous conditions, battling blizzards on the heights and crossing rushing streams in bitter cold, they turned their backs on the woodlands, resolved to discontinue their search for the "Ghost Ridge," as Walt had named it, until the flowers of May nodded and swayed in the warm spring breezes.

Jesse Savage no longer tried forcing his attentions upon Alice Randall, but he continued to drive Grant Randall home from Richwood at odd times. Whenever he and Ben chanced to meet face to face, no greetings were ever exchanged. Ben considered him the most loathsome of creatures. Savage glared at him sharply. He was the type of human who would go to his grave seeking revenge on a person who had refused to yield to his stupid demands.

In mid-February, word drifted through the countryside that Jess Savage had returned from a two-week trip to the bayou country of Louisiana. Local gossip had it that he had come home accompanied by a middle-aged, widowed, Creole woman, and her grown daughter, who was said to be of striking beauty. Wise old heads began to nod knowingly, and their deductions were not long in becoming household gossip.

"Look like Jess Savage got himself another bed-feller," they reasoned. "Come late summer, though, and there'll be another unfortunate girl shipped home with a one-way railroad ticket in her hands and an unborn baby in her belly."

When the whisperings came to Alice Randall's ears, she shriveled in on herself and went about as if she were living a bad dream. Ben tried to jolt her out of it, but his efforts were for naught. With each passing day, the girl he loved drew further away from him, completely ignoring all overtures, and there were times she refused to talk with him at all. Eventually, wearied to the point of distraction, he began to live life as it came to him, day to day. As with all who have loved and lost, solace came to him in the hour of his extremity, and he emerged from the darkness of his despair a man at peace. In the rebirth of his courage, he remembered his father's words and decided to conduct himself accordingly in the future.

Lynn Randall, on the other hand, never paused in her campaign of conquest. She exhausted every means at her disposal letting him know that she would never alter her behavior as long as desire for him possessed her. Whenever Lynn was near him she was displayed her wares in a way that sent his blood dashing madly through his veins. During the months he had known her, Lynn had developed into a luscious young woman who possessed all the seductive beauty and charm of any of history's greatest sirens. Her figure had gradually become fuller and more rounded in the places of womanly charm, if that were possible, and as winter slowly merged into spring, Ben began to look forward to the time when she would flaunt her loveliness. And when that day came, he promised that he would possess Lynn Randall's gorgeous, untouched young womanhood as passionately and as completely as he had ever possessed any of the uninhibited young beauties he had known along the lower reaches of the Mississippi River.

In April, the snow melted off the great ridges, and the waters came cascading down the slopes and draws in flashing, gurgling streams. As the warm sun increased the speed of the thaw, and warm spring rains fell, the Cranberry River awoke. One day, it was an ice-locked waterway, its discolored waters flowing beneath armored sheeting. Twenty-four hours later, it had transformed into an awesome millrace, sweeping along at frightening speed. Jagged pieces of ice occasionally reared up out of its angry waters. Every tree within striking distance of those cakes of ice suffered damage.

As April closed, flowers began to appear in the meadows, fields, and woodland, and the melodious song of birds was heard almost every day. The winter was over, and in its stead came the glorious miracle of springtime. In May, the leaves unfolded from swelling buds, and the plants, long dormant, woke to the call of the seasons. In the middle of the month, Ben and Walt, by mutual agreement, decided for forego prop cutting for the day and take a stroll in the woods, instead. Upon their return, they stacked their timber cutting tools and began preparing for the coming hunt for ginseng. On the stroll that day, they had come upon many herbs related to ginseng that were up and unfolded "full tilt."

"Well, partner," Walt said. "There she be. Reckon from now on, we're wasting time at this prop business. The seng's here again. I'm for hitting the woods as soon as we can get our paraphernalia kicked together. How about you?"

"Same here," Ben replied. "Only let's take it kinda easy at first. This prop cutting has softened up our walking legs. It's only the middle of May. That May apple, rattleroot, wild ginger, and other weeds we seen today just unfolded. They were all on fairly low ground to boot. Back there on them high ridges, and up in them coves, I'd bet you a fin that things are still pretty dead yet. Some of them old hogbacks are a good two thousand feet higher up than we are down here by the Cranberry. At the start of the root season, that kind of altitude can make one whale of a difference. Let's take a little jaunt tomorrow and look the situation over. The ground's still plenty spongy, and the streams are running lots of water yet, and probably'll be rough to cross. We got to consider these things, pard. Got the whole summer ahead of us now. There ain't no need to rush out halfcocked."

Grinning broadly, Walt nodded. Ben was an old hand at the ginseng game, and Walt had always followed his lead. As the warm days of May gave way to the still warmer days of June, the partners gradually settled into the routine of root hunting they had followed the season before. They began to range deeper, into new territory, and occasionally would be absent for a week at a time.

On the first Sunday in June, Lynn returned home from Sunday school with a boyfriend on her arm. She introduced her companion to Ben with a glint in her eyes that was not lost on him.

"Oh, Ben," Lynn cried gaily, as she and her friend strolled up to the front porch, hand in hand. "Shake hands with Wayne Lanner. His folks are neighbors to the men you and Walt went bear hunting with last fall. Wayne, this is Ben Waters. Get acquainted, you two."

"Glad to meet you, Wayne," Ben said easily, as he rose from his seat on the porch steps and shook hands with the tall, freckled young man. Wayne Lanner looked to be in his late teens. He had the lanky body, big feet, and ungainly movement of a young dog, blue eyes, a long, thin face, and a thatch of red hair that bristled from under his Sunday hat. One look at the boy's innocent, honest, trusting face was enough to convince Ben that Wayne would never be a match for Lynn. She was only using him to get attention. Excusing herself after a while, Lynn rose from her seat, and picking up a church paper she had brought home from church, moved to go into the house. At the doorway, she paused and cast a feminine glance at Ben while she shook a finger disapprovingly.

"Serves you right, Ben Waters," she chided. "Remember what I've been telling you? I'm fed up with you ignoring my charms. Now you've lost me to another. A girl can wait around just so long. Toodle-oo! I told you so." And she disappeared into the house.

As June sped by, Wayne Lanner became a constant caller at the Randall home, becoming more enamored with Lynn with each passing day. She played with his affection as deftly as any professional siren could have done. As time went by, it was customary for him to hear her bid Wayne good night rather early, every Saturday night, as he sat on the doorstep of the cabin up the old logging road.

He lived alone on the days he and Walt were home from roaming the forestlands. Walt had never shared the cabin with him, and now he was glad that he didn't, as on every Saturday night he listened to Lynn's teasing voice and mocking laugh as she flirted and petted her new boyfriend on the front porch of the Randall home. On those warm summer nights, Ben lived with the growing conviction that before many weeks had passed Lynn would come to him some night after she sent Wayne Lanner home. And when she did come, and flung her passionate young body into his arms, he knew that he would never have the strength to resist her any longer.

Every word she said to Ben, and every look she bent upon him, there came again that same old, unspoken challenge and thinly veiled promise if things yet to come. It was there, plain as day, in her every word and action. Ben's heart would beat with the roll and boom of thunder, and his blood would race with the fury of an active volcano, as he listened to her voice and laugh.

One Saturday night in early July, at about ten o'clock, Ben once again sat and listened to the sounds of courtship coming from the Randall front porch. He and Walt had returned that afternoon from a four-day hike into the country beyond the Cranberry shed. Two hours after they had arrived home, Walt had driven off in Ben's car, bent on an all-night courting spree with his best girl Flo.

After seeing his friend off with a wide grin on his young face, Ban bathed and shaved, and after eating a hearty supper, sat and relaxed on the doorstep in the summer night. As time passed, the storm crept closer, occasionally lighting up the skies with jagged streaks of lighting. At such times, the accompanying thunder rolled and boomed, not unlike a giant was rolling huge boulders across the sky.

At intervals, between the thunder, Ben would catch the sound of Lynn's laugh quite clearly. The air was deathly still, as is often the way before a summer storm, and the slightest sound seemed to travel an incredible distance. The sound of the storm's approach drowned out all other sounds, and its roll and sweep seemed to fill the universe. Eventually, the first few pattering drops of rain began to fall, and with rasping sigh, Ben arose from his seat.

Walking to one side a few paces, he unbuttoned the front of his trousers, exposed his privates, and urinated. Stepping back to the doorway again, he was just about to enter when he heard light running steps coming up the old logging road from the direction of the Randall homestead. Closer came the steps, and in another moment, he heard them on the flagstone walk which ran from the roadway to his cabin door. Peering sharply into the night, Ben faintly saw a figure hurrying towards him.

Just then, the yard was lit up as plainly as midday for a few seconds by a great flash of lightning. Ben recognized that figure, and the potential of this visit flashed over him. Ben stepped out of the doorway to meet Lynn.

"Why, Lynnie," he cried, taking her by the hand and leading her into the cabin. By now, the rain had begun to fall quite heavily. "Is anything wrong down at the house? Is someone sick? Here, let me light the lamp."

"No, Bennie-boy. Don't bother to light the lamp. It's better this way," she replied.

"Is someone sick?" Ben asked again.

"Nothing wrong down there. Nobody's sick," she replied then, in a voice he remembered from the summer before when they had gone strolling up the Cranberry, placing a special emphasis on "down there."

"I don't think I understand," he continued, every word almost choking him. But he knew, even as he said it, that he was lying. "If everything is okay why did you come running up here through the rain in the middle of the night?"

"Shame on you, Ben Waters. Don't try to pull that innocent stuff on me. You know perfectly well why I'm here, lover of mine-to-be."

"Lynnie, Lynnie," he implored, in a last gallant effort before capitulating. "Girl, do you realize what you're asking of me? Are you sure this is what you want and the way you want it?"

"Positive, dear man," she whispered. She was standing so close to him that he could feel her hot breath fanning his cheek. She fumbled about herself as though rearranging her clothing.

"What about Wayne Lanner? Would this be fair to him?"

"Forget the overgrown kid," she admonished sweetly, reaching upward in the darkness and laying a small, cool hand on his lips. "He's only a boy, with no experience at lovemaking. I want you to love me like I know you can, you big, ugly, long-nosed devil. Wake up. Be a man, Bennie. Make love to me tonight, all the way."

"What about Alice?" he asked, shaking like a leaf.

"Alice is plain nuts these days, and you know it," she said.

"She's in a shell like a turtle, and we can't afford to wait around for her to come crawling out. We've got things to do, exciting things."

Reaching out to her, his hands touched nothing but bare flesh. She was nude. He remembered the rustling sounds of a few moments before, and smiled to himself. She was following the same old patterns. She knew the power of her glorious young womanhood, and she was using it to gain her desires.

With a knowing smile, he put his hand on the nude girl. She gave a low, throaty laugh, full of feminine triumph, and flung her naked body into his arms. Wordlessly, Ben gathered the trembling girl close. All the pent-up fires of passion burst their bonds, and he fondled and kissed his clinging companion in a way that brought gasps of delight from her lips.

Finally, tearing her lips loose from his, she whispered, "Take me to the bed, lover man. Then make love to me all the way. And please, Bennie-boy, please, let yourself go. Don't wait a minute longer. I'm dying for it. I've wanted you so badly and needed you for so long."

Without another word of protest, he swept her up in his arms and turned towards his bed. The hour of his temptation had come and he was bowing before it as he knew all along that he would. To deny it any longer would be an insult to his manhood. Moments later, her voice was raised in agonized ecstasy.

"Ah," she gasped, her breath coming in pants. "I'm in heaven and hell, at the same time. Oh, no, don't stop now. I'd just die dead if you did. Every move you make, I'm sure it's gonna kill me if you keep this up. But please do, oh, God above, please do."

"I couldn't stop now, even if I wanted to, which I don't, you hot little baby," he gasped.

"Damn you, Ben Waters. Damn you all to hell," she moaned as she pulled his face down and kissed him. "It's good. Oh, so good. I love it. I love you, too, lover man of mine. I'll never let you go. Never, no never. I'll—ahhhh."

She clung to him as tightly as her strength would permit. Her shapely legs were high in the air, spread wide, and thrashing wildly. Her heels beat a sharp tattoo in the small of his back, and she bit down firmly into the muscles of his right shoulder with her strong white teeth.

An hour later, he walked her home. Overhead, the storm had cleared, and the stars blazed down upon the young lovers. As they strolled along, she kept her arms locked around his waist. Often, she would pause in their walk and kiss him with a ruby mouth, trying to drink him down. Between kisses, she whispered sweet and shocking things in his ears. Ben's head was whirling like a schoolboy's on his first date as he kissed Lynn good night at the door of her home.

Chapter 21

*T*he long days of July ran into weeks, and then one day it was August, which sped by as though on magical wings. Ben and Walt searched the wilderness on the headwaters of the Gauley River with intensity, though their returns were disheartening. Abundant ginseng was found occasionally. As the weeks slipped away, they began to fear that they would eventually fall short of their goal unless their luck ran differently than it had in the past. At last, September was ten days away. The partners had walked themselves bow-legged, but they were still no nearer to finding Ghost Ridge than they had been the fall before. However, Ben persisted doggedly. Walt stuck by his side like a burr, trusting his leadership and judgment in all things.

Lynn came to the little cabin many times after that stormy night. Always, she came at night, after she had sent young Wayne Lanner home. It became a customary thing between them nearly every Saturday night. If they did not get together on Saturday night, Lynn would slip out of the house and come to him some other night during the week. Shortly after their first night together, she told Ben that she and Alice now had separate rooms. Her room was the one he had occupied for some months. It was off by itself and had an outside entrance, as well as an inside one. This was ideally suited to her needs. She could slip out of her room anytime and come to him with little danger of being detected by her family. Now all Ben had to do was leave his door unlocked at night. This arrangement was set up, and the deal was sealed with a lingering kiss. Ben would often wake late at night and find her in bed with him completely nude, kissing him.

In those hours of passion, the lovers repeatedly, and so completely, exhausted each other, that after the crest of their passion had passed, they would lay in each other's arms as limp as wet dishrags. Lynn   was a never-failing source of delight and thrills, as she responded to Ben's every touch and movement. Their embraces always caused Lynn to cry out and always left her exhausted and wildly disheveled. On the night of their third meeting, she had dismissed her boyfriend long before midnight, and ten minutes after he had driven away, she was naked in Ben's arms on the bed in the little cabin. No sooner were they prostrate upon the bed than she rolled into his arms and began pouring her pent-up desires upon him.

"Lynnie, baby," Ben said, as he cupped a hand over one of her firm breasts and gave it a squeeze. "It's heaven on earth to make love to you this way, but nature has a way of exerting itself."

"What's the matter, Bennie-boy?" she asked, snuggling close to him and running a hand over his chest and down his abdomen. "Are you afraid I'll tell Allie?"

"It's not that, you little witch. However, if you do tell her about us, I'll tell her that if she hadn't drove me away I wouldn't have fallen into your arms. Anyway that's not what's worrying me."

"Tell me your troubles," Lynn coaxed. She raised herself on an elbow, leaned over, and claimed his lips.

"Lynnie, here's the rub. These stolen moments are wonderful while they last, but in nearly every case, the girl almost always becomes pregnant before too long."

"Is that all that's troubling you?" she asked, giggling.

"Ain't that enough? If you get a kid in your belly, I'll do the honorable thing and marry you."

"Nothing doing, Ben Waters," she snapped with a barely audible catch in her voice. "It's not that you'd leave me in the lurch. I'd stake my life on that. No, Bennie, my lover, you really don't love me at all when the cards are down. I'll not try to explain how I feel about you. I'm afraid you wouldn't understand. We both know that we're attracted to each other. Now that we've finally gotten together, how about we just have our fun, and forget about everything else? I think it'd work out best for both of us in the long run. Okay?"

"But honey, suppose you do become pregnant? What then?"

"Forget about it," she said. "I'm taking a precaution against that every day."

"I don't understand," Ben replied, mystified. "We use no protection when we give ourselves to each other. And as far as I know, you haven't been to see a doctor for medicine to prevent pregnancy. Even if you did contact a doctor, a request like that would be kinda hard for a single girl to explain. He'd know you was absorbing a little pun-jab on the sly."

"Of course the good doctor would know that, silly," she chided playfully. "It'd be a waste of time trying to fool him, and I'd be the last one to try. Now please, forget your fears and let's make love. After all, that's what I sneak up here for. There ain't anything else I know that would get a girl so hot and bothered that she'll leave her bed and go looking for it in the middle of the night. I say let's have fun while we're still young and able to enjoy it. We can worry about the consequences after the fire's out."

"Be serious, Lynnie. I don't want to be the cause of you getting a bad name."

"Bad name, my hind eye," she retorted. "That's the very least of my worries. You're holding back when we're lovemaking. If you are, I beg of you to let go and give me everything you can give. Please don't hold back. If you are, you're doing it needlessly. Every day, I take a hot bath in my room and brew myself a cup of tansy tea. No fuss, no muss."

"What in the hell is tansy tea?"

"Listen, lover boy, and learn about homegrown birth control. Tansy is a strong smelling flower raised by housewives in their gardens. Tea made from the leaves of this plant will prevent any woman from having a baby. With tansy, she could bed down with a dozen men every night, and not have a care in the world. All she need concentrated on is enjoying her nooky. My mother has raised this flower ever since I can remember. I don't know whether she ever used it for that purpose, but I wouldn't be surprised if she had. Anyway, it's growing in our garden right now, and I've become quite a tansy tea drinker lately."

"Tansy will prevent a woman from having a baby?"

"Exactly."

"Impossible," Ben snorted in disbelief.

"It's true," she said firmly. "How do you suppose the married women in these hills can take on a strange piece now and then without an off-color duck to account for, and still be able to keep their husbands in the dark? Tansy tea is the answer. Around here, women ain't always got a doctor's neck to fall on in case anything goes wrong. That's one of the disadvantages of living way back in these hills."

"Suppose it don't work in your case? Things are known to fail at times, you know."

"All right, you old worry-wart," she laughed. "Suppose I do get knocked-up? So what? That won't mean disgrace for either of us. I've had that situation figured out this long while."

"Okay, Miss Smarty Pants. Consider letting me in on your magic solution."

"Ben Waters," she giggled, "you're all wet. I ain't got pants on, as you very well know. That's one piece of clothing that would be in our way something terrible."

"All right, all right, my beautiful nudist. What's the answer?"

"Wayne Tanner is the answer if it ever comes to that, which I bet it never will."

"What about Tanner?" Ben demanded. "Has that over-grown kid been getting any ideas?"

"Ha, ha," she laughed softly. "Ain't that the natural reaction of you men around us girls? Is he any different from you, in the long run?

"Don't act coy, girl. You know exactly what I mean."

"Don't tell me you're jealous of my beau's attentions."

"Hell, yes, I'm jealous, Lynnie," Ben roared. "When I stop to think about us, my head whirls round and round. Maybe I oughtn't to say this, but you're my girl now. I know I haven't played fair with you, but I'll come out of the fog that's been blinding me yet. Just give me time, girlie. Just give me time. It makes me squirm all over inside at the thought of that punk kid laying a hand on you. That might sound silly, but that's the way I feel about you."

"Gosh, Bennie-boy," she said. "Gosh Almighty, but it's good to know you feel that way. I hadn't the slightest idea you felt that way. Honest, I didn't. I don't know whether to laugh or cry, but let me give you a great, big French kiss. You deserve one after saying a thing like that."

"Look, gorgeous, stop beating around the bush. Tell me the truth. Has this Tanner kid made passes at you?"

"Not yet, he hasn't, but who knows when he might? He's a man, same as you. Forget your jealousies and listen to my plan in case I get a hump in my back and a knot in my belly. This Tanner boy wants to marry me the worst way. So far, all I'm doing is petting with him and generally stringing him along. It's a dirty trick, but that's how it is. I only took up with him in the first place to make you jealous. It worked all right, and I'm glad. I never had so much fun before in all my life. If we do hit home base while lovemaking, I'll have to use my head instead of my rear end.

I'll pretend to be overcome by this boy until I can't resist him any longer. I'll see that he gets behind my panties a couple of times. If he's a bit backwards about getting started, I'll even help him along. On some dark night, I'll break down and confess that he's to become a father. Wouldn't that be great? Him fathering your child? If I know that kid, he'll puff up like a toad at hearing of the little bundle that's going to arrive, rush me off to a preacher, and get the knot tied before I have time to get bigger around the belly. That's the only sensible thing to do. It'd be foolish to let jealousy ruin a perfect out. Little Lynnie has all bets coppered. There's nothing to fear. Let's just let the chips fall where they will. I once read that people get lots more fun out of life when they do it that way."

"Enough, you sly little schemer," Ben laughed, slapping her naked buttock with his open hand. "I ain't overly fond of him getting behind your panties. However, if it becomes necessary, what can I say or do? One thing I do know. That would be a lousy trick to pull that boy."

"He'd never know the difference, lover man," she whispered softly, using her hands to excite him.

"All right, all right, you she devil," he gasped. "From now on, we'll make love high, wide, and handsome—as long as my strength holds out, that is. At the rate we're going, that might not take too long. You're really some pumpkins in bed, and no mistake."

"Better than those Mississippi River bitches you bragged about?" she asked quickly.

"Oh, much better," he replied, and he believed that he was telling the truth. Lynn Randall was truly the most remarkable girl he had ever known. She was completely feminine one minute, tomboyish the next, sweet as honey one minute, bitter and biting the next. Sunshine one minute, tempest the next. Cool and indifferent one minute, blazing with passion the next. Clear as crystal water one minute, life's greatest mystery the next. She was God's fairest creation and his most incomprehensible one. She was a woman. Utterly loveable, beautiful, and desirable, indispensable to nature's plan for reproduction, but beyond the understanding of any man.

The summer days rolled on, and during this golden season, Ben and Lynn kept their secret love trysts. Whenever they were around other people, she never betrayed her interest in him. However, in the velvety softness of the summer nights, alone in the darkness of the little cabin and sharing the privacy of his bed, Lynn Randall became another person.

At such times, she became a human tigress, consuming him in a tornado of passionate kisses, clinging arms, undulating motions, and panting, terminating at last in an eventual climax.

Chapter 22

*A*s the summer season drew towards its zenith, Alice grew more relaxed. Watching her, Ben shook his head in hopeless regret, but as time wore on, success continued to elude the hunters. Ben began to accept things over which he had no control. Eventually, he gave Alice up as lost to him. September was a third of the way behind them, and during the entire season, he and Walt gathered enough ginseng to pay more than a third of the mortgage. Ben began to accept that defeat was scarcely more than a month away. They had done remarkably well, but a thousand dollars would never be enough to stave off foreclosure.

On September 15, a Monday, after it had rained for a day and night, the hunters postposed going into the woods until the following day. At noon, Grant Randall hitched his mare to the buggy, and he and Mrs. Randall drove to the general store at Holcomb. An hour later, Walt pulled out to see his best girl Flo, leaving Ben and the two sisters at home on the wide front porch. Alice took a chair to one side and began reading a church folder. Ben and Lynn began playing checkers.

While they battled across the board, she laughed merrily at every move she made, followed by an intimate, obscene gesture meant for his eyes alone. Fortunately, Alice was sitting with her face turned away from them, so Lynn felt safe carrying on. By the eternal, he breathed, she was capable of being all things to any man at any time.

At three o'clock, an automobile came up the driveway. From their seats, the three young people could see far down the Cranberry, but they couldn't identify it. The approaching car was old, dilapidated, and sounded as though it was going to fall apart at any moment. It ground to a wheezing halt in the front yard, and a young woman alighted. The driver, a bewhiskered man of indeterminate age wearing a huge, floppy, straw hat, remained inside the automobile. As the young woman walked up to the gate, Ben studied her with a keen eye. When she came to a halt below the three on the porch and raised her head, his heart gave a great leap. He recognized her and knew her visit was not a social call.

She was of medium height, but unusually comely. Her skin was creamy white, with just a hint of a tan. She had dark hair that swept down below her shoulders in a rippling tide that glistened like ebony. Her eyes were great, dark pools of misery, sadness, and shame.

"Is this the Randall home?" she asked softly. Her voice was decidedly southern.

"Yes, it is," Alice replied as she rose from her chair and stepped to the edge of the porch. A quizzical look crept across her face. "What can I do for you?"

"I'm looking for Alice Randall. Is she at home?"

Ben glanced at Lynn. Her face registered keen interest and curiosity.

"I'm Alice Randall," Alice replied. "Won't you come up and sit down?"

"No, thank you," the girl said. "I didn't come here today to talk. I come on an unpleasant mission."

"What do you want then?" Alice asked.

"I'm Lila LaGrange, from down Louisiana way. Me and my mother work for Jess Savage. Does that name mean anything to you?"

Alice uttered a choking cry, and reeled backwards a few steps, almost falling. She recovered her composure, but her face was as white and immobile as marble.

"Miss LaGrange," she said, in practically a whisper. "Why are you here? Is it to laugh in my face? Is not my cross hard enough to bear?"

"I didn't come for what you think," said Lila.

"Why did you come? You must have a good reason for this visit."

"I had to come. I had to see the girl Jess has sworn will soon be his wife."

Alice fought for mastery over her face. When the tide of emotion had passed, she sank down the top step. Ben watched her emotional display with an aching heart. He had guessed what was coming, and would have given anything to spare Alice the blow, but he was powerless to prevent it. So he sat, looked, and waited.

Lynn cursed and moved from her seat to the edge of the porch. Fixing an unfriendly eye on the girl, she said, "Speak your piece then haul outta here fast."

"Look and see," Lila cried.

With a trembling hand, she flung open her coat. One look at her bulging abdomen told the story better than any words. She was at least six months pregnant. Then with a moan, the girl sank down on the lower porch step, covering her face. Alice and Lynn ran down the steps and gently led her up the steps and to a chair on the porch. The girl dried her eyes and smiled at them wanly.

"You folks are right kind," she quavered. "I'm so worried these days. The good Lord above only knows what's to become of Ma and me."

"You poor thing," Alice said, drawing her chair up beside that of the unhappy girl. "We see the condition you are in. You're like me—fairly bursting with bitterness. Tell us your story. Maybe talking your troubles over with others will lighten your shoulders a little. It won't do any harm to try. Please tell us. We all want to help you."

"Perhaps you're right, Miss Randall," Lila replied. "I'm all pent up with my troubles. If I burst, though, it won't be the result of bitterness." She placed hand on her bulging abdomen.

"We know what you mean, Miss LaGrange," Ben said. "Reckon we know who's responsible for your condition, too. Jess Savage and his hellish ways ain't any stranger to us."

"Maybe I oughtn't to tell it," she whispered, as though talking to herself, "but I really want to confide in someone who'll understand and sympathize. I'm at the end of my rope, and don't know which way to turn anymore."

"Tell us your troubles, Lila," Alice said, "and maybe I'll tell you mine. Jess Savage ain't exactly the type of man I'd choose for a husband. Not by a long shot. He's got us Randalls over a barrel with our pants down, if you know what I mean. If I become his wife next month, it'll be because I, too, am between a rock and a hard place and don't know of any way out."

Without preamble, Lila began to speak. Her story was as old as time. The February before, Jess Savage had come to the bayou country of Louisiana looking for a housekeeper. When word if his need reached their ears, she and her mother had gotten in touch with After one good look at her, Lila recalled, he accepted their offer.

Her father had died two years previously of a fever, and she and her mother had barely managed to eke out the most miserable kind of existence. The proposals of marriage Lila had had since her father's untimely death were anything but attractive. All that the men of the bayou country looked for in a wife was that she be young, strong, good in bed, able to cook passably well, keep house, and naturally bear children. Her beauty, if she possessed any, was of secondary importance because beauty would fade in time. They considered heavily the more lasting qualities in a woman whenever they went hunting for a female bedfellow.

As soon as they were settled in Savage's home, the man's behavior changed. He began to make advances. When Lila tried to resist, he became violent and threatened to throw her and her mother into the road without a cent in their pockets. He even swore that if they gave him any trouble after he threw them out, he would sic the law after them. When she related how Savage had had his way with her, Lila LaGrange blushed scarlet and bowed her head in shame.

"That's how it's been for me all these months," she finished tearfully. "I've shared my bed with him every night for over five months. He forbade me to sleep with my mother after he had his way with me. One night in early March, when I went upstairs, I found him in my bed, waiting for me. Mother had said she'd be up soon, so I didn't think anything of going to bed without her, but the minute I entered the room, I knew I was in for something terrible. Quick as a flash, he slammed the door shut and locked it. Then he grabbed me and dragged me towards the bed. He was stark mother naked. I fought him, but he laughed it off and fairly smothered me in his arms. He was as strong as an ox, and I couldn't get away from him. I just didn't have the strength. At first, I thought about running away, but he swore that terrible things would happen to me if I tried that. After I knew that I was going to have a baby, he sort of promised to see that I was properly taken care of when my time came. Lately, though, he's been awful. Now he constantly threatens Ma and me with all sorts of awful things if we don't hit the road. Yesterday, he laughed in my face and said he'd had his fun with me, but the show was over. That was when he mentioned your name, Miss Randall. When I asked who you was, he grinned like an alligator, called me a bad name, and said you was the girl he was going to marry next month. I just had to see you. So today, after he went into Richwood, I persuaded one of the hired men to drive me out here. For God's sake, don't marry Jess Savage.

He's not a man, really. He's an animal. I ought to know. He and I have slept together for close to half a year now."

"Oh, monster," Alice gasped as Lila bowed her head in humiliation. Ben swore roundly under his breath, and kicked one of the porch posts.

"That dirty, low-down…" Lynn cursed, using one of her most colorful expressions.

Lila turned as pink as a rose and stared at her, round-eyed.

"So," Lynn continued, "you've given him what he wanted, and you have his kid in your belly, but he wants to break up his love nest and get rid of you and your mother. It that it?"

"That's exactly right."

"Why don't he marry you and give his child a legitimate name?"

"He swore he'd see me and the baby in hell before he'd stoop to marry a half-nigger."

"He wants you to leave?" Ben asked. "Even though you haven't any money or friends to turn to for help?"

"That's right," said Lila. "Every day, he hounds us to go, but I don't know where to go or how to go. I'm a thousand miles from where I grew up, and I ain't got a red cent to travel on. In my condition, I couldn't walk very far. I don't know what's going to happen to Ma and me. Lord above, what's to become of us?"

"Well I'll be a lop-eared son-of-bitch," Lynn exploded. "I say take a twelve-gauge shot gun and blow the bastard's brains out. It would be a waste of gunpowder, I know, but maybe it'd be worth it."

Alice patted Lila's shoulder then told how Jess Savage had the Randall household at his mercy and his scheme to ensnare her in exchange for her parents' home. Afterwards, Lila rose from her chair and smiled sadly.

"Reckon I'll be heading back now," she said. "It's been awful   nice of you folks to receive me like you did and listen to my sad story. Remember what I told you, Alice Randall. Steer clear of that two-legged water moccasin. He is poison all the way through."

"What're you going to do?" Alice asked.

"Nothing, unless I have to. Jess Savage brought me up here of his own free will. I didn't force him. Now that he's used me, he wants to cast me aside like an old shoe, but he's not going to get away with it this time, by heavens."

"How can you prevent it?" Alice asked. "How can you expect justice at his hands?"

"I don't know yet, but I'll find a way," Lila cried. "Good-bye, Miss Randall. It's been real nice meeting you folks. You're good, all the way through, May God bless and keep you from this evil."

Later that evening, an hour or so before sundown, Alice came up the cabin and insisted that she and Ben go for a walk to the Cranberry. He consented, though her request struck him as unusual. For months, she had turned a deaf ear to his overtures. He asked no explanation for her unexpected request.

As they strolled, she chatted in a voice that was artificially light and gay, and she had an arm tucked into his whenever they could walk abreast. At the fork in the river, she stopped and sat upon an old log that lay on the upper side of the trail. She looked up at him from out of a face with a strange mixture of emotions—hate, vindictiveness, love, shame, and sorrow.

"Ben," she said, "I'm so mad I could burst wide open."

"Life has some queer twists at times, Alice," he replied as he sat down beside her.

He was at a loss as to what to say. She had to surmount her hurdles by herself. She alone held the key to freedom. If she chose to use her God-given rights as a free woman, all was well and good. Ben was weary to the point of distraction of the reason for her sacrifice. His love for Alice still smoldered. He had fought a losing fight for her heart and hand, and had turned to the comfort of her younger sister's ready arms.

"That dirty, low-down skunk," Alice said. "He's sure been living up to his reputation, hasn't he? Has that man no decency or honesty? That poor, fatherless girl. Now that she's ceased thrilling him and is carrying his child, he wants to cast her aside without a thought or care. Ain't that a beautiful way to treat a girl whose honor he has defiled?"

"Alice," Ben said patiently. "Did you expect anything else from that geezer?"

"I don't know, Ben, I don't know," she said sadly. "Last winter, when I heard that this girl and her mother had come up to work for Jess Savage, I tried to convince myself that it was all just idle gossip. Now I know differently. My eyes were really opened this afternoon. What a shame a nice girl like her fell into his clutches."

"Lila LaGrange is a nice girl," he agreed, "but being a nice girl wouldn't influence Savage. No doubt, her niceness made him more determined than ever to use her to satisfy his lusts. Such men are like that, you know."

"And I suppose," she cried bitterly, "he's still expecting me to come to him as fresh and untouched as the day I was born?"

"That's the idea."

"I won't do it, Ben. I won't do it," she cried. "When I go to him, it'll be exactly as he comes to me—a used article."

"Alice, what are you saying?" Ben asked.

She turned and flung herself into his arms. She transformed from a blazing-eyed girl, consumed with anger, to one that was soft, warm, and clinging with burning lips. Ben was flabbergasted. As soon as he could tear his lips from hers, he demanded to know the reason for her strange behavior.

"Make love to me, Ben," she whispered as she clung to him.

"Why now, Alice," he demanded harshly, "and not all these past months when I fairly begged you not to turn away from me?"

"Because I want to know your love while I'm still un-wed and still a virgin."

"You want me to make love to you all the way, as though we were man and wife? Is that what you mean?"

"Yes, yes," she panted, hiding her face against his chest.

"But why, Alice? Why do you suddenly want my love now, when always before you preached that we forget and smother our love for each other? What changed your mind?"

"Lila LaGrange," she hissed.

"Oh, I see. You plan to use me the same as Jess Savage used her. How about that?"

"Oh please, Ben," she begged. "Don't talk to me like that."

"It's true, ain't it?"

"Not in the way you think."

"Then you've given up this insane idea of marrying him to save the homestead?"

"I didn't say that."

"What did you say then?"

"Isn't it explanation enough to say that I love you? Isn't that reason enough?"

"Not by a long shot, it ain't," he replied scornfully.

"But it's true, Ben. It's true," she whispered wistfully as she pulled his head down and kissed him passionately.

She had given him quite a shock. However, knowing from experience that the ways of the opposite sex are beyond discernment, he had come to accept that it is best to take life as it comes and let tomorrow take care of its own problems. He had also long since decided to accept people as he found them, and not as he would have them be.

"I don't believe you, Alice Randal," he scoffed.

"Oh, Ben," she cried, standing. "I love you with all my heart. I know I haven't shown it lately, but I do. I can't marry you, Ben. I've got to see his deal though so that my parents will have a home in their old age."

"Alice, I've about lost patience with you. Here you talk of great love for me and yet tell me that you must marry a man who is lower than any snake that ever crawled upon this earth. Does that make sense?"

"It does to me."

"Poppy-cock," he snorted. "Now you want me to lay you, just as though you was some hot-pants hussy. What am I supposed to believe?"

"I can't help how it looks on the surface, Ben," she whispered. "I can't help you believe me. I only know how I feel about you. Please try to see my aide of it. I love you, yes, love you. I must marry that scoundrel, but before I do, I want to give myself to you, the man I love. What more can I say? What better reason could I give?"

"Alice," he groaned. "I'm as mixed up these days as you are. You're only doing this because of that poor LaGrange girl. For months now, you've been as cold towards me as a dead fish."

"No, Ben, my love," she maintained. "I know I'm acting like a shameless hussy, but I can't help myself. For many months, I've had this thought locked deep in my heart. Seeing that miserable girl this afternoon only hastened it's coming to life. That's the truth as surely as there is a God above us."

"Hush," he pleaded. "You poor, mixed-up, martyred girl. I just can't believe you're on the level. How can you love me as you say you do and let anything short of death come between us? How could you love me so and then want to cheapen that love?"

"I'm a woman, Ben Waters," she cried brokenly. "There's no other explanation I can give."

"All right, all right," he thundered. "Enough said. I won't do it. I've still pride as a man. Let's go home."

Suddenly, her hands busied themselves with her clothing. In less than a dozen heartbeats, she slipped out of her cotton dress and slip. Ben watched Alice Randall, mesmerized. Then she stood before him in all of her nude loveliness. Once more, she stretched forth her arms and made her plea again.

"Come into my arms, Ben, my love," she implored as wave after wave of crimson suffused her lovely features. And as he leaned towards him and pleaded, her beautifully contoured breasts heaved and quivered, drawing his gaze like a magnet. "I'm determined not to go to Jess Savage a virgin. I will give myself to the first strange man I can seduce first. Again, I ask you, my love, make love to me. I love you. Oh, God, how I love you. Please come and possess me, all the way."

Like a man in a dream, Ben Waters leapt from the log on which he sat and gathered Alice close to his breast with arms that trembled. Wordlessly, she clung to him. Without further protest, he led her up the slope to a great square of moss that grew soft and springy beneath the leafy branches of the gnarled jack-oaks.

Chapter 23

*T*hree days later, Ben and Walt descended a tributary of the Williams River thirty miles to the east of the Randall homestead. For the past two days, they had been working the watershed. Up one side and down the other, into every hollow and draw that led back to the hogback above. The topography was uneven and rough. Great ledges, cliffs, and huge, jumbled rock formations confronted the hunters. The slope to either side of the stream was almost perpendicular at times, almost as though they were traveling down a canyon.

Their luck had been very discouraging, but being the seasoned hunters that they were, they accepted this as part of the game, and searched on without protest. At about midafternoon, they came to an unusually formidable spot. The stream they were following appeared to drop out of sight ahead. The deep, rumbling roar of a waterfall smote the air, and the hunters looked at one another with lifted eyebrows. If it could not be circled, they would have to back track to a spot where they could take to higher ground until the falls were past.

However, they were relieved to see that they could safely bypass the obstacle. Crossing the stream, they ascended the right hand slope, and twenty minutes later, they were looking up at the falls. The water there took at least a thirty-foot plunge. It came roaring over the ledge and flashed down in a solid column to land on huge, greenish boulders. A pool of considerable size and depth had been dug out by the force of the water. As they gazed upon its shimmering surface, Ben felt reasonably certain that a number of fine trout called this wild, beautiful pool home. The fish darted here and there, as they strove to escape notice.

Bens gaze was drawn to an unusual phenomenon on the left-hand slope, approximately fifty yards downstream. A sizable depression swept back from the creek, like that which is often found where a spring gushes forth. Even at a distance, Ben heard the rushing babble of water that rose above the clamor of the stream. Ben followed the stream down until he stood opposite the phenomenon and looked on it in wonder.

Instead of normal drainage, the flow here was equal to the stream they were descending, a hundred times the quantity of any spring he had ever seen. It roared and gurgled out of the mountain from a great, cavernous hole. Huge blocks of rock formed the ceiling of the subterranean waterway. The whole mountain slope above it was one long incline or rocks that appeared to stand on end, and every which way, like mussed up pieces of a jigsaw puzzle. Trees, vines, ferns, and other vegetation had overgrown the slope until it appeared impassable.

Walt grinned widely. "Say, pard," he drawled. "How do you like that spring?"

"Walt," Ben said reflectively. "That's a hundred times over the biggest spring I've ever seen." His eyes took in every detail of this phenomenon. "Great day in the morning," he breathed. "If I wasn't looking at this thing with my own eyes, I wouldn't believe it."

"Whoa, boy, whoa," Walt laughed. "Let's not go overboard. Ben, old pard, that water yonder ain't a spring at all."

"Honest Injun?"

"That's right."

"Then what in heaven's name is it?"

Walt pointed to the distorted mountain slope. The lofty barrier soared up and up. "See that mountain over there?"

"Plain as daylight," Ben answered. "What's that got to do with the spring?"

"Plenty," said Walt. "Look, Ben, see how jumbled up that whole shebang is? Long years and years ago, when these mountains were pushed up out of the bowels of the earth, somewhere back over that ridge that's facing us is a creek. It was, what you might say was, "cut off." Then it had to find an outlet through that mountainous ridge of jumbled rock. Sounds impossible, I know, but water'll do strange things sometimes."

"Walt, what're you trying to tell me?" Ben asked. "Did you say that the water pouring out of that ghostly looking hole over there is coming from a stream or creek across the ridge?"

"It can't."

"Why not?"

"The creek over there flows along just so far, then it runs right smack up against a whole mountainside of rock. When that happens, the only thing left for Mister Stream to do is go underground, and that he does."

"Thanks for the explanation," Ben said with a shrug. He hadn't the faintest idea what Walt had been trying to tell him. Seeing his friend's look of disbelief, Walt gave a dry little chuckle, and picked up a piece of dead tree limb. Squatting down on his haunches, he took the stick and drew a long furrow that terminated against a rock that was half-imbedded in the sand.

"See this furrow?"

Ben nodded. "This represents the ridge. Thousands of years ago, when them mountains were formed, that stream over there just got cut off. That's all there was to it. It's odd, I know, but something like this ain't unusual. Such formations are called sinks."

"So there's a good-sized stream of water over that ridge," Ben said. He looked preoccupied.

"That's how it is, pard," said Walt, "but what say we amble along? We ain't finding any seng standing here chewing the fat."

"Hold, partner," Ben commanded, holding up a hand. Something just occurred to me. If there's a stream over the ridge we're facing, I want to go over there and explore it from one end to the other."

"Why so?"

"Listen, and see if what I'm thinking doesn't make sense. Suppose it's actually there. If so, there's bound to be a ridge on either side that'll be virgin territory. If there happens to be a fork in that stream that could well be what we've been searching for these many months. That ridge I crossed when I was lost is here somewhere. Maybe this is it. We'll never know till we go. Let's hit it and work it out from hell to breakfast. We've enough grub left to last us four more days. What say we make camp tonight on the stream across that ridge. In the morning, we'll have the whole day ahead of us to explore. We'll follow the stream till it goes underground. Then we'll head upstream, work the ridges on both sides, and keep on the lookout for one in the middle. Okay?"

"Okay with me, pard," Walt answered as he adjusted his pack straps for the long climb ahead. Two hours later, the hunters stood on the crest of the first hogback. The ridge was anything but promising as far as ginseng was concerned. The crest wasn't more than fifty feet wide across the tip and was practically solid rock. Stunted laurel grew here whenever it could find a foothold. There was no other vegetation.

After resting from their climb, the partners began the descent on the other side, making much better time than they had coming up. Slightly more than an hour later, they left the ridge they were standing on for the banks of the stream on the other side. This watercourse was identical to dozens of other streams they had traversed. Ben saw nothing about it to differentiate it from its fellow streams.

Night was near at hand when they came to the place where the stream went underground. The phenomenon was heralded by a low rumbling sound, which came to them like the roll of distant thunder. Walt gave a low whistle to attract Ben's attention and pointed downstream. Twenty minutes later, the hunters stood on the slope gazed down on a remarkable spectacle. The stream's course was obstructed, but a colossal barrier of broken rock formation stretched from one slope to the other and ascended. The mountain stream disappeared at the base if the formidable rampart out of which strange sounds rose. A weird hissing, bubbling, moaning, groaning roar came from the hole. And as he stood and gazed, spellbound, into its shadowy depths, Ben shook as one afflicted with a fever. The place fascinated him, even as it terrified him. When the hunters crossed over to the other side and began working back upstream, he was relieved.

Night was falling fast when they stopped to make camp. After the camp was set up, and the evening meal cooked and eaten, the partners sat, smoked, and talked at great length about what the morrow might bring. At the discovery of the unusual mountain formation, Ben had begun to feel excitement coursing through his body. He had a feeling that the next forty-eight hours would bring many answers, and he acknowledged that come what may, he had fought a good fight to keep the title to the Randall homestead in the hands of its rightful owners.

Later that night, while his friend snored peacefully, Ben stared up at the stars twinkling down though the foliage around their lonely camp. Sleep eluded him, even though his bones were weary. A gentle breeze had begun blowing. Faintly came the distant growl of the stream that flowed by their campsite as it plunged into the subterranean channel for its trip under the mountain. At times, the voice of the stream was a whispering sign. It seemed to be trying to convey a message.

Eventually, he dropped into a fitful slumber. He dreamed he was waste deep in dark water. Its clamor beat against his eardrum with a roll and beat that was like the knell of fate. Suddenly, the waters sank into the ground, and Ben dreamed he was on a windswept ridge; and the mocking laughter in the wind buffered and beat him. Then the scene changed, and he dreamed that he had a commanding view of ridges that swept down and away from him on every hand, each with a natural saddle, but not one of them housed a laurel thicket or a black walnut grove.

The next day, the hunters explored miles of the mountain slope and ridge, but though they found ginseng in paying quantities, the Ghost Ridge eluded them. On the second day of exploring the mysterious watercourse, they worked their way up the main stream. Just before they stopped for lunch, they came to where the stream forked. The partners exchanged hopeful glances, and each help up a hand with two crossed fingers.

"Maybe that's it, pard," Walt said as he pointed to a long sloping spur that swept down from the heights, and its bold outline drew the eyes of the hunters irresistibly. It was a formidable picture indeed.

At the junction of the forks, the sides of the dividing spur were practically straight up and down; with numerous outcroppings all up and down their frowning faces. Scattered hemlocks, cedars, and small laurel clung to its sides with admirable tenacity. After they had partaken of a scanty lunch, the hunters resumed their searching. During the remainder of that day, they worked the left-hand branch of the forks. Another night was spent on the banks of the "Lost Stream," as Walt called it, and the following day they finished hunting the ridge on that side.

Chapter 24

*T*hat night, they camped at the forks of the Lost Stream. After all camp chores had been attended to, they held a war council. Their food supply was running low, and unless success attended their efforts within the next forty-eight hours, they would have to abandon the hunt and head home without delay. To be caught in those mountain woods without food could prove fatal.

The following morning, they gauged their depleted food supplies and promptly cut the hunting time they had allotted themselves in half. When the sun rose again in the eastern sky, they would have to turn home, Ghost Ridge or no Ghost Ridge.

Tightening their belts, they started up the right hand branch of the stream. High noon found them far up at the beginning of the tributary. For five hours, they ferreted out every nook and cranny that they came upon. Even the smallest hollow and draw was given careful attention.

During the last half-hour, they had been gradually climbing into a section that spread away from the tiny creek and swept out and up, not unlike the sides of a tremendous natural saucer. Great round patches of laurel began to appear as the hunters ascended to higher ground. Eventually they drew to a halt and ate sparingly of their dwindling food. The noon meal consisted of a can of pork and beans and a dozen salty crackers, washed down by a drink of water from the stream they were following. After lunch, they pressed on.

At last, they stood upon the crest of the ridge. However, off to the right was a continuation of the slope they had just ascended. Heaving a sigh of disgust and disappointment, Ben lifted his arms aloft and headed that way. Walt fell into step behind him. They walked along silently with bowed heads, in single file.

For the past four days, they had eagerly searched out the head of this lost stream, while they hoped against hope that the ancient hills were ready to reveal the great ginseng patch. With dragging steps and bowed heads, totally disinterested in their surroundings, they walked wearily on. Eventually, Ben drew to a halt and raised his head, looking around. Like an electric shock, it dawned upon him that he had been through this country before, under different circumstances.

The hunters had been steadily ascending. Now they stood at the gateway to a natural saddle in a rugged ridge that loomed ahead. Great blocks of stone lay around in scattered profusion amongst patches of big laurel. Ben dropped his eye and saw a game trail leading straight up the gentle slope amongst the huge rocks and laurel bushes. Swinging around, he grasped his friend's arm in an iron grip, though his hands shook violently from excitement.

"Walt," he croaked, and at the sound of his voice, Walt looked around. "As I live and breathe," he raved, "I think we've come to the end of a long, hard trail."

"Ben, what in hell's wrong?" Walt asked. "You're babbling like a man who has flipped his lid. Don't you feel well? You ain't sick, are you, pard?"

"Walt, Walt," Ben shouted as he pointed with a shaking hand. "We've hit it. As God is my judge, I truly believe that that saddle ahead is the one I struck last summer. It's where I found the big ginseng patch."

"What makes you think so?" Walt asked, frowning as he peered around at the mountain terrain. "What's got you all steamed up? It don't look a bit different to me than dozens of other ridges we've looked at before."

"I know all that, but it's the place," Ben cried. "I'd know this spot in a million years."

"It looks the same as any other."

"Not to me, it don't," Ben maintained. "See that saddle up ahead? And see this game trail that leads straight up into it?"

"All right, all right," Walt said briskly. "Say no more. Let's go see. It won't take us long to find out either way." Swinging around Ben, he began walking briskly up the slope towards the rocks and laurel.

"Walt, for God's sake, wait," Ben cried hoarsely as he hurried to catch up with his friend.

Walt stopped and looked at him. Taking him by an arm, he insisted that he sit down on a large, mossy rock. When Walt spoke, his voice was full of feeling.

"Pard," he said softly, "what spooked you? This ain't like you at all. All of a sudden, you're as white as a sheet, and as nervous as a cat on a tin roof. What's wrong, Ben?"

"I don't know, Walt," Ben replied earnestly, removing a huge red bandana from a hip pocket of his jeans and mopping cold sweat from his brow. "Maybe we've suffered so many disappointments that the sight of the saddle ahead unnerved me. I reckon that's why I feel so shaky inside."

"Could be that's it," Walt agreed. "Offhand, though, I'd say you're kinda taking this whole thing too seriously. Maybe you've been trying too hard to throw a monkey wrench into the Savage deal. Let up a little. You're only human. Why don't you just sit here, relax a bit, and let me take a look-see at that place up ahead. That way, you wouldn't be keyed-up like you are now. It'll only take a few minutes to look it over. You'd soon know one way or the other."

"No, Walt, no."

"Why not?"

"I couldn't."

"Talk sense, pard. You've got me all balled up. You're shaking like a virgin bride on her wedding night, and you still refuse to let me soften the blow. Does that make sense?"

"Be patient, partner," Ben implored. "If that patch is up there, I want to be by your side when you see it for the first time. This might sound batty, I know, but it's true. Last summer, when I stumbled onto that patch, I was more dead than alive. For over a year now, we've been searching this wilderness for it, and now that I believe we've found it, I get buck fever. I have to go in there with you, Walt, even if I fall flat on my face. I feel better now. Let's go before it hits me again. I must know soon. This uncertainty is more nerve wracking than anything else."

"Okay, partner," Walt agreed with a good-natured laugh. "If go you must, then go it is. I'm ready to travel anytime you say the word. However, it you don't feel up to it, my offer stands."

"Never," Ben roared as he rose from the rock. Squaring his shoulders and straightening the straps on his pack, he picked up his ginseng mattock and faced the mountain saddle. He spoke from between set teeth. "Let's travel." He started up the game trail, Walt close to his heels. In the matter of moments, they were in the mouth of the great natural saddle in the mountain ridge.

Close at hand, the unusual formation was larger than it had appeared from below. As they strode deeper, the saddle widened considerably, the great blocks of pebbly rock gave way, and the round patches of laurel began to consolidate until they were confronted by the laurel bed that covered the floor of the saddle. The patch of laurel presented a solid formation like the dense, rank growth of a tropical jungle. The game trail led straight into that wall of evergreen and disappeared from view. Ben turned on his heel and faced his friend.

"Ah," he cried, and the timbre of his voice sent shivers up and down Walt's spine. "This is it. Lead off into them laurels now, Walt, and directly you'll see a sight that'll spell finish to Jess Savage's low-down plan. I'll be right at your heels. This game trail leads straight through the laurel patch."

Walt looked into his friend's shining eyes and turned about, squared his shoulders, and plunged into the laurel thicket. Working his way forward, he found to his surprise that the laurel bushes parted at his touch, and he easily moved ahead. Ben was right at his shoulder. When they had shouldered their way along the game trail for perhaps a hundred yards, Walt stopped dead.

"Pard," he cried. "I see something red shining through the laurel ahead. Do you suppose that's it? They could be ripe seng berries. The berries are ripe now, you know."

At his words, another cry burst from Ben's lips. He pointed ahead. After one look, Walt plunged on. He saw the spreading branches of huge black walnut trees high overhead, not fifty feet in front of him.

Suddenly, the hunters burst through the last of the laurel and into a great park-like place. Dozens of big black walnut trees stood there and beneath their lofty boughs grew the great ginseng patch Ben stumbled onto fifteen months before. The entire floor of the space under the trees was thickly covered with ginseng stalks. Four-, five-, and six-prong stalks stood waist-high over every foot of the open space. Long seed stems thrust their heads above the gold-tinged leaves of the ginseng plants. The hand of fall had already begun to make its presence known. The seed stems were topped by clumps of seed that were ripe, ruby red, and as big around as good sized oranges. Walt was momentarily struck speechless. Disbelieving, he strode amongst it and stared around in bug-eyed amazement. Ben was leaning against one of the ancient walnut trees, watching him with an amused smile. In the moment of their triumph, Ben automatically reverted back to his former cool, calm, and collected self.

"Great day in the morning," Walt   whispered. "Man, oh man, what a sight. Ben, old pard, I want to apologize before I collapse for all the doubts I've had about the existence of this patch of seng. It's here all right. If I was to make a rough guess, I'd say there's a ton of dry root here if there's an ounce. Maybe more. I was wrong, pard, dead wrong. I'm sorry I ever doubted you."

"Forget it," Ben laughed. "Perhaps I'd have done the same thing if a stranger was found half-dead in my back yard and told me a wild cock-and-bull story. Anyway, the important thing is that we've found it. Everything is in the bag now. We've licked these hills, and ferreted out their closely guarded secret. It took us over a year of sweat, blood, and cussing to do it, but what the hell. Nothing important comes easy."

"What're we going to do now that we've found the patch?" Walt asked.

"Head for home," said Ben calmly. "We're almost out of grub."

"But what of the patch of seng?"

"It'll keep till we get back. This seng has stood here for God knows how long. It'll stand a while longer till we can get back and dig it out."

"I know that, pard. But that ain't what's got me worried. How are we going to know where to come? This spot gave them soldiers the slip years ago, and the same thing happened to you. It could happen again."

"Not this time, my friend," said Ben.

"Oh, no?"

"No."

"And why not?"

"Because, Walt, when I walk away from the seng patch this time, I'm going to blaze a trail. That's why not."

"Well, by the great Horn Spoon," Walt said, "that's what I call using your head. All we'll have to do is follow the blaze back. Simple as A, B, C, but how soon do we start for home?"

"Right now. The sooner we get home, the sooner we'll get back and begin digging this out. So come on, partner. Let's be on our way."

Immediately thereafter, they were on the move. At the edge of the laurel bed, on the side opposite side from where they had entered it, they consulted the compass they always carried. Setting their direction due west, they started out, and Ben scalped a small patch of bark off a   tree every fifty feet or so with a small mattock he always carried when out ginseng hunting.

The following day, the sun had set when the hunters arrived home, weary and footsore. At the news of their discovery, Grant Randall and his wife were fairly beside themselves for joy. Lynn received the good news with a wide grin then danced a little gig and yelled like an Indian. How full of life and joy she was as she cavorted about, taking advantage of the excitement of the moment she flung her arms around Ben's neck, pulled his head down, and kissed him on the lips. Grant gave Ben a hearty slap on the back and roared with laughter.

Alice, however, received the news of their good fortune in an entirely different manner. Her face became very pale and strained. With a gasp, she threw her hands into the air and slipped to the floor in a dead faint. Ben helped carry the unconscious girl to her room and stood by until Lynn and Mrs. Randall had revived her then he excused himself and left the room. After supper, he repaired to the cabin up the old logging road, and for more than an hour sat in the doorway and gazed into the yard. At last, he rose and retired for the night.

Hours later, he was awakened by the subtle touch of pair of small, cool hands and two soft lips. Strong arms embraced him, while a familiar voice coaxed him. He was unable to resist her charms, and her beautiful young body was as fresh, fragrant, and satisfying as green leaves.

Chapter 25

*O*ctober sixteenth dawned bright, clear, and cold, with the frost coating the meadow that stretched down to the banks of the Cranberry. The entire Randall household was astir. That day momentous things would come to pass. In the next few hours, they were going to meet Jess Savage at the bank in Richwood, and wipe out the debt on their home. The week before, Grant Randall notified Savage of their desire to meet him at the Richwood Bank, and received a curt reply agreeing to the meeting. As yet, Jess Savage had not the slightest inkling of the Randalls' ability to redeem their home, and they were determined to keep him in the dark until the last minute.

The preceding twenty-one days had been full of hard work for Ben, Walt, and Grant Randall. With careful planning and herculean effort, the three men got the big patch of ginseng dug and out of the woods by the tenth of October. Ben had insisted that they sell a portion of the ginseng roots green. It would take close to a month for the great roots to air-dry. And just then, a month of waiting was out of the question. So on the twelfth of the month, he and Walt loaded his ancient touring car with burlap bags of green ginseng root and drove to Charleston, the state capital. They were able to negotiate a good price for their ginseng with the same dealer they had sold roots and furs to the previous year. The buyer was very generous. They sold enough of the ginseng, undried, to bring them a little over four thousand dollars. They needed to make two trips to Charleston because Ben's old automobile could haul just so much at one time. They sold him over a thousand pounds of green roots, plus the ginseng they had dug and dried previously that season.

"Man, oh man," he said as he looked on the great pile of roots on the floor of his stock room. "That's the biggest pile of seng roots I ever seen at one time. This ain't none of my business, I know, but I'm willing to bet that these roots came out of the big patch them Rebel soldiers stumbled across seventy-five years ago. Am I right?"

"Old timer," the hunters laughed as he handed them a check, "as for where these roots came from, we ain't saying one way or the other. I'll say this, however. If anybody thinks that tramping them ridges is easy, let him or her try it. After a few days in there, they'll change their minds. Got to be shoving off now. We'll have another bunch of roots in a couple weeks or so. Keep the price up. If you don't, we'll find ourselves another buyer. Ha, ha!"

True to their promise, they had notified Ben's father of their find and invited him to come out and help dig the big patch. However, Amos Waters wrote back that couldn't possibly get away from the farm chores. He congratulated the young men on their success and wished them the best of luck in digging and marketing their find. Grant Randall couldn't believe that at last he had the means to free himself of the debt to Jess Savage. Twenty-four hours after Ben and Walt walked out of the woods with news of their find Grant had thrown off the haggard look he had worn ever since Ben met him. Overnight he developed the look of a man dragged from brink of disaster.

"Boys," he said to them on the day after their discovery. "Thank God for letting you attain your goal. The next big problem is getting it dug and out of the woods before the sixteenth of next month. I'm going back in them woods with you boys and help you dig out every last root of that patch if it kills me. I know, Walt, that I've been one hell of a father these past eighteen months and longer. Worry has dragged me downhill. Now I'm asking the good Lord above that through his guidance and you boys; stick-with-it-ness, that all that is behind me. What a load off my mind. I'm dead set to help you boys all I can."

"Pa, you don't realize how much you're sticking your neck out when you say that," Walt laughed. "That patch of seng is one hell of a ways back in them woods, and there's a whale of lot of it to be dug. Maybe you'll change your mind once you get in there and see it."

"That I doubt," said Randall.

"Mr. Randall, we'll be glad to have you help us," Ben said. "You're more than welcome. It'll be a little hard on you at first in the woods, but I believe it'll do you a world of good."

"Fine," boomed Randall. "I'm against tipping our hand to Savage before the sixteenth of next month. What say to playing mum until the last minute? That way, that two-legged skunk'll get the surprise of his rotten life. If he sets foot on this place before the court gives him permission to do so, I'll fire his ass outta here so quick it'll make his head swim. That would do my old heart a world of good. It shames me something awful when I see how far I'd slipped. That's why I'm asking to help you boys all I can. Why, I even tried to discourage you from looking for seng at all. The least I can do now is to help."

Randall lay to with a will and worked like a titan, early and late, while the big patch of ginseng was dug, and as he worked and sweated at getting the great old roots out of the ground, the droop went out of his shoulders and the cloudiness out of his eyes. At night, he retired to the shelter Ben and Walt had built at the edge of the walnut grove so tired he could hardly move one foot ahead of the other.

Nevertheless, the next morning, he would be up early cooking breakfast, as though he had not worked himself almost to the dropping point the day before. Ben was delighted to find that Grant Randall was no slouch when it came to cooking on an open fire. He could whip up a filling, tasty meal while Ben and Walt were trying to decide what to cook.

That the young men appreciated his presence and his help pleased the elder Randall no end and he doubled his efforts to remain in their favor. He worked as though trying to do the work of two men. As the bright fall days passed, and the three men slowly but surely came nearer to completing the task, Ben realized that Grant Randall was putting forth a supreme effort, trying to redeem himself.

Not a whisper of complaint passed his lips. He was bright and cheerful, regardless of the conditions. As Ben watched him working day after day, great admiration and respect for the man came to him. Grant Randall might not have been a good father for a time, but all men deviate from the path of perfect parenthood at some point in their lives. Such deviations are expected, because no human being under the sun is perfect.

Ben was best qualified to handle getting the ginseng roots out of the woods, and he used two horses to accomplish it. After the first three days of digging, he was kept busy packing the roots out. It took a day to bring a load out, and a day to get back to the patch. He would walk out, leading the two loaded horses. He rode one of the horses back in and led the other. Back at the patch, he helped them dig for a day, and the following morning he loaded up the two horses and headed for the homestead again.

Whenever he came home from the woods, Alice greeted him in a glad, half-embarrassed way and followed him about with her heart shining in her big, dark eyes. She was free at last, and from her actions, Ben divined that she wanted to be his wife, but as he traveled the long miles back and forth from the big patch, Ben knew that the flame of love he once felt for Alice no longer existed. The long months had taken their toll. His yearning for Alice Randall had dulled to a common attraction. Now that she was a free woman, free to make her own decisions and choose whom she would romantically, Ben was undecided. Only time, he knew, would erase the doubt he harbored and set him straight in his thinking. He eventually decided to drift along until he could be honest with himself and declare his feelings for Alice Randall, whatever they were.

With Lynn, however, there still existed the same free and easy relationship as before. Every time he bought a pack load of roots home, she came to him at night in the little cabin up the logging road. These nighttime visits were as regular as clockwork, and he had begun to look forward to her visits with an almost feverish anticipation. She was like a narcotic, and Ben knew he had to get Lynn Randall out of his system completely before he could be happy with any other girl, regardless of who she might be.

On his third trip out from the patch, Lynn came to the little cabin and woke him out of a death-like sleep with a subtle, demanding touch. As usual, she was in bed with him, as naked as a newborn baby, snuggling close to him under the blankets. Her body was deliciously warm against his, and as smooth and pleasing to his touch as new satin.

"Lordy, honey," he groaned. "I'm dead tonight. Can't we forget about it this once? I'm just not in the mood."

"Shh, darling," she whispered as she began applying skillful hands and passionate lips.

"Relax, Bennie-boy," she continued. "Don't fight it. You want it just as badly as I do. Of course, you're tired. So what? I've been tired plenty of times and expect to be again in the future. What I'm about to give you will make you sleep like a sleeping pill. It never fails. Just relax, and I'll guarantee you'll enjoy every minute of it. I'll even do all the work."

Ben could contain himself no longer and clutched her to him. Quicker than it takes to tell, they were locked in an embrace. Minutes later, they lay limp, but satisfied, in each other's arms and talked.

"Lynnie, baby," Ben began, after a few moments, "I'm all balled up in my thinking these days."

"How?" she asked as she lay in his arms with her head pillowed on his shoulder.

"How I feel is hard to put into words," he replied.

"I see," she said. "Maybe my great big seng-digging lover is tired of our lovemaking. Maybe he wants to cast me aside like an old hoe. He'll be in big money when he sells all them roots. Is that what's troubling my lover? Is he worrying about how to get a girl off his neck once he's had her and grown tired of her? Is that what's troubling you?"

"Then come clean, Bennie-boy," she said. "Please stop beating around the bush. If I'm no longer welcome in your arms, just say the word. I can take the hint. We only started this affair for thrills. So give it to me straight, honey. If you're trying to break it off with me, let me know. I'll step aside, as much as I'd hate to. The least I can do is bow out of our relationship like a good sport."

"Shut the gab and be quiet," Ben growled. "If you don't, I'm liable to spank that cute little round, wiggling butt of yours. It's not what you're thinking at all."

"Oh, no?"

"No."

"Poppycock," she replied. "If that's not it, then what has you on the fence?"

"I said be quiet," he growled, "or I'm liable to rape you."

"I won't be quiet, Ben Waters," she retorted, "and right now, I'd rape real easy. So take care, my good man. It isn't wise to make rash statements like that, especially when you're in bed with a naked girl. I'm just the type to take you serious and insist that either you put up or shut up. From the way you've been acting tonight, I'm beginning to think you have some bitch on the string. Honestly, though, I don't think you'd need one, but a girl can never tell about a man's sexual desires. Some men are plumb hand to satisfy."

"Lynnie, please," Ben said tiredly. "I beg of you to be quiet about my roving eye, and listen. I'm all mixed up inside when it comes to Alice and me."

"Yeah? Well, I'll be a monkey's uncle. Come off it, will you? What gives? Aren't you two going to get married?"

"I don't know," Ben replied miserably.

"You don't know?" she asked. "Why not, if I may be so bold? For months, you wouldn't give me the tiniest tumble because you was so moon-eyed over my sister. I don't get this at all. How come you're at sea now? You and her can get married anytime you want to now. Jess Savage is out of the picture for good, or soon will be. So why the sudden doubt? Be honest with me, Mister Waters. Has our little shindig changed your mind?"

"It's this way, Lynnie," Ben answered as he reached up with a work-hardened hand and tenderly stroked her beautiful blonde head. At his touch, an almost inaudible sigh escaped her lips and snuggled closer.

"For more than a year, Alice thrust my love aside for her duty to her parents. I tried every argument in the book to change her mind, to no avail. Eventually, I accepted my love for her was a lost cause, and some of its fervor died inside of me. I decided to live life as it came to me. The love I once felt for her has been smothered too long. It just doesn't exist anymore. I'm all at sea in my mind about me and her, but I've done some serious thinking on the matter in the past weeks. When the day comes when I know where I stand, I'll take it from there, but not before."

"And in the meantime," she asked, "will you and I continue to have our fun?"

"I reckon so," he replied. "Right now, I can't think of anything I'd get more enjoyment out of." Then he began to fondle her breasts, bringing gasps of delight from the beautiful nude girl. In moments like these, Lynn Randall was as animated as a highly charged wire, and Ben was caught up and carried away by her emotions. It was contagious, and he found himself utterly powerless to resist it.

"Thank God," she whispered fiercely. "I'm so glad, even while I'm deeply sorry for Alice. That swinging gut of yours is just what the good doctor ordered. So believe me, Bennie-boy when I say I'm not about to give it up unless I have to. In the meantime, you just drift along, and I'll drift right along with you. What fun we'll have as we drift along together.

Chapter 26

On the sixteenth of October, 1934, Grant Randall, his son Walter, his daughter Lynn, and Ben Waters, dressed in their Sunday best, arrived at the Citizens National Bank in Richwood, West Virginia, at quarter till twelve a.m. At the last moment, Alice and Mrs. Randall begged to be excused from accompanying them, pleading nervousness. Lynn, however, said she wouldn't miss seeing Jess Savage's face for the world.

Upon their arrival at the bank, Grant Randall asked for an audience with the bank president. In a moment, they found themselves ushered through a glass door that bore the following words in heavy gold lettering.

Arnold Creston, Pres.
Citizen's National
Richwood, West Virginia
Private

When they entered the room, a short, stocky, balding man of advanced years with a florid face and shrewd, beady eyes rose to his feet from behind a huge desk of black walnut, and met them with a smile and out-stretched hand. He was wearing a double-breasted, blue serge suit that fitted him as though tailored. A diamond stickpin flashed from his tie, and a heavy gold ring shone on the middle finger of his right hand.

One look at this bland, affable man was enough to convince Ben that before him stood an individual who would sell his own granddaughter down the river without compunction, should the deal prove profitable. The man's appearance and friendliness was only camouflage to conceal his true self. When the banker spoke, his voice was a carefully modulated bass, the kind that befits a man in his position.

"Well, well, Mr. Randall," he beamed. "Such a pleasure to see you again. And this beautiful young lady, I presume, is one of your daughters. She must be the youngest. Her name completely eludes me at the moment. This strapping young fellow on your right is certainly a Randall. Walter Randall. Am I correct?"

"That's right, Mr. Creston," Walter replied easily. "I'm Walt Randall." He didn't like Creston. He remembered how easily Arnold Creston sold the mortgage to Savage. One look at that money-hungry face was enough to convince him that he hadn't changed. "I'd like to introduce a very good friend of mine. Mr. Creston, meet Ben Waters."

Arnold Creston acknowledged the introduction and invited everyone to sit down.

"Now then," he began, smiling, "what brings you folks to Richwood? Can I be of service?"

"Mr. Creston, it's about the mortgage on our home," Randall said. He looked for like a man who had suffered defeat at every turn of the wheel and had come there to try for some last mercy. Grant Randall had seen through the banker's superficial exterior, recognized it for what it was, and decided to play the role of a poverty-stricken farmer. Then he would produce the certified check Ben and Walt had brought home from Charleston and laugh in the banker's face.

At Randall's words, a shadow of false sorrow crossed the banker's face, and he threw his pudgy hands into the air in helplessness. "My dear man, the matter is out of my hands and has been for some time now. Due to pressing financial difficulties at the bank, I was forced to sell a number of liens. Unfortunately, the lien on your property was among the lot. Therefore, your best bet would be to talk to the man holding the mortgage in question—Jesse Savage."

For a moment, Grant Randall sat hunched over in his chair. With a gnarled hand, he slowly stroked his chin, while deep furrows serrated his brow. He was the picture of despair. When he raised his shaggy head, he did so in such a way that he faced away from Arnold Creston. Winking broadly at his son, daughter, and Ben, he turned back to face the banker once more.

"Yes, Mr. Creston, you're right," Randall said. "Jess Savage now holds the mortgage on my home, but that isn't the worst of it. The lien falls due today. Savage is to meet us here in a few minutes, and that man is as hard as nails when it comes to money matters. He'll foreclose on me as sure as there's a God above us. That's why I came in to see you before he appears. Will you take over the mortgage on my home again? You'll be saving an old farmer from the clutches of a cold-blooded schemer."

"Please look at this from my standpoint, Mr. Randall," he began. "I'm running a bank here, not a charitable organization. It's impossible to help you. Jesse Savage might be in a bargaining mood. He' a bachelor, you now, and you have two beautiful, unmarried, daughters. A son-in-law of his financial standing should not be objectionable, especially when you consider the fact that you and your entire family are practically homeless, as of today."

"Uh-huh, I see," Randall replied, stroking his long jaw and eyeing the banker with a speculative eye. "Then you won't help me, is that it?"

"Utterly impossible, my good man," the banker said. "There's too many risks involved, not the least of which is your age. Too many winters and summers have rolled over your head, Mr. Randall. I must protect my position. Business acumen, you know."

"All right then," said Randall, as a wave of red slowly crept over his face. "Have it your way. Call Savage, and tell him I'm here and ready to talk business. Also, call Sheriff Craig. I want him in on this little set to."

"Must we have Craig in on this?" the banker demurred. "Such procedure seems highly irregular."

"To hell with your procedures," Randall roared. "I want Craig present when I tangle with Savage. Either phone him to come here, or I'll hold our meeting in his office. Take your pick."

"Okay. Keep your shirt on," the banker conceded as he complied with Randall's request. After had had finished phoning, he excused himself, and stepped out of his office.

As soon as the banker left his office, the Randalls and Ben settled down to await the men in question. Fortunately, they did not have long to wait. Within twenty minutes, the banker had reentered his office, accompanied by Jess Savage and Sheriff Craig. As Savage entered the office, he swept the room with an eagle-like glance.

He's looking for Alice, Ben thought. Look, damn you, but you'll look in vain. That poor girl is out from under you forever.

As Savage's eyes rested on Ben, a wave of crimson washed over the man's features, and his heavy jaw snapped shut with a click. Even though the girl he wanted for a bride was absent, he looked satisfied with his mastery over the situation. The tall, lanky sheriff, however, was calm, cool, and easy to everyone present then feasted his eyes in admiration on Lynn, who was seated beside Ben with her shapely legs crossed, and her dress carefully draped in such a way that her dimpled knees were in full exposure.

Gad, Craig muttered. I'd love to lay that hot little bitch a few times. What wouldn't I give to be twenty-five again, and have her on her hands and knees, with nothing on but a collar button. I'm old man today, but she could put the lead back in my pencil again in gig-time. That's the way with her kind. They always have been, and always will be mantraps.

When everybody was seated, the banker cleared his throat. "Craig," he said, "the mortgage on Grant Randall's property is due today, and he hasn't the money to liquidate even the interest due on the mortgage, let alone the mortgage itself."

"What's that got to do with me, Creston?" the Craig asked, a puzzled frown creasing his brow.

Creston sighed. "Jess Savage holds that mortgage. If Randall expected to retain his property, he must pay Jess Savage the face value of the mortgage, with the interest accumulated, compounded semi-annually. That's where you come in, sheriff. You are going to be asked to serve foreclosure papers on Grant Randall before this day is over, unless the pays Jess in full, which is very unlikely. He has come here with hardly two nickels in his pocket to rub together. He's flat broke, busted. He came here today, confessed his situation, and begged me to pull him out of his mess."

"Grant Randall came in today and asked you for financial assistance?" the sheriff asked glint in his piercing eyes.

"He did," the banker said. "I was forced to turn him down."

"Uh-huh, I see," Craig said as he pursed his lips and spat a stream of brown tobacco juice into a large brass cuspidor. Wiping his mouth with the back of a leathery-looking hand, he directed his keen eyes upon the bank president. "You turned Grant down cold turkey, eh?"

"You're absolutely right."

"Couldn't see your way clear to help him out at all?"

"No."

"Not even for the interest on the mortgage on his home?"

"Not one thin dime," the banker said with cold finality.

"Uh-huh. I see," the sheriff muttered to himself. "Just where does that leave Grant? Looks like he's sort of out on a limb. What did you suggest he do to save his home?"

"Make a deal with Savage," was Creston's answer.

"Just what kind of deal did you have in mind, Mister Creston?" Sheriff Craig asked.

"Any deal that would be satisfactory to both parties," the banker growled. "I'm not interested in this matter either way. It's professionally impossible for me to help this man. If Jess here turns him down, I reckon it means his neck. If these men can work out a deal amongst themselves, that's up to them, and none of my affair."

"Naturally," Sheriff Craig said dryly. "Well, men," he continued, turning to Grant Randall and Jess Savage. "Let's get on with it and wrap this up as quickly as possible. I have work to do at my office, so unless I'm rushing things unduly, I'd appreciate getting the ball rolling."

Jess Savage again swept the room with satisfaction and jumped to his feet. "Randall," he gloated, "you've finally reached the end of your rope. Too bad, my friend, too bad. I've enjoyed our little game of cat and mouse over the last eighteen months. Even so, I'm really glad it's over. You can't stall me any longer. All right, what's it to be? Pay up, meet my demands, or get off my property. Take your pick. Only make it short and sweet. I've waited a year and half for this, and my patience was wearing thin."

"Look now, Jess," Grant Randall said.

Ben's heart gave a great leap of admiration. Damn your lousy hide, Jess Savage, Ben cursed. You don't know it yet, but the gig's up for you. Your tune will change mighty quick now.

"My back's to the wall," Randall said. "Surely you're not going to throw two old people out of their home. I just can't believe that you're that kind of a man, Jess."

"Come off it, farmer," Savage said. "You're wasting your time. It won't work. You know what we agreed on more than a year ago. I'm holding you to that agreement. Meet those conditions, and you ain't got a single thing in this world to worry about. On the other hand, if you can't pay the lien in full, and refuse to meet the conditions of our agreement, then you and your entire family will be out on the public road before you're another week older—lock, stock, and barrel. Where's Alice?"

"Alice and her mother are at home," said Grant Randall.

"Sick, or to cowardly to show her face?"

"Sick, yes, but mostly at the sight of you," Randall growled.

"Hell you say," Savage snarled. "Well, let me tell you, once that finicky split-tail is under my roof, I'll cool her coffee. You can tell her that for me."

"Alice Randall is not under your roof yet, Mister Savage," Ben said.

Jess Savage turned like a flash, and an inarticulate cry of rage fell from his lips. All the hate in the world was mirrored in his eyes.

"You damn meddling bum," he roared. "Keep your two cents' worth out of this. I'm not standing for hogwash from you. The sheriff is right here, and I'd like nothing better than to slap a charge against you that'd skin the pants off your dirty ass and land you in jail. There'll be trouble, sure as hell, if you start something."

"Hold your horses, Jess," Sherriff Craig growled. "Get on with business. That's what I'm more interested in right now. To hell with your personal grievances. Settle them later. Get this mortgage deal over. I want to get outta here."

Jess Savage swallowed his rage, and turned a deaf ear to all of Grant Randall's pleas that he show leniency. At last, with a harsh laugh and a muttered curse, Randall thrust his right hand into an inside coat pocket and drew forth a worn, cowhide wallet. Taking a small yellowish slip of paper from the wallet, he handed it to Sheriff Craig.

"Here, Craig," he said. "Look this over. Reckon that little strip of paper will get my home outta the red. I tried today to find even a small amount of compassion in my fellow man, but it was a waste of time. In all my born days, I ain't never seen two harder men than these two. Savage and Creston. What a pair. It'll be sweet to be free of the likes of them. Now tell me, Craig, old friend. Do you think that hunk of paper I gave you will see me through?"

"I'd say positively," said Craig as a thin smile crossed his leathery face.

"Gentlemen," the banker said. "What's going on here?"

Jess Savage eyed the sheriff and Randall suspiciously, while a pale shade crept over his ruddy countenance. He hurried to the banker's side and whispered into his ear. The sheriff thrust the slip of paper Randall had given him across the big walnut desk.

"Read it and weep, friend," Craig said. "Then you'll know what's going on."

Picking up the slip of paper, the banker looked at it then shoved it under Jess Savage's nose. Rage had replaced his smug, unruffled countenance.

"You stupid ass," he snarled at a flabbergasted Savage, who was standing at his elbow with an open mouth. "I thought we had this Randall deal wrapped up as tight as a drum. Would you be kind enough to explain this certified check?"

"It's a forgery," Savage gasped. "That check can't be legal. I'd stake my last dime on it being worthless. It's got to be. Where could this pack of hillbillies scrape together more than four thousand dollars? Such a thing is utterly ridiculous."

"But supposing it isn't?" the banker roared. "Then what?"

"Don't cross bridges until we come to them," Savage answered. "We ain't lost out yet. Why don't you phone the bank in Charleston that this check is drawn on? They can tell you whether it's genuine or not. I say it's a phony."

The banker turned to his telephone and asked to be connected. In less than five minutes, the operator phoned back to tell him that his party was on the line. After he asked about the check, he replaced the receiver and bent wrathful eyes upon Savage, who was waiting anxiously.

"You bungling idiot," he rasped. "That check's as good as gold. I might have known you'd muff this deal."

"You're damn right that check's good," the sheriff spat. "Enough of this monkey business. Looks to me as though your little deal has backfired. Produce that mortgage, Jess Savage, and do it on the double. Right here and now, you're signing over all claims you may have on this man's home. If I hear much more about the deal you and Creston cooked up, I'll clap the both of you in jail. I'm convinced that selling the mortgage on Grant's home was not unavoidable, Creston. It was a deliberate attempt to strip him of his earthly possessions. Don't you think I'm aware that the young timber on his thousand acres will be worth a fortune in a few years?"

"My business methods are my own affair, Craig," the banker said coldly. "I'll thank you to keep your nose out of them. You've nothing on me, only your suspicions."

"My suspicions are enough to convince me that I've got you and this ring-tail figured right," said Craig. "Come, Savage, let's have that mortgage. I'm anxious to see if you've forgotten how to sign your own name."

Under the sheriff's piercing eye, the mortgage was produced and signed over to the original landowner. All during the proceedings, Arnold Creston glared at Jesse Savage. When everything was properly signed over and witnessed, Jess Savage rose and announced his intention to leave.

"Go home, Savage," Ben thundered. "Go home to the girl who's waiting for you, who by all the laws of nature should be your wife."

"What you mean?" Savage gasped.

"Lila LaGrange," Lynn cried.

"You lie," Savage whispered. "I don't know who you're talking about. You're trying to frame me. I'm an innocent man. I'll have the sheriff here arrest you all. I'll even—"

"Hold your tongue, you lying scoundrel," Walt Randall roared. "A month ago, the poor girl came to my home one afternoon when I was away and told Lynn, Alice, and Ben here all about the low-down way you tricked her and her mother into coming up here with you last February. Then she told them how you forced your attentions on her shortly after they arrived at your place and how you forced her to sleep with you ever since. All that time, you threatened these poor people with all sorts of terrible things. Don't bother to deny it, you weasel. You know I'm telling the truth. At this very minute, that poor girl is out at your home, heavy with your unborn child. Go to her and do the honorable thing. For once in your rotten life, be a man."

Jess Savage's face turned a thousand hues of guilt. With uplifted hands, he staggered backwards a few steps. Meaningless, scrambled sentences fell from his lips in frantic denial.

"That dirty, low-down slut," he croaked. "Put the finger on me, will she? I'll fix her clock but good for this. When I'm through with her, she'll be glad to say that some local hillbilly popped her corn. Bitch-of-a-bitch, I could kill her with my bare hands for blabbing her guts."

With a frightful curse spilling out of his hate-twisted mouth, Savage grabbed his hat from the banker's desk and dashed out of the office. On his way out, he slammed the office door, making the walls rattle and cracking the frosted glass pane in the door from top to bottom.

Chapter 27

*T*hat fall, the Randall household gradually settled back into a relaxed, unhurried way of life. During those tranquil autumn days, Ben found himself leaning towards that way of life, not because he was a lazy man, but because the people of the hill country seemed to derive so much more pleasure out of everyday living than those who were constantly hurrying through life as though their very existence depended upon activity. As the fall season advanced, Ben and Walt began preparing for the winter trapping season. By November first, all of their ginseng roots were dry and sold to the dealer in Charleston. The big patch from the walnut grove netted the hunters better than twenty-five thousand dollars.

"Gosh, partner," Walt said as the partners examined their bankbooks on the day they sold the last of their dry ginseng roots. "With all this money, I'm beginning to feel like a financier."

Ben smiled, but refrained from comment. An idea was formatting in the back of his mind by which he hoped to be able to erase a portion of his debt to the Randall family. They saved his life, and rehabilitated him. And as he thought on the subject, he decided to wait for a favorable opportunity. During the week of Thanksgiving, the opportunity he had waited for presented itself, and he decided to take advantage of it. That afternoon, he and Walt returned from laying out the last of their trap-line and setting the traps. Repairing to the cabin up the old logging road, Ben had bathed, shaved, changed his clothes, and cooked and ate his supper before going down to the Randall residence for a friendly chat.

The evening shadows were falling when he sallied forth. The weather was clear and cold after a day of blustery snow squalls. And as Ben walked, he experienced a buoyancy of spirit from the clean, cold air. He was cheerful and at peace with the world and himself. True, his love life had not gone as he had hoped that it would, but other things had gone remarkably well for him. The things he had experienced there on the Cranberry would remain in his heart until his dying day.

He had faced death and felt its cold breath upon his brow. He had known his first real love and suffered bitter disappointment. He had also known the love of a wonderful mountain girl and realized the fulfillment of a dream he had nurtured since his boyhood—finding incredible quality and quantity of ginseng.

As he drew near to the Randall home, he saw Grant Randall splitting kindling and stopped to talk. It was the opportunity he had long waited for, and he immediately acquainted him with his desire to assist him in getting his thousand-acre homestead back on paying basis.

"You see, sir," Craig explained. "It's the very least I can do for you people."

"Well, son," Grant Randall answered, "I reckon us Randalls would ordinarily feel lower than a snake's belly for accepting pay for a favor, but in your case, I'm willing to make an exception. You've always been welcome in my home, but I also know that a man's got to settle things where he imagines a debt is concerned. Do in this matter as your heart dictates. No member of my family holds you in the slightest obligation to us. What we did for you in your hour of need was done with no strings attached."

"Your hospitality humbles me, Mister Randall," Ben replied. "Tomorrow is Thanksgiving Day, and I just got to do something nice for you. That way I can be thankful, and not feel like a hypocrite while I'm doing it. You folks saved my life. I've got to live with myself, you know."

"As you will, my boy, as you will," Randall said, smiling.

Walt strode out the front door and out across the yard to where Ben and his father were talking. He was decked out in his Sunday best, his dark hair combed meticulously, with a shine on his shoes that a person could see himself in. A keen look of anticipation for the evening's courting radiated from his every word and action. He came up Ben and his father and asked about the serious faces. Without preamble, Randall acquainted his son with what Ben proposed. Walt smiled, but slowly shook his head.

"It's no soap, Ben, old partner," he chuckled. "Now please, don't argue with me, 'cause I mean it. We're partners, you know, and have been for more than a year now. Therefore, any debt you say you owe we'll split down the middle. That's right. Partnerships always work that way, so as a full partner, I demand my rights when it comes to money matters. Any financial deal you cook up with Dad, I'm in on—fifty-fifty. I'll be going now. Flo's waiting for me with hot pants, I hope. Got a big date all lined up for tonight. I sure hope she doesn't disappoint me. Reckon I'll be trying out that flivver tonight that I bought in Richwood last week. If it's as good as your old stand-by, Ben, I don't need to worry about it breaking down on me in the wrong place. Well, time's flying, and Flo's waiting. See you later, partner. Be in late tonight, Dad. So long."

With a pleasant smile, Walt raised his right hand and strode to his recently purchased automobile. The car was used, but in good condition. Grant Randall turned to Ben and regarded him.

"Son," he said. "There's something I've wanted to speak to you about for quite a spell now."

"What's on your mind, Mister Randall?" Ben asked.

"It's about Alice and you," Randall said.

Ben's throat contracted. He hadn't once mentioned his love for Alice to her father since he and Walt had removed the obstacle that stood in the way of their marrying. Now he shrank from any explanation for his delinquency in the matter. Could he admit that he no longer cared for her as he once had? Could he hope for understanding if he confessed that the reason for his change of heart towards Alice was because he had been carrying on an affair with his youngest daughter?

Not one father in a thousand would regard him favorably after such a confession. Better, by far, to hold his tongue and come up with something logical and reasonable for his delay. He raised his head to defend his delinquency as best he could, but Grant Randall was speaking again and looking at the surrounding mountain ridges as he did. Ben could not detect anything in the man's face to indicate that he had noticed his hesitation. Randall was calm and serene as he puffed on his pipe.

"You know, last winter," he said, "you asked me for her hand in marriage, and I turned you down. Forgive me, boy, cause in them days, I was blinded to everything but the mortgage hanging over my head. Thank God, it's gone and I see clearly once more. Son, Alice is yours, as far as I'm concerned. Take her as your wife with my blessings, if you still want her. If you two marry, I wish you both the best that life has to offer. Here's my hand on it."

"Mr. Randall, I'm at a loss for words," Ben said as he shook the older man's hand. "I'm glad to the bottom of my soul that Jess Savage's evil scheme came to naught."

"So am I," Grant Randall said. "I can't explain it, Ben, but I have the feeling that that man's race is about run in these parts."

"What do you mean?" Ben asked.

"Savage has shot his wad," said Randall.

"Sure, he lost out on the deal he cooked up here, but I'd be willing to lay you odds that our dear Mister Savage is up to his usual skullduggery elsewhere."

"I don't know," Randall said. "You see, son, he's lost face since last month. People tell me he's been getting meaner and meaner. They also tell me that he treats that woman and her daughter something awful. It wouldn't surprise me none to hear that he's net his just desserts. Women will stand just so much brutality, and no more. If all I hear is true, that poor woman and her pregnant daughter are desperate. He wants to throw them out, and they've no money and no place to go. That's hell, boy. Believe me, that's hell. The man's playing with dynamite, but he's too bull-headed to realize it. In a situation like that, anything could happen."

"You're right," Ben agreed, remembering Lila LaGrange's flashing eyes and belligerent tone. "However, Savage would have to have a house fall on him before he saw the light."

"So be it, my son, so be it," said Randall as he bent down and picked up the kindling he had just split. "Enough about that no-good. For him I have scant compassion. I'm thinking about that poor widow and her unfortunate daughter. May the good Lord point a way to their deliverance from evil hands. Let's go inside. It's a bit chilly out there. From the pinch in the air, I'd say it'll freeze hard tonight."

Nodding silent agreement, Ben followed Randall inside. During the evening, Alice spoke little, but her eyes were big and expressive as he laughed and chatted with the family and talked about the plans he and Walt had for trapping furs that winter. Lynn, however, regarded him with the innocence of a child, and Ben marveled at what an accomplished actress she was, but that was Lynn's way, and he accepted her.

Hours later, wrapped in slumber, he dreamed that she came to his bed once more and crept into his arms. Then he dreamed that Alice confronted him with blazing eyes and told him that she knew all about his seduction of her little sister. When he tried to defend what had been going on between himself and Lynn, Alice slapped his face, turned her back on him, and vanished. He awoke in the cold, grey light of dawn, bathed in icy sweat, and for more than an hour, lay in bed while pangs of conscience gnawed at his vitals. Finally, cursing life's disappointments and broken dreams, he rose and began dressing for Thanksgiving Day.

Ten days later, Grant Randall's prediction concerning Jesse Savage came true. Word flashed across the countryside that he had met a violent death at Lila LaGrange's hands. According to the report, the girl shot him to death with a double-barreled shotgun, defending herself and her mother. Savage had ordered the widow and her daughter from his home, and when they refused to go unless he paid for their transportation and agreed to support Lila and her child, he flew into a rage and proceeded to beat the girl unmercifully. When Savage turned on her mother, Lila rushed into the hallway, grabbed up the shotgun he always kept there, leveled the gun at Savage, and pulled both triggers. The blast from the loaded gun nearly tore the man's head from his shoulders.

"If ever a person deserved a self-defense verdict, that poor Creole does," said Sheriff Craig. "It's one helluva mess. For him, I feel nothing but contempt, and I'll do all I can to see that the LaGranges get justice."

Jesse Savage died as he had lived, vainly and ingloriously, and the community mourned not his passing. Instead, a scene of relief prevailed. He had treated everyone in the community as though they were beneath him, and he had finally paid for his stupidity with his life.

A fortnight later, at midnight, Ben Waters paced the frozen ground in the yard before the little cabin up the logging road. The news of Jesse Savage's death had upset him more than he cared to admit. Of late, he had begun to feel that he should leave the mountains before the situation between Lynn, Alice, and himself blew up in his face, but even as he considered leaving, he knew he could not go. Unseen shackles bound him to the Randall homestead on the Cranberry. He had become a prisoner of love, passion, or desire. Whatever held him in its gasp was stronger than willpower to resist it. And so he paced to and fro and cursed himself for his weakness.

A crescent moon hung low over the ridges to the southwest. It cast long, slanting shadows over the landscape. The skies were cloudless, and the stars shone bright and clear. Ben turned his face to the heavens and flung a silent plea for strength into their star-spangled glory. But his cry for help was ignored. The night winds moaned in the branches of the maple tree that loomed dark and eerie over his head, and the moon and stars shone on. What did it matter to those far-off lights that one weak worm of the dust had cried for help? He was one tiny cog in the gigantic wheel of the universe, destined to live out his life on the earth.

Ben paused in his pacing and canted his head sideways to listen. A familiar step had sounded on the rocky road leading to the Randall home. At the sound of that step, his head fell to his chest, and he began to shake as a leaf in the wind. Lynn Randall was coming to his bed again, to claim and consume him in a way that would leave him wrung out. He could no more resist her than he could fly over the soaring mountain ridges.

"Oh, God," he whispered. "What am I to do? Is there no deliverance from my quandary?"

The chill night breezed fanned his brow, and his answer came. "Stand up," his father had said. "Stand up and be a man. Let no female put anything over on you, regardless of who she is or whose sister she may be." That was his solution, and by putting this philosophy foremost, he would eventually find peace. And as for his association with Lynn Randall, he decide to keep on as before until time presented the solution his romantic problem.

Flinging up his head, he called her name and rushed to meet her in the deepening shadows.

The End

1979 – Jane and Harold, his first dance.

1972 – Giving Janice away at her wedding.

Early 1950's – Jane and Harold

Fall 1969 – Nancy, Janice, and Harold at the park.

Harold H. Milton

January 16, 1990 – Janice and Harold on her birthday.

1980 – Janice and Harold.

Janice and Harold on Easter.

Janice reviewing Harold's books for publishing.

June, 1986 – Nursing graduation.

Harold's birthday.

Harold at the fireplace in their Bay Village home.

Janice with Harold on his birthday.

Fall, 1969 – Jane and Harold.

Harold'sgrandparents,AlfredFarleyandLucindaMillerFarley.

House on W. 19th – Cleveland, Ohio.

Harold and dog, Heidi.

Harold's birthday.

1995 – Harold with great-grandaughter, Madison.

Harold and Madison.

Harold and daughter, Nancy.

Orville Blanton

Orville Blanton with baseball.

1980s – Harold and Janice in the woods.

1993 – Harold gets his GED.

1994 – Harold in Vegas.

Jane and Harold after Nancy's death.

Harold with his GED.

www.ingramcontent.com/pod-product-compliance
Lightning Source LLC
Chambersburg PA
CBHW032142020726
47496CB00003B/674